SARA'S
MONEY'S
GONE

Other novels by David Ross

The Saleswoman and the Househusband
That Boy's Facts of Life

David-Ross.com

SARA'S MONEY'S GONE

DAVID ROSS

ONE

August 31, Thursday

Washington's sun beat down harder and harder all morning, until it was a late summer bog-broil. All Jake could do was lower his cap and aim for whatever cover there was on the tree lined streets. He had to sweat it out, walking by rows of beautiful old brownstone or brick townhouses, their slick antique doors and window frames painted in red, white, pumpkin, whatever. The rich were hiding somewhere inside those air-conditioned houses in a town where Jake couldn't afford to hide.

All he could do was walk, wondering why the air smelled like sweet burnt dust -- from laundry vents? Jake thought he remembered that smell from other walks, other times, but he had to ignore it. He needed a plan, now. He didn't have enough work, so he had to get out of town, soon.

Getting to the broader, airier flats of Wisconsin Avenue, Jake saw a young mother walking thirty feet ahead hand in hand with two kids. As always, commercial Wisconsin sat pretty with its set piece cafes and restaurants and boutique clothing stores. Rich locals signed petitions to keep out cheap chains and those were the rich bastards who used to pay Jake's way. It was their pretty-pretty Wisconsin, along with pretty-pretty M Street, in posh residential Georgetown. And Georgetown sat in the middle of Washington DC, smoldering.

Even moving slowly, he gained on that woman and those two kids. Jake didn't know them, he just wanted to. He noticed the mother wasn't looking in any store windows. She watched her kids, pacing herself to their attempts at momentum. The toddler staggered, one hand attached to her, while the slightly older one pulled ahead, dramatically less happy with each step, complaining back at the fire giant in the sky.

Jake assumed she was their mother. Whoever or whatever she was they stopped at a car with an Illinois license plate. He wanted to find out more about them, ask that woman where she was going, but obviously he couldn't. It was important to keep walking, to tell himself they were strangers, nothing more. The car was a small dark blue Honda jammed into a parking place. If Jake owned a car, if he could afford one, it would be the same -- cheap and no nonsense.

She leaned forward, her long brown hair flowing down as she nudged the children into the back seat, kissing the tops of their heads, speaking in that hallowed soul-of-the-universe voice.

"Okay, here we go. Rest in the car. We'll have lunch in a little while. Okay."

Her focus must have broken for a second. A form was near, a tall, thin, graying, middle-aged man was close. She glanced, reached in quickly, strapped her toddler into his car seat and backed out, unbending as she closed the back door of the car. She stuck herself in the driver's seat and Jake was past. He heard her doors lock and her car start behind him.

He kept moving, sorry. He'd given them as much space as the sidewalk allowed and he just had to finish his morning walk and forget that family. Jake had his own family -- Sara and only Sara. And Sara didn't want to move away from Georgetown.

Head down again, Jake asked himself when they could move on. Even if his fourteen-year-old daughter loved Georgetown they had to move on if he didn't have enough work.

He rumbled at the sidewalk, "Nothing we can do."

Halfway along M Street, still in a full body sweat and still far enough from anyone to hear, his rumble was hoarse. "No more than three more months of hanging around."

At the small antique brick warehouse midway along M Street he turned down a narrow alley, and as usual a couple of tourists watched. He might be one of the odd few who belonged in places like that and he was entering a private side door. It looked like two types of important buildings dominated central Washington -- monumental government buildings and elegant old private residences, with commercial buildings serving as connectors.

What Jake entered was the failing connection between him and his surroundings. The 1817, flat-faced, with large original sash windows, all symmetrical, two and a half story, Federal styled brick building was ultra-cute and attracted attention, but he was desperate for customers, not gawkers. Up one flight of nineteenth century mildewed concrete stairs he turned left to pull at the heavy sheet metal door that let him into his apartment. He pulled at it to enclose himself, wheezing, "We have no choice. Three more months, tops."

Bright overhead lights opened up the cavernous white hallway where, down at the end, he unlatched another old metal warehouse door, squinting at all the lingering space of his studio. It was glowing even more than usual. It always had a glow, the light in the studio. Jake could never not see the midair bloom that came from broad white painted brick walls set against the long, smooth, dull black soapstone countertop and set against thirty feet of slightly worn, dark gray painted warehouse floorboards. He just no longer knew what to do with the business he put together and kept together for fourteen years. It never made a lot of money but now it wasn't making enough to pay for itself, and he was forty-seven. He was trained to be an art conservator -- something that Goddamned esoteric. He wasn't trained for anything else, and he was getting older, blinking at the relentless sun as he stepped to one of the walls, the one dominated by a row of five black, steel framed industrial windows. He leaned over the counter and lowered the long pale green canvas shades. The windows and doors were put in sometime around eighteen-ninety to modernize the back of the second floor of the warehouse. Now those architectural details were quaint antique-modern-industrial.

The point was it was so damned hot. The studio air was gamy, very gamy and that was very bad for the art, so he aimed his phone's app at the big air conditioner on the far wall. It would take almost half an hour to cool down the space. If people knew he skimped on air conditioning he'd get no work at all.

He made his way into his bedroom across from the studio, grabbed a change of clothes, headed back, midway down the hallway to the bathroom, peeled off his sweaty clothes and got in the shower. The cool water felt great, but he had to keep it short and get downstairs, so he got out and got dressed. Stopping at the top of the hallway outside Sara's metal warehouse door, he paused. She was at school –her first day of high school. How was that going?

He walked downstairs and pulled at one more heavy, creaking, old gray metal door to Arthouse Framers. Finally, cool thin air drifted everywhere in the open, two thousand square feet of frame shop. He had to ignore Fiona and the two guys she worked with over on the left. Even the idea of fey nineteen-year-old banter repulsed him just then. He aimed himself at Simon who was at his usual spot near the front with a customer. Simon's text early that morning said a collector was due in at ten-thirty.

She looked familiar, that woman with Simon. Hearing loud voices behind him, Jake turned, and there was Fiona bouncing up and down in her inside-out Georgetown University T shirt with a lot of small holes cut in it, front and back, and wearing a large-brimmed straw hat, a hat covered with large plastic red and yellow flowers. Exhibitionists were everywhere now, or it felt that way surrounded by university students.

He turned back to Simon and the customer. Simon pointed.

"This is Jake Holtz. Jake runs M Street Art Conservation upstairs. He can answer your questions. Gwen Minot."

Her narrow, smooth hand slid into his briefly. She was probably in her mid-thirties and Jake made a point of not staring into her eyes, wanting to but wanting to be polite. She had a few inches of plush black hair springing up and out, and very dark skin and stood there in real clothes not teenwear. Jake tried to breathe her in, the mature woman in well-tailored clothes. Maybe she had serious money if she looked like that in her elegant light blue cotton dress and finished it like that with very minimal, fine leather sandals. Maybe she had art that needed treatment.

Simon gave her Jake's brochure -- a few glossy pages describing the art conservation work he did, his educational background and a partial list of clients. She stored that information in her small tan leather bag, and everyone looked halted, anticipating some other person's next move.

Jake found himself grinning at Gwen as her mouth pulled at her cheekbones, grinning back, opening her round, soft face and deep brown eyes. She was gorgeous. And she really did look familiar, maybe from town.

"Ms. Minot's an architect and an art collector and has some prints. And drawings? Did you say that?" Simon became old-fashioned formal when he had a serious customer.

"No, please, it's Gwen. Yeah, I only have a few things that might need work."

Simon was fixed on her, and it took quite a bit of charm to do that to Simon. Unlike Jake, Simon had a lot of work to get to and a great wife and there was that wedding ring on Gwen's finger.

"Okay. That's fine," Jake said quietly. "I can just look at whatever you bring in. Works on paper. And usually, I can tell you right away what would be needed, and the time and cost involved."

Gwen Minot smiled and left.

CHAPTER TWO

September 1, Friday

*O*n my way. Just got out of school. Day 2 as stupid as day 1

As she texted, Sara imagined her father wiping down the kitchen sink. His love for things like that old white marble sink made her wonder what else there was in the world for them to polish.

Ok. See you soon.

Soon? Where was he when he sent that? Not nearby, she hoped. Sara always enjoyed walking in the city and the three mile walk home should be an exercise in inner and outer discovery. She hoped. She'd been living in Georgetown for three months and today was her second day of ninth grade. She was living with her father and going to high school in town. Those thoughts gave her goosebumps because the only thing right about her life, that she saw on her inner GPS screen, was living with her father in Georgetown. She always wanted to live in Georgetown. What could be cooler than living right smack in the middle of the nation's capital? It was obviously so much better than living twenty miles out there in pissy North Bethesda with her mother, that reminding herself

13

where she lived now, almost always washed away the anger, hurt and frustration from her mother leaving the way she did.

Meanwhile, walking quickly, she was far enough along Wisconsin Ave to be free of potential threats, like those high schoolers and their jerky hustle, their aggressive chaos. The older high schoolers were so damned big. Maybe that was why it felt like there so many more kids than teachers in that huge building. It was ugly-hot outside, but the stale machine-made air in that school was used up or reused too many times or something.

Craning her neck, she couldn't see her father anywhere. She told him he didn't have to meet her, but like the day before he'd probably lurk somewhere along her route home. Cars and trucks and buses thundered by as the harsh, sometimes newer, cheaply built buildings near her high school were away, behind her. Now, even small amounts of money transformed the nineteenth century three-story brick buildings around her into treats. It only took trees, painted brick, painted trim and doors, new windows and the mood of style. *The Mood of Style* was the name of a DC blog Sara looked at a few times recently.

* * * * *

Jake stopped to text again.

I'm on Wisconsin halfway.

A dozen steps on he waved at her unique form fifty yards away. She started to wave back, then lowered her hand. They closed their distance.

No one could come close to lifting Jake's spirits the way gangling, five-six, curly-wavy light brown hair to the waist,

Sara did. Her face wasn't pushed out through all the baby pudge yet, just most of it. This was one of those emerging times. Her hazel eyes darkened at the awkward public meeting of father and daughter, something Jake chose to ignore trying to hug her.

"I can walk alone here. I'm not ten years old, Dad." She turned, barely tapping her side once against his, and they started walking.

"Yeah, but see the thing is you're still just a little bit too young and it's a long walk." He remained straight-faced and she bit her bottom lip, raising her head, eyes closed to the sky.

He turned to her, matching his pace with hers. "It's a city, even if it looks civilized."

"In like, a year and a half, I'm driving."

"Driving? What, a city bus?"

She snarled, "No. A Harley. Actually, I want a scooter."

Jake worried he was in for a rough afternoon.

"Anyway, "he said. "It should start to cool down in a few weeks and, yeah, later, when the weather gets colder and rainier, you'll have to take the bus. You'll have to use your city bus pass."

"Um."

He knew she knew that. They made their way silently. He had to hope her traipsing around the city unnerved her less than it unnerved him.

The building, along with the ten inch, black steel letters, all individually screwed into the old bricks, *M S T R E E T   A R T H O U S E   F R A M E R S*, stood out and Sara gazed up at it as she approached, maybe still not totally used to the setting. They walked to the side door.

Upstairs, Jake pointed to the closed studio door. "Can we talk for a minute? The air's on in there."

Simon owned the building, but no matter how many financial weaknesses Jake had he knew he designed a far from boring place. It didn't have a living room, with the tall wide hallway, kitchen, bath and two large bedrooms and then the studio absorbing all the space. The galley kitchen had a long antique white marble sink he put in and a thick, stainless-steel countertop. Another bit of thick burnished stainless steel made a tabletop hinged to the chair rail on the wall. The two bedrooms were big, both twenty-one by thirty-four feet. Sara always said she loved it all for her weekend visits, until last June. That was when plans were made for Sara to move in.

But Jake knew his best space was the studio. Its large sink in the far corner and the binocular microscope in the other corner stood out as sculptural accents. And there was all that ceiling way up there with birch veneer plywood between the rafters, all sealed with tung oil varnish that made a deep honey-russet tone and set off all the white walls and dark gray floors below.

Sara climbed onto an industrial, dark steel stool and he stood next to the other one. She yawned, then sat still.

"So, how was school?"

"Okay."

He exaggerated a frown.

"It was."

"Meet any potential friends?"

She slowly filled her chest with air. "Maybe. There are like, some nice kids or whatever."

He remained standing, hands in his pockets, motionless, expectant.

"It's fine, Dad. It's only the second day and the place is so gigantic and we all got knocked around all day looking for our classrooms and lockers. We all went to assembly first of all, just like yesterday. The principal might be a little brain damaged."

Deep nerves rattled in Jake because Sara seemed genuinely disgusted. He managed to stay steady. "Okay, and the teachers?"

"Okay, I guess."

He kept on message. "I know I said this last week when we were talking about you not seeing your old friends anymore, or not much anyway. I mean, we have to be honest. They're all off to a high school somewhere else. It'll take you some time to adjust. Right? You have to tell me how things are. Please."

She stiffened. "Why do you want me to say I'm having problems?"

"No, stop, please. I don't. I just don't want you to avoid me, too much. Keep your privacy but talk to me when you want to." He hated feeling like a nagging, needy parent.

Sara's face went dull. "God, you're so filled with guilt. Please, Dad, get over it? We have to move on, motherless. Meanwhile, all my friends' parents are divorced, and you and Mom have been divorced for how long? My whole life. I'm moving on."

Jake was getting enervated. He should have eaten more for lunch. He folded his arms. "Hmm. All your friends' parents are divorced?"

"Yeah? It's like, most of them in North Bethesda and, God, it can't be any worse in Georgetown." She stretched her body to one side, still seated. "Don't worry about me taking drugs or joining a cult or getting some venereal disease. It was easy to steer clear of the losers…the pissy degenerates in North Bethesda. Same here." She twisted her torso again, to the other side. "I have to get through it somehow, eventually.

I just don't want to be a teenager, Dad. Please don't laugh at that. It's so boring being a teenager, and I'm only fourteen."

It took him a few seconds to truly believe Sara just made that speech and ended it that way. Jake often felt himself lurching from cautious to wound-up by his daughter and now he burst into laughter.

That stopped her twisting. Her glare broke down to more and more of a smile. "Stop, Dad, really." She groaned, "I know that's a ridiculous thing to say."

Jake had to force himself to stop laughing. It took him a few seconds. "It isn't. Damn. It isn't at all. It's just so filled with personal insight."

"Indulged child syndrome, Dad…you telling your only kid how brilliant she is. A bunch of my friends in North Bethesda are indulged children too. Then you wonder why we're all rude brats."

"You're not a rude brat. You'd better not be. You're not a rude brat."

"Indulged child syndrome again, Dad."

"Okay, okay." He grimaced. "Whew! I can't win that debate."

"Nope." Sara's grin warmed.

Jake sat down. "Ugh. Okay. Um." He pulled back his shoulders. "I think we should talk about college, just for a minute. Okay?"

She was expressionless and he had to slog along. "I just want to talk about it because you're starting high school. And we haven't really talked about it because college is way off in the distance, four years away. And because I don't want you getting caught up in all that crazy college pressure out there." He stopped to get her reaction.

Sara leaned forward on the stool, elbows on her knees, aiming her face at him, looking alerted to something. "I know

I have to get scholarship money or financial aid or whatever. I know that."

A darkness hit him. What threat level was Sara living under? He didn't know where any money was coming from, so he could only imagine how insecure Sara's future must seem to her.

Her eyes were on his hunched form. "I'm good at doing research, Dad. I've researched things online. And, I mean, indulged child Mom dropping the stupid news on us when she did and me stuck with the huge high school for this year might not help much for college applications in a few years."

He stood up. Sara had a way of suddenly purging a theme. Jake thought they were talking about what not to worry about – college. Then she added the money issue. Then it was also a conversation about Sara's mother leaving suddenly in June, too late for Sara to apply to any of the alternative public high schools in DC.

There was plenty to worry about.

As sanguine as possible, Jake said, "We'll do what we can this year and, with any luck, be fine. But please don't be disrespectful toward your mother."

He sat again. "You're saying your high school doesn't care about college?"

"Same as most schools. I know, even the Charter schools pretend to care, but really most teachers are just worn out by years of brat kids coming and going. Yeah, I looked it up and they only get a few kids into good colleges, whatever good means…like the ones ranked in the top one hundred. And hell, we all know college ratings games are all nuts. I just want financial aid for a solid degree, then I want a solid job."

It always amazed him how much she delved into things going on around her. He'd been planning to slowly get her to realize the expense of college and the fact that financial aid was so competitive and that she'd need lots and lots of it. She was somewhere beyond delving into all that?

Was she delving into life after college? At fourteen?

"Don't tell me you know what you want to pursue as a career."

She didn't blink. "Medical research. I've told you that. I just know. I shouldn't know yet, I know. I might change my mind, but I need something to look at in the future." She pointed her face at the long, dark floorboards, thinking. He wanted to hug her. He always wanted to, but this hyper-attenuated very young adult in front of him seemed too possessed to interrupt.

"All right. You're doing really well. And you can change your mind, or not."

"My grades were okay last year. I will get good grades this year. I'm taking honors courses and the teachers will be better than stupid Ms. Lucas last year."

"Okay. Good. You're taking *all* honors courses?" He tried to remember the coursework they discussed in the past.

"What? No, not history because of the C I got last year from Ms. Lucas, but almost everything else is honors. It's fine. It is."

"Right. Of course, it is. You got almost all A's last year. Fantastic. And I will help you with college applications, years from now. Just please enjoy high school? Okay? That's my advice. It's good to plan for the future, obviously, but you're only in high school once. Okay? I mean, work, sure. Do your best, but learn about the world and pay attention to, you know, calmly learning what you're good at and like."

Sara began looking downright exasperated, like she really, really wanted the conversation to end right there. She stood up and rotated on her heals, and so he stood up. Apparently, no point in belaboring the parental advice. She asked him about the etching lying on his counter and barely listened when he described what repairs it needed along the torn margins. She rocked back and forth from one foot to the other. He stopped speaking and, sure enough, she said she was hungry. At the door, she said she'd been looking forward all day to a bowl of that miso she bought over the weekend.

Jake bobbed his head, indicating go, see you later.

Sara cooked her soup in the kitchen and ate across the hallway in her room. He waited and then went to the kitchen and ate an apple and some nuts, reading some news on his phone. He washed his hands and returned to poking at the margins of the sickly old etching with his narrowest scalpel.

Around four-thirty they walked downstairs and out into the long-heated day, with tired, fermenting pavements and buildings off-gassing into the late afternoon late summer air. The smell was burnt vinegar not laundry vents now. And if the anxious mission of, *no more than three more months*, owned him, he had to hide that from Sara. She had enough to worry about. They walked along in the shade as much as they could to the air-conditioned Browsers' Bookstore farther west on M Street. Conversation was kept to the minimal and banal so they could both save their energy and hope to get on with things.

CHAPTER THREE

H is phone was ringing in his pocket. A few minutes after ten Jake stepped out of the shower to reach into his tan khakis hanging on the bathroom door. Simon said Gwen Minot was downstairs with the two works of art she wanted Jake to look at. Jake tried to unscramble some thoughts, standing on the wet cream-colored travertine stone tile floor, trying to dry off. What works of art? Did she mention particular works? His skin was damp under his cotton khakis and pale blue cotton, button down collar shirt. His hair was still damp. Those clothes were his summer professional enough mode, and they were fine, but he didn't want patches of wet coming through looking like sweat and he didn't even try to get socks on his damp feet. He just jammed barefoot into a pair of Mucks.

Trundling downstairs, caught in a rush of movement, trying to piece himself together, winded, he coughed out, "Sorry. You got me in the middle of a shower."

Simon laughed. "You should have told me."

"Oh, I'm so sorry. I should have called first," Gwen said through clenched teeth, her shoulders up.

"No. No problem at all. Really. Who takes a shower at ten in the morning? Uh, but I'm clean."

All three laughed roughly, shuffling around, Gwen coughing and then turning back to her artwork. "So they're both by William T. Williams. One's a drawing and the other's a hand-colored etching."

Jake bowed his head. "William T. Williams. I saw an exhibition somewhere…can't remember where."

"Yeah, I love the guy's art." Gwen was holding the leather edges of a large canvas portfolio.

Simon stayed back a step. "Okay, well maybe the best thing would be for you to take them up to the conservation studio and Jake can talk to you about what treatment they need. I mean, we've already covered the matting and framing issues. Would that make sense?"

She nodded slowly back at Simon, not looking sure.

As always, Simon had work to get to, so as he helped Gwen tie the three strings of her portfolio, Jake waited, wondering what to say, his stolen glances telling him Gwen Minot was uncomfortable. Normally, he'd just look at artworks there and then, in the frame shop, but he knew -- Simon was sending her up to the big-league studio. She'd see how professional and cool the whole operation was and bring in more art. People were impressed a few times in the past, but Jake remembered this woman telling them the last time she didn't have much more art.

"I do have a camera, a monitor on up there," Jake said. "I have to record things when clients are there for my security too. But we can stay here."

Gwen's polite smile was already more of a rictus gape.

Jake added, "Really, we can just stay here."

Something about Jake's emphasis, or maybe not wanting to insult him, seemed to reverse her view. "No, that's fine," she said quietly. "I'd like to see the conservation lab or studio."

He was unconvinced but moved along. They shuffled between the separate matting and framing tables, out through the screeching metal door in the back of the frame shop. He turned as she flinched.

"Sorry. Yeah, sorry. I have to oil that." His echo was short lived in the hollow, dusty stairwell as their shoes scrapped, him leading up the concrete steps, all his vital signs upended. Did he close his bathroom door? He wasn't expecting someone upstairs. At least he did turn on the air earlier.

Inside, the four big overhead copper lights opened up the large old industrial white plaster hallway and his phone's app turned on a camera in a corner ten feet above them. His bedroom and bathroom doors were closed, fortunately.

She was faced forward ahead, stopped, waiting.

He aimed his face, uselessly. "That's the studio door at the end on the right."

Into the studio and, sure enough, Gwen stayed silent. After he pointed his phone at the camera in the corner above the microscope Jake remained a few feet away, his eyes on her portfolio that she placed in the middle of the open stretch of black soapstone countertop. She untied the strings and pulled out the two artworks. Both were colorful abstractions, almost Color Field in style, the larger one around twenty by thirty inches, and the other one a bit smaller. They were beautiful and Jake said that, still a few feet to her side.

"Yeah, I'm afraid they got damaged in the last move my husband and I made."

Jake got a foot closer and leaned toward the larger drawing, following the soft white paper's three-inch fold with his finger an inch above the top of the image. The smaller one was dented all along one side.

"I see this a lot. But at least it's a soft wove paper and might flatten a bit under some damp blotters and weight…if you want. It would be a two-hour charge." He straightened up and put his hands in his pockets, still looking down at the art. He could have told her that downstairs.

She glanced at him. "Great. Let's do that. Thanks."

"Okay. Great." He got his treatment agreement form from a shelf under the counter, and she signed it, him indulging in a quick eyeful. She had on jeans today with another pair of elegant leather sandals and a short sleeve dark orange thin collarless shirt. Her neck was noticeably narrow, linear, contrasting with the smooth curve of her face. That hint of Chanel Number Five started reaching him when she arrived downstairs.

She handed him the signed form and he thanked her. No earrings on her, no jewelry, except an impressive diamond wedding ring. Although Jake didn't know a thing about jewels, so he realized he was just assuming it was impressive.

She began to look around. "This studio's so amazingly beautiful. How long have you been here? I forget what your brochure says."

"About fifteen years."

She widened her eyes. "Wow. Yeah, I thought about going into art conservation at one point in college."

"Really?" What happened?"

"Oh, I forgot, I guess. I don't think I would have been good at it at all. I don't have the finesse. I'm too clumsy. That's why these things have creases." Her smile that had been hesitant before, filled up her face.

Jake laughed and then she did.

"So, is this northern light?" Gwen looked at the expansive row of industrial windows.

"Yeah. Well, north-east facing. So almost the same indirect light most of the day."

"I bet you designed all this yourself."

An obscure gleam in her perfect brown eyes drew him way in as he huffed, "Uh, well, I did, with help constructing it from Simon." He looked away, adding, "But I have to admit the windows and doors, the raw materials, were here and that was a huge start."

She arched backward, looking up at the tall wooden ceiling.

"Yeah, Simon had to help me with that," he said, leaning on the counter with his left hand, at least five feet away. "So do you collect anything other than twentieth century and contemporary art? I don't want to get too nosy."

"No. I do. I actually like older stuff too. It depends. I mean, when I go to museums I find myself looking at nineteenth century stuff. I love French paintings and drawings and prints from that whole century. But who doesn't?"

"Liars and illiterates. I'm the same way."

"You're a cliché too."

"I am. Yup. Yup, not hip-cool to say your favorite painter is Cezanne or Mary Cassatt. Right? But I'm sticking with them."

"Good!"

Their tame remarks reverberated as they both took a few seconds to stop smiling aimlessly.

Jake filled in, "You had to go to Paris or somewhere in France apparently to get inspired back then. Right?"

"Then New York, Chicago and LA in the twentieth century. Jazz and movies."

"Wow, yeah, exactly. Wow, jazz and movies. And paperback novels." He pushed off the counter and stood upright, galvanized.

"Now where for inspiration?" Gwen stayed positioned toward the counter, her head turned to him.

He had to think. "Uhh, anywhere. Everywhere online. Right?"

She turned to him and put her hand on her hip. "Yeah, endlessly."

He paused, wrinkling his face. "We're talking about hellbent decadence and violent disorder, right?"

She bent at the waist and laughed with a perverse crackle that sank into the center of her -- her body shaking and her eyes watering. He joined right in but with the contented, groaning sound he made when he was caught by the laughter of someone else. He barely moved as he watched her.

Yeah," she sighed, taking in a deep breath and shaking her head. She breathed out slowly, gathering herself. "Anyway, anyway. At least you can get some creases out of my little bits of art on paper."

"Creases, right. Tiny, tiny creases in a world rupturing apart."

Now, his starkness wasn't funny or clever and seemed to poison the air for any more gentle canoodling. He longed to indulge in canoodling with the phenomenal woman in front of him, but he wasn't even smiling anymore. He couldn't.

"Anyway," he said, feeling the ugly anxieties of his life showing as he was stopped, adding nothing. The unwieldy quiet got them redirected by her steering herself away, no longer looking at him. And with their tasks complete they thanked each other and made their way downstairs, saying nothing until he pointed to the side door. "That's an option."

She opened it, the creaking metal adding harshly to the coursing street sounds, as she stepped outside. Half turning to him she said, "Thanks."

All movement was happening on its own and he didn't want her to go. "Thank you. I'll call you when they're done, in a couple of weeks. Thanks."

"Great. Whenever. Thanks," she said, still in profile.

She walked away and he closed the door and puffed out his cheeks as he scraped along alone up the stairs. There were a few flirtations in the past with women in his studio, but nothing like what just happened. His heart was banging but it had been the whole time with her.

After turning off his cameras he walked in small circles in his studio, looking down, reliving her perfect hair, all those naturally silky coils, fine, soft tufts springing three inches, some four inches, up and out, urging him in, in, in.

He put her works of art between damp blotters into the press and went for a walk.

* * * * *

Gwen arrived home wanting to readjust after meeting with that Jake Holtz. She'd take a few other works she thought needed conservation treatment but those would be pretty much the last major things needed to complete the house, unfortunately. It was unfortunate he was so damned attractive, so she just started wandering around her rooms, her sumptuous rooms, to convene with herself. It was her day off and she should wallow in her house. No appointments with the Arts Council, no cleaners because it was Tuesday.

She walked slowly through the rectangular kitchen, the rectangular dining room, rectangular living room and rectangular library. She always told Larny it's not finished until it's finished. It's endlessly iffy until finally it all comes together in some mysterious way and forms. So, how were her rectangles?

Yup, finished. The original proportion of length, width and height was perfect when they bought the house. Restoring it all allowed her to bask in it now, satiated, looking, absorbing the daylight filled Georgian rooms, settling in her favorite, the living room.

All that architectural bliss seemed to be giving her time and space for her brain to drift. She noticed her brain drifting the last couple of days, and each time she found herself hovering in a space at least partially occupied by Jake Holtz.

But he was a stranger.

She stood still and rallied herself, grunting, "Time for the exception that proves the rule principle, Gwen."

She needed that main principle of hers, discovered when she was only nine or ten from some dialogue in a TV show she barely remembered now. The principle had to be applied at regular intervals later. She had to raise herself or die young and knew that early on, and she had to think as clearly as a kid could, making her next moves out into the world. The *exception that proves the rule principle* always worked as a basic frame of reference, keeping her from getting caught-up in some distraction in a world of crazy, dangerous distractions. To understand something or to produce anything positive, you had to understand the way distractions were only exceptions. And exceptions were very, very good at proving some rule.

Right then the rule was the gorgeous hunk of architecture around her. So Gwen tucked into her window seat in her new-old living room. All the work, all the mess, was worth it. She only bragged to herself but the whole townhouse was incredibly stunning. She loved it almost as much as the house she designed for Larny and her in Georgetown, which was saying something. That took her five years to finish because she did the whole thing, exterior and interior, between projects designing other people's houses. The Georgetown house was new and so was most of her work for clients and she wanted to try an old house restoration. So, the big antique house she was sitting in now fulfilled that wish and more. She looked down and felt the soft, dense material below her. It was a floral embossed crimson velvet cushion under one of the two huge twelve-over-twelve Georgian windows in a room built in seventeen-ninety.

She stood up, looking around. The beautiful fireplace with the large mustard-yellow Georgian mantle was the main feature in the room when they bought the house and it still was, but much more complimented now by the walls and floors. The special oil based deeply penetrating varnish gave off a luscious dark oak shimmer to the thick, centuries old floorboards. The pale pink glossy paint on the high plastered ceiling complimented soft sheen, dark original cherry wainscoting covering the lower portion of the walls, with flat sky-blue walls above.

The rest of the downstairs' painted plaster walls – glossy gold in the library and glossy peach in the kitchen – gave a sensual hum to the sensational place, in her humble, well-honed opinion.

At night she might light a room or two with candles for an hour. Larny soaked it up too. Some wine, a fire in the hooded open fireplace, and there didn't seem to be any end to the satisfaction of designing and then living in places like her Old Town Alexandria townhouse, one of the oldest architectural grandees in the old area.

Then there was the exception. She saw Jake before, somewhere in Georgetown, she thought. But since meeting him she was in a state of euphoria one minute and self-disgust the next. It started the first time she saw him in the frame shop. He seemed to look stunned at her too. The way he looked at her, God, what was that? She was thirty-six years old, not nineteen. She didn't even know the guy. But he was so damned attractive in some way. That long, lean, strong body and high cheekbone face, and his smile, with that mature, distant, polite way of his was gorgeous, wild gorgeous.

She sat down again, same spot, trying to relax, calm down. She shouldn't have gone up into his apartment. She knew that. Why did she just go along with their suggestion, that Simon and Jake? Stupid.

She'd always known all the splendors of money and top-drawer education offered no magical protection from life. Admitting that kept her wary, her brain sharp, she hoped. She sure as hell never bragged. Princeton and Yale had so many stupid, stupid braggarts. *Jaded jackasses,* Larny loved calling them. Pathetic to watch so many of them, sure enough, make piles of money after graduating and then fall into drugs or depression, or just self-righteous smugness.

Meeting and falling deeply in love and eventually marrying Larny while they were both in graduate school was her luckiest break by far. She knew that. For the two of them, she and Larny were the on-going proven rule.

*   *   *   *   *

It was Tuesday afternoon, only two hours after Gwen Minot left when he ground his teeth and reminded himself out loud that she was married. Jake saw his immediate, tormented future. There was an acidic back he had to get off a World War One poster the Simmons Gallery brought in. There were one or two other jobs he'd do while taking the blotters off Gwen's artworks and looking sideways in raking light to see the wrinkles more accurately. He hated having to wait two weeks to see her again, but there was no rushing damp paper with creases. Meanwhile all he'd get paid, all he estimated, was two hundred dollars. Who'd pay more than that to flatten some minor creases in soft paper? Pretty much no one. That was the problem.

There was nothing else to do so he went downstairs. Simon was in front to one side talking to an old couple and Sean, Luis and Fiona were all at two merged tables putting posters into cheap metal frames. The posters were sold from five large wooden boxes next to the door. Simon sold around a thousand posters a year, mostly to students -- about a quarter of the posters framed, another quarter mounted to a backboard and the rest just rolled in a tube.

Jake walked through, heading to the front, away from Simon. It was a few months back when he stopped interacting with people in the frame shop. Sara arrived and the full-time emotional and occupational effort of bolstering their lives upstairs spent him. Actually, it was hard the last couple of years for him to join in the ongoing, buoyant enterprise downstairs. Simon was doing really well, and Simon was always busy. They'd been roommates the first two years at George Washington University, a couple of miles away in Foggy Bottom, all those years ago. They bonded right away, partly by laughing about the obvious university-diversity set-up -- Jake was white and Simon was black. Simon was from Bethesda, half an hour away and Jake was from Frederick, Maryland, an hour and a half away. More bonding was easy once they explored what they had in common, both being from Mid-Atlantic, middle-class suburbia. It was college bonding.

They faded apart after graduation as Jake moved to Delaware for graduate school and Simon started working at his father's frame shop. It wasn't until Jake was thirty-two that he approached Simon, suggesting a conservation studio above the frame shop. They hadn't seen each other for over a decade but Simon bonded with Jake on that idea right away.

The area above the frame shop was used for storage or offices or as an apartment for two centuries but it had atrophied. Jake and Simon were eager to renovate what they could, and since Simon's father died a year before, Jake and Simon shook hands on a future that was open to new prospects.

Now Simon was always busy, and it was not because of Jake's conservation studio. Jake stood at the front of the frame shop, beyond the creamy white quartzite counter, all the way to the window to the right of the extra-large metal front door. He didn't want to go out and walk around town. He should stay there in case someone came in and needed work. He put his brochure in galleries recently. He was also trying to pay more attention to his social media accounts and had put up more pictures of his work. You never knew if someone might turn up without calling or texting first.

Meanwhile, Sara was at school in her second week. He tried asking her how things were going but she resisted, so he backed off. She'd say something if there were a reason to, he hoped.

Not able to go anywhere, Jake let his mind travel out the window. There was a lot of activity on the street at nine-thirty in the morning. Post Labor Day, tourists were thinner on the ground, but students filled any empty spaces. Pockets of the District, like Georgetown, were officially back to being adolescent Collegeland as Washington's many universities opened their doors. M Street in September was always nothing but those students clustering and marauding. Along with Wisconsin Avenue, it was where Georgetown University students shopped, ate and drank, but it was in the center of Washington and it was beautiful and stimulated whatever gathering-consuming skills adolescents had, so other university students would gather around too. Over the coming months the clusters would break into smaller fragments, until the sidewalks would be mobbed at times, but with more couples and fewer groups and more and more single students, looking nervous about something like an exam or a bad date or eternal desolation.

How would Sara do surrounded by so many older adolescents? Sara already hated being a teenager.

CHAPTER FOUR

September 8, Friday

Gwen was coming in and Jake waited downstairs at four with the frame shop occupied, sure enough, by clusters of students buying posters.

On time, she squeaked through the large metal front door, with its large spring hinges jangling. She had a small portfolio under one arm and Jake pointed to the far end of the frame shop's stone counter, trying to avoid the damage potential of the throngs around them.

"Yeah, I have five drawings." Gwen turned her head to Jake who was pleased she was there and pleased she had more work. But both of them had stooped shoulders and with strained glances around, projected their concern about the noisy, crowded space.

Jake's warning to himself, from days of sober thinking, to avoid taking Gwen, married, phenomenal Gwen, upstairs, died as soon as Gwen phoned him Thursday afternoon saying she had some art for him to look at and she didn't want to wait until the two Williams works were flat and dry. Now Jake made brave attempts to look nonplussed as they packed-up and moved along, electrically charged air clinging to them.

Switched on lights and cameras led to the studio. Jake took a breath to relax and aimed at the assignment in front of him, a group of five French nineteenth century drawings -- two by Tissot, one by Boulanger, one by Raffet, and one by Delaroche -- garden scenes, street scenes. They were mostly small. The largest sheet was no larger than fourteen by eighteen inches. It was an impressive group. The problem was foxing. She actually used the word, foxing, and Jake was impressed once again. Not many people used that word and he said that.

"It's from mold in the paper, right? Sometimes metallic salts in the paper? I learned that from dealers and curators who say those little dark spots are called foxing."

Jake was making an effort to not puff up, but he was sinking into those brown, brown eyes. "Why do I think you could just do this yourself?"

She shrugged, smiling and he resorted to his standard speech. "Uhh, the thing is, I can try to put the paper on the suction table and spot bleach some of them where I'd very carefully use a small Q Tip with some bleach on it. I can be very careful not to get too much in the paper, so rings won't form and anyway the less bleach the better. But it might only be moderately successful. See, the paper here is all, you know, fairly old, so it has over a hundred and fifty years of dirt in it."

"Yeah, I love it when the British call things like these, *time stained*. Isn't that great?"

Jake barked out a laugh, waving his head along with her.

She aimed herself at the counter again. "But so, tell me, do you think it's not worth doing that spot bleaching on these?"

He stepped closer to the works to finish saying what he did think. "Yeah, spot bleaching should be the last resort and it'll only get rid of bits of the discoloration and can leave rings as I said, although not if I'm careful. But look." He leaned over the counter, pointing at the drawing closest to him. "Most of the foxing isn't in the image on this one." He moved his finger over the next one. "This has less all around. This one has it again, mostly in the margins. This one, same thing. This one's a bit of a mess."

He stood straight up, biting his bottom lip the way he did when he was deliberating. She waited and he said, "If you want, I could do a couple of things, like spray some of them with alkaline water, then dry them on blotters and remove some of the soiling. The foxing will get reduced, too, but if the paper gets back into a damp environment again, which is inevitable eventually, it will happen again…spots."

"What kids used to call pimples. God. I'm sorry. I try to keep these things clean and dry."

He put his head down and coughed out a laugh.

She said, "I'm a bad custodian."

Now, Jake gagged, lost, laughing along with her. After a few seconds he managed to say, "Ugh, damn. Bad custodian. That's the best damned thing anyone's ever said here."

She made a pinched face. "Really?"

Face beaming, he said, "Absolutely without a doubt." He tried to keep from grabbing her by turning back to her artworks. "Anyway, what I'm trying to say is, I can get these things looking better and more stable with about four hours billing work on some water treatment and about four hours on a bit of spot bleaching where it seems to interfere with the image. You know, instead of murdering the paper with chemicals."

She smiled stiffly. Normally his camera neutralized most of the closeted intimacy of his studio, but in Gwen's presence the camera was neutralized. He didn't move or say a thing and she pursed her lips and gazed at the artwork laid out. "Great, that sounds terrific. I don't want to frame these. I want to just mat them. That should take care of them, acid-free mats. I'll email Simon. But thanks so much."

He nodded and she stepped back and sighed, looking around one more time. "God, you could be a designer yourself from the looks of things. Can I see your kitchen? Sorry, I realize how weird and pushy that is. Go put some things away first if you want to." She forced a smile through blushing.

Jake was sidewacked. "My kitchen?"

She pulled her head back while lowering her eyebrows, and he wanted to smooth over her embarrassment. Thinking fast, he said, "My kitchen. All right, tell you what. Let me go get my daughter. I can let you two introduce yourselves while I put a few things away in my little, oddball kitchen."

Gwen's face tightened and her chest caved in enough to notice. "Oh, you have a daughter?"

"I do. She's home from school, in her room across from the kitchen. She's fourteen, almost fifteen."

Jake watched Gwen's eyes grow fuzzy as some distant voice inside her rose. "Wow. That's great. Yeah, what a great place to grow up."

All the flirting was abruptly rocked by one true confession, one major, true confession. And he knew he had to follow through. "My daughter, Sara, lived in Bethesda with her mother until last June when her mother moved away. So now I get to have her with me all the time."

It felt so right laying that out for some reason. Pride? He had a daughter, a life? He was showing fidelity to his daughter? He just knew any actual structural reinforcement in the world started with his life with Sara.

Meanwhile, Gwen's body stiffened even more. "I'd love to meet her sometime. I don't have to see your kitchen. I was being a goof."

Jake was a couple of steps toward the door. He wanted to see Gwen meet Sara, and without a doubt, Sara should meet someone so cool and accomplished. But Gwen's face remained unusually blank, so he stopped.

"I can just gently ask her what she's up to. I'm afraid she's bored. Is that okay?" He spoke with enough dead-on sincerity to convince her, apparently, because Gwen relaxed her face and nodded. He left.

Jake knew Sara had an endless fascination with adults. It might have been her aspiring to be one, or it might have been her curiosity about the big world out there. It was one of the most unusual traits in Sara he picked up on when she was very young, even five or six, and maybe more astonishingly, in the last couple of teen years. Introduce Sara to an adult in the studio or on the street and she fixed her eyes and made every effort to connect.

Sara was sitting on her bed with her back against its nineteenth century walnut headboard, a tapestry covered cushion lodged in the small of her back. She was looking at something on her computer and didn't flinch when her father invited her to meet someone.

They entered the studio, and everyone became very formal, Gwen stepping forward to shake Sara's hand, after which Sara smiled and stood straight, hands behind her back. Very briefly, Jake thought of turning off his camera, but instead of assuming Gwen was suddenly no longer a client, left it on.

He told Sara about Gwen being an architect and art collector.

Gwen asked, "What about you, Sara? Discovered any subjects you especially like yet?"

"Um, well it's like, just the first year of high school but I like science, I think."

"Do you? Great. I liked science."

"When did you know you wanted to be an architect?"

"Oh, early in college, I guess. I just took a couple of art history and architectural history courses and got excited."

Sara bobbed her head slowly, looking less than fully satisfied, and Gwen stepped it up. "To be honest I went into history to start with but wasn't wild about the courses. Then, after a while I discovered how much I loved the history of architecture and design courses. Then I went to graduate school…maybe too soon."

Sara stayed silent, so Jake asked, "Too soon?"

Gwen rotated a few inches to face him, her neck extended, her voice taut. "Yeah, I went straight from college to graduate school. And I think, now, it might have been better to wait a couple of years. I mean, I worked for an architectural firm after graduate school and that was intense and not always in a productive way. Yeah, a bunch of my friends took breaks and seemed better for it. My husband took a break after graduate school and worked low pressure dumb jobs for a while."

"To avoid burnout?" Sara asked.

Gwen turned to her. "Yup. But at this point I've been working by and for myself for about seven years and that can get just a little bit too, what's the phrase…self-inclusive?" She pointed her eyes to the side sardonically.

"Self-inclusive," Jake parroted. "Damn, that sums it up. And I know." Jake wanted to hear more. "Let me get another chair." He stepped to the corner and carried the third old metal backed, wooden bar stool to his daughter and grabbed the one he sat on for work. All of them settled several feet apart as Sara answered Gwen's question about how high school was going. Sara's few unenthusiastic words reached an ambivalent denouement with, "At least it's not too far away."

Gwen sighed, "Georgetown does have its merits, beyond its great beauty. So many things to do. Bookstores, cafes, parks…the Canal." Her eyes stayed on Sara, whose intense expression began to match Gwen's.

Jake wanted everyone to relax. "And students," he joked, and added, "Tourists."

Gwen's face flushed and she looked frustrated. Jake stood and reached up to pull down two pale green shades to block some light and create some movement. As he did, he told Sara about Gwen living in Georgetown for years and Alexandria now.

"Um, right." Gwen bent her head back and up toward Jake, then back to Sara. "So I know there's something great about both places."

"But, like, where would you live if you could live anywhere?" Sara asked.

Gwen's body remained stiffer than Jake had seen before. "Live anywhere, wow. I guess Nigeria. Went there twice. Austin, Texas. Wells, England. Rome. I've been to Rome a few times. Alexandria, Virginia. Do I get more than one place?"

Sara shrugged, smiling.

Gwen asked, "So is your point that we can't have everything?"

"I'm not sure I had a point. But that sounds like a good one."

Jake grinned and stood up, disappointed, because Gwen was standing. Sara slid off her stool to join them just as Jake suggested Gwen view his kitchen before leaving. Gwen agreed, miming a self-caricature with a clenched, toothy grin and closed eyes. Then she shook Sara's hand.

"Very nice meeting you. You know, I've had a hankering to go to the National Gallery of Art and I was thinking of going in a couple of days…Saturday. Want to meet up there, you and your father? Do you like art museums? I'm sure your father does."

The suggestion took Jake by surprise, but Sara reacted with instant enthusiasm, saying yes, she liked art museums and yes, she'd like going with Gwen. The new triad's magnetic field whirred down the hulking, brightly lit, shiny white hallway and stopped at the kitchen doorway with Sara excitedly saying good-bye across from them and closing her large metal bedroom door.

*　*　*　*　*

All through dinner Jake had to listen to Sara describe Gwen's ultimate coolness. Jake wasn't feeling cool. He felt like he had a fever. It was like some combination of being drunk and having pneumonia.

He nodded and ate with every emote from Sara stoking his need to recover, refocus. If Gwen brought in a bit more art, he'd be able to pay some bills. So he had to concentrate and hope for the best, for the interim, for the next few weeks. What he couldn't do was imagine Gwen and him and Sara in two days at the National Gallery. At the end of dinner Sara said, again, she couldn't wait to go there, and Jake only nodded again, his head aching, his heart falling down an empty elevator shaft.

Now, in his room finally, he went straight for the Internet. He figured Gwen was too cool-understated to have much of a presence on social media and sure enough her Facebook page was a conservative and low-profile business account. And he wasn't about to ask to friend her. That would seem freakishly invasive. Typing her name on a Google search produced a result after a few additions, like, *Washington* and then, *Alexandria, Virginia.* There was an independent school blog writing about something called Bardon School. Jake wondered if that name sounded familiar as he clicked on the item.

Bardon steering committee greets new recruits. Tanya Cottingham is greeted by Gwen Minot, Chair of the Bardon School Steering Committee on June third. As an upcoming first year student, Tanya is currently completing eighth grade at Franklin Middle School in Baltimore, Maryland and was chosen as one of five recipients of this year's, **Gwen Jackson Minot Scholarship***.*

There were two pictures of Gwen and some other adults standing around a young black girl, everyone smiling – the girl looking nervous and shy. The name was coming back to him. Bardon School was some fancy boarding school somewhere. He'd heard of various stately people, like a couple of presidents in the distant past, attached to that name. Gwen's mystique was going from scary to intimidating. With a few serious relationships in his past, he knew the first stage in being in love with someone was exhilarating and overwhelming no matter what. He shook his head and sat forward. Late summer would turn to late fall before he knew it. By Thanksgiving – at the latest -- he had to move somewhere for work. Still, he wanted to look.

GWEN JACKSON MINOT ARCHITECTURE

It wasn't surprising her website was elegant with beautiful fonts and colors in a clear and simple layout. Her background was described briefly. She had a BA from Princeton and a Master of Architecture degree from Yale. There were photographs of a few exquisitely beautiful buildings. One was a rusted steel and lime rendered house in Arlington, Virginia. Along with the exposed red rusted steel, it had a wooden shingle roof and large horizontal windows. There was another house in a suburb of Alexandria, Virginia that was a gorgeous combination of long, thick slabs of rough granite for siding below vertical black charred boards leading to a rusted metal roof. There were some additions to other buildings and then historical, renovated rooms – some Victorian, some older, some twentieth century.

There was a client list at the end. Jake poked at the site for fifteen minutes.

He sat back in his mid-twentieth century red leather armchair, stretching slowly, twisting his chest and neck, looking around his space, his rental space. He stopped seeing things after so many years, but with a bit of effort now he could see his apartment was real enough, just not up to the level of Gwen's designs. His large bedroom amplified the architecture already there. Maybe Gwen genuinely liked his apartment. He looked up to his ceiling where the ribs of the building, the long white painted rafters, repeated themselves again and again to the wall opposite, over thirty feet away. By painting the brick walls and wooden ceiling white, Jake managed to enhance the room's volume and also set off the oil-based painted dark gray, long, wide old floorboards. His ornate, gothic revival antique walnut bed at the far wall and his two patina-rich pine chests of drawers came off as almost cozy in the abundance of airy indoor space. His Georgetown apartment was the only thing he ever designed, fifteen years earlier.

He leaned an elbow on the arm of his chair and rested his head in his hand. His computer nestled on his chair's other arm. The only light at nine-thirty at night came from an old, college days, IKEA floor lamp Jake had next to his chair. He spent a lot of time in that bedroom. Once he didn't have a living room, he started sitting in his bedroom chair in the corner, reading or looking at his laptop. The old chair was next to his bedroom's two front windows. Some books were piled on the floor next to it and he had more stacks of books in the closet next to his bed. It was all feeling old and stale these days, since young and vibrant Sara moved in a few months ago, and since looking at Gwen's designs two minutes ago.

Gwen's web page said her husband's name was Lawrence. Against his better judgment, Jake grabbed his computer and typed in Lawrence Minot, Washington DC and sure enough a few things showed. Google had Lawrence Minot in an old article in the Washington Post, writing about him giving money to Colgate University. The article, with a picture on top, said he was on the board there. Jake only skimmed three more articles about him and then a blog came up: *L. Minot's Business Review*. Lawrence Minot's basic resume was there at the top. Colgate as an undergraduate, then Yale for an MBA and a law degree.

Jake meandered online clicking on dead ends until sure enough, another article in the Washington Post wrote about a fundraising effort. Colgate University, after two years, successfully raised over one hundred million dollars for its endowment, *through great personal effort by Lawrence and Gwen Minot.* It said, "*The Minots put five million dollars into the pot to get things started.*" Jake turned off his computer.

He sat still and tried not to let his feelings of insecurity fester but fester they did.

It was too early to go to sleep. The collectors in Jake's past weren't as beautiful or Goddamned charming as Gwen -- or as rich. He turned his computer back on. He went to the Bardon website. Over eight hundred acres in Delaware, established in 1747, it was the fourth oldest boarding school in America. There were stunning pictures of stone buildings, old and new, with fields of green around and between. He veered off, searching for more articles on Lawrence Minot and, of course, there were more. The guy owned his own company. The story of her chiseled, strong-jawed, handsome husband, who at thirty-nine was CEO of a company unknown to Jake, Tiros Data, was enough to dig a huge moat beyond which Gwen actually lived her life.

He searched for something online to take his mind off her. Normally it was an effort to read news items without more and more of them, one after another, avalanching, so he went right to YouTube. He clicked on the first thing he saw under early TV shows. It was an archaic TV episode of, *Rin Tin Tin*. The mid nineteen-fifties show was so dated and raw, it worked to distract him for twenty minutes.

He shifted semi-consciously into bed.

* * * * *

Growing up, Sara always loved her weekend room in Georgetown, but now she felt it was more hers, a lot more. Whatever she brought with her from North Bethesda belonged, lodged with her now, in some way more stubbornly and more permanently. The quilted bed cover, paid for from babysitting money and claimed as a souvenir on a middle school outing to Lancaster Pennsylvania, never looked right in the bland little nineteen-nineties house her mother bought after Sara was born. It made perfect sense on her antique walnut bed now. Her nineteenth century school desk fit perfectly in the corner of the room with the ancient, wonky Windsor chair her father gave her years ago. Sara was very proud of the museum posters she had on the walls. She bought those downstairs over the summer.

She walked from her bed to her desk, looking out one of her two huge windows onto M Street. Outside was the highest level of refined street bustle, of trees and handsome, solid buildings, all coated in city nightlight sparkle.

Feeling a weekend kind of sharp-edged renewal, Sara's assessment came to things being so far, so good with her father leaving her alone the right amount. It wasn't like her mother actively tried to smother her in the past, all of the time. It was just the unrelenting uncoolness of her mother that sucked up all the air. But now the potential was always there for sadness from Dear Old Dad. And, well, so far, he wasn't so sad around her, like she was a wounded stray kitten or worse, a rejected orphan in the storm. All Sara knew right then, at that point in her life, was she had to raise herself. Her father would help her, but she knew when she turned fourteen, before her stupid damned mother had to self-gratify somewhere else, away from her only child, that her mother, her teachers, her friends and maybe even her father, were all out for themselves and the sooner you faced that, the better.

She swung her head and upper torso back and forth, weaving herself in broad swaths away from part of that so sad analysis. No. No. Her father was not just out for himself. She loved him and he loved her. Did anyone outside see her swing back and forth?

There'd be some time in the future when she'd analyze what went wrong with her mother, but since it wasn't Sara's fault, and Sara was sure enough of that to move on, then she should postpone thinking about it. She really just knew that. She knew she was young and had time. She even knew any decent psychologist would say she was repressing something major, or filled with denial, or something. She had to postpone worrying about that too. Maybe it was good they couldn't afford a psychoanalyst.

Feeling adequately self-coached for the moment, she turned away from the window in front of her desk and looked around her room. It was a very, very cool room and it was hers, even if she and her father didn't own it.

CHAPTER FIVE

66 "Today the day you're going to the National Gallery?" Larny kissed Gwen on the back of her neck, standing behind her. She was momentarily mesmerized. Even in the morning, in the kitchen, her neck being kissed opened a few hormonal floodgates somewhere deep inside her.

Still, she managed to remember what she couldn't forget for the past twenty-four hours. "Yeah, at ten, when it opens."

Larny removed himself to sit across the table and then pour soy milk into his cereal. Gwen watched, poised in her usual place in the built-in booth next to the window -- all planned and project managed by her. She was finished with her cereal.

"Coffee's really good this morning. I like the old coffee plunger." Larny was in his own contented zone. The weekend might explain part of that, but Gwen had to assume it was genuine when he consistently expressed his love for her architectural work. He was contented in Gwen's design.

His phone gave off its jingly version of Coltrane from his jacket side pocket. Larny grumbled, "Ignoring it, I am, on a Saturday."

"Let's just stick with the old coffee plunger." She said, devising a conversation. "Maybe it was fate that broke the new, elaborate machine."

"Yup, fate. Fate hates elaborate new things, like the elaborate new guy, Jonas, we hired."

"Still not a good hire?"

"Nope, I really don't think so. It's really, really not getting better. He's still so damned emotional." Larny sat straight, sipping some coffee. "He got lunatic category weird again at yesterday's meeting, asking odd questions, practically shouting. Damn. I don't know. I really don't know. I almost feel sorry for him. Almost. I feel sorrier for the rest of us. It has everyone on edge."

Gwen looked at Larny. He was on edge? He didn't look like he was on edge.

Larny ate. The coffee was really good, she thought, now that Larny mentioned it. A few words revolved around the weather being a tiny bit cooler finally and plans for dinner at Aaron and Joe's new condo at seven. Aaron and Joe were very excited about their condo and Gwen was worried they might ask her for help redesigning it. She didn't want to do little interior decorating jobs but would swallow her pride for friends. Gwen didn't say any of that to Larny.

She was looking too forward to going to the museum and she couldn't help reasoning that the new hire, Jonas, was all the more reason for Larny to want to get into his quiet office today. He spent something like half of their Saturdays at his office and had for the last few years. She seldom felt put-out by that because he always checked with her first and he usually got back home by late afternoon. At least he didn't play golf or whatever.

He was sitting there reading some blog on his phone, eating his organic, whole grains, nuts and berries cereal. She introduced him to that cereal, along with the rest of his healthy diet and exercise. She introduced him to architecture and art. He introduced her to lasting saneness, to both feet on the ground, the ground that grew him. No gangs, no drug deaths, no prostitution, no murdered parents in Larny's background. He was the exception to the rule of prevailing decadence and destruction in the world at large. There was no better way for him to be there for her the way she needed. She knew that.

It didn't hurt that he was entirely hunky, although she wished he hadn't put on that smooth dark blue silk jacket with that smooth white cotton shirt today. The attraction hurt.

They both got up from their breakfast booth at the same time and rinsed off their dishes and put them in the dishwasher.

Ten minutes later Larny hugged her, kissed her cheek and was heading out finally.

Gwen took in a deep breath and went upstairs to get dressed.

*   *   *   *   *

Jake asked Sara if she wanted to walk. She did. He wanted to save cab or Uber fare but didn't say that. He saw her peripherally, giving off the look of an alert adolescent animal on a new hunt as they weaved through central DC.

Ten minutes later he said, "I haven't been to the National Gallery for over two years. It's been, what, four years for you?"

She nodded. He knew he was talking to himself. Maybe he wasn't the only one nervous about this date with Gwen. Walking and not talking was fine.

The forty-five-minute hike numbed some of his nerves and it was a windy enough day to keep Jake from overheating. They got there in time to see Gwen pulling up in a taxi fifty feet ahead on Fourth Street. They all waved and walked toward each other.

A few hellos and smiles and they entered the I M Pei East Building of the museum, into the atrium of marble, topped with a ceiling of tall, jagged glass triangles each framed in shafts of gray metal. Like everyone, they looked up. It was the sensation of a lot of light through a lot of pieces of outwardly pointed glass. Floating between them and the infinite ceiling was a giant Calder mobile.

"You know, I always want to come here because I love this old modern entrance but what about you and Sara? We could go across to the West Building if you'd rather look at nineteenth century or older pictures." Gwen buttoned up her thin dark green cardigan as she said this.

Jake shook his head and looked at Sara, who said, "No, this is great for me. Can we do both?"

That surprised Jake. Sara seldom lasted longer than an hour in a museum. Gwen looked happy with Sara's response, and they headed upstairs, all declaring their desire to start with the early twentieth century galleries.

"Chronology, Sara," Jake said, smirking at her.

She nodded. "Thank you. Tell Ms Lucas that's how to teach history!"

Jake laughed, wanting to add a one-liner or two, verbally hug Sara, but didn't want to exclude Gwen who was watching and listening. She didn't know about Sara's complaints about her middle school history classes being erratic and incomplete.

They began their gallery sweep. There were paintings by Picasso, Braque, Kandinsky, Klee and others. Gwen, Jake and Sara stood and stared together at times, apart at times, and sitting down at times. They moved on to mid-century American abstract expressionists and then, after an hour and a half of looking at paintings, went downstairs to the museum's *Cascade Cafe*. It was crowded but after shuffling in line, they found a table and sat down.

"My father and I like frozen food and so this is very strange and exciting for us."

Jake wasn't surprised by Sara's quip, but Gwen hesitated, with a cautious smile at Sara, then said, "Frozen food?"

"It's okay," Jake said. "We eat fresh salads and things. I hate cooking and so does Sara, so yeah, we do eat a fair number of frozen entrees."

Sara laughed loudly, "Frozen entrees!" She garbled something incoherent, aiming her head to the side, down at the floor and laughed more. Gwen and Jake watched, grinning, until Sara stopped, shaking her head, saying, "Frozen entrees. That's what they call them."

Jake still didn't know how to include Gwen, whose expression was just a bit rigid.

"Anyway, we try to eat well. Seriously. Organic salads and fruit and nuts and whole grains and not too much sugar."

Sara was still stifling laughter about frozen entrees.

Jake asked Gwen if she liked to cook, and she nodded and described her diet as generally healthy. They drifted off to actually eating. Jake was enjoying his hake sandwich on sourdough toast with lettuce and red peppers. Sara seemed content with her tomato and kale soup and Gwen poked at her Greek salad. Gwen didn't seem content. Jake noticed her sitting stiffly with her legs crossed at a sharp diagonal to her torso. He hoped she didn't regret the museum date.

Sara probed a bit. "Did you grow up in Georgetown?"

"No. No, I grew up in a very poor neighborhood in Baltimore."

"Oh." Sara blushed and shifted her eyes down to her plate.

"And survived. I was lucky."

"Seems like more than luck was involved," Jake said. "I saw your resume." That embarrassing revelation burst out before he could stop it.

"Um, well, thanks. I got some very serious help."

Sara looked like she was trying to nonchalantly sip some soup and Jake was no longer trying to eat. He took a sip of water.

Gwen still wasn't eating. "We all need help sometimes, and some of us get lucky and a bunch not so lucky."

Jake and Sara were obviously stalled, not knowing what to say, and Gwen added, "I was recruited by a boarding school for high school, and I did really well there."

A childhood of poverty wasn't on her resume, but Jake nodded, feeling like a creeper for already knowing too much about Gwen and wanting to know more.

"So, like, you lived there?" Sara asked.

Gwen smiled. "Yup."

Jake and Sara just nodded.

Gwen elaborated. "It's obviously not for everyone but I needed to get away from a bad family situation and, yeah, I loved the school, Bardon School in Delaware. Yeah, a woman from Bardon showed up at my middle school in Baltimore and my principal there pulled me out of class and sat me down and they showed me clips on a laptop of the campus and students and teachers and all that. I was totally confused of course and didn't get what the school was or what they were offering me. They gave me some brochures and asked me if I'd like to think about it, but also suggested I go there to see the school."

"Was it beautiful?" Sara asked.

Gwen's eyes seemed to fade away as she managed a tepid smile. "It was like nothing I ever knew existed. It was so beautiful."

"Were, like, the people nice? The kids?" Sara showed her age.

Gwen nodded. "A lot nicer than some of the kids in the high school I would have gone to. Kids in gangs. You only need a few of those kids and everyone's in trouble. But I missed my friends, a lot. At first especially."

Jake got in, "At what point did you say yes, you wanted to go?"

"Uhh, I think the end of the two days I stayed there visiting. They were nerve-racking days, but then I went back to my squalor in Baltimore."

Sara's eyes were focused on Gwen, but she began eating her soup again, and Jake took a bite of his sandwich.

Gwen ate some salad, her expression solemn and tense. She wiped her mouth with her paper napkin. "It was all free. Everything was paid for. I was young and naive in my way, but I knew that was too good to pass up."

"Your parents didn't mind?" Once again, Sara asked what was on Jake's mind.

"Well, my father was shot and killed before I was born, and my mother was an addict by the time I was two and died of an overdose a year later. They were both teenagers. I was their only child, I think. My aunt raised me and, no, she thought I should grab it. She had two kids of her own and no one to help her."

Sara lost all the blood in her face and Jake groaned, trying not to by clearing his throat. Gwen didn't seem to see or hear them.

No one ate. Gwen's face was contorted, locked in an inward gaze even when her eyes aimed at Jake or Sara. Her voice was low and engrossed. "When I was in my last year at Bardon, I took an advanced history course called, The Cold War and Poverty, and over and under population was the subject one week. I became glued to it. The link between population shifts and economics fascinated me, and I read all I could about it…fairly confused the whole time. But, undaunted, I wrote a paper on it at mid-term, and I got a B. I wasn't thrilled, I guess because I was used to higher grades, and I'd worked hard on that paper. Then the teacher, Clara Munson, pulled me aside after class the last day of term and explained my grade. She said she believed my paper was just a bit overly optimistic. I think I claimed middle class cultures usually have fewer children, and then those cultures were able grow economically. Anyway, I got an A in the class, so why was she pulling me aside, talking about that paper? I thought I knew why. There were kids of all races in the school and even a bunch from poor backgrounds, but I was in her class, and I wrote the paper and Clara Munson grew up middle-class and is black. So she said to me, 'It might be important to not blame the children. They aren't responsible for the misfortunes or misjudgments of their parents.'"

Gwen stopped herself and cast her eyes on Jake to make her point. "Clara retired last year. She's a good woman and she didn't want me to feel like I didn't deserve to be born."

Jake felt his head recoil, revulsion filling him. It was all he could do to not reach for Gwen.

Seeing Jake's emotional reaction, Gwen sat back and seemed to try to relax a bit, lowering her shoulders, not speaking for a few seconds. The dazed father and daughter cohorts across from her had nothing to add or subtract just then, and it turned out she did. She poked her fork at her salad, looking up sporadically. "Anyway, I didn't say much to her and just left after thanking her. I saved my words for my school therapist." She moved her eyes from Jake to Sara. "A lot of the kids at the school spent an hour a week with a therapist."

Jake wanted to let Gwen eat but also felt the urgent need to ask more questions.

"So, was it good that you got a chance to talk over things with the school therapist?"

Gwen bobbed her head, chewing. Swallowing, she said, "Yeah. Oh, that's for sure. She listened patiently and listened patiently, until she finally, very unobtrusively, steered me toward whatever my inner demons might be. After a year or two I figured out one thing that was bugging me. I was haunted by being the product of social engineering, selected very arbitrarily by some people. I was plucked out of the world of so many unlucky people. Why me?"

Gwen pointed her face at Jake adding, "There were tons of nice, smart poor kids who were missed in the lottery game. It all seemed contrived and freakish to me. Life in the modern world, that is."

Jake was flummoxed and Sara looked stuck speechless, and Gwen suddenly gaped at them, widened her eyes and crooned, "Sorry. Well, aren't I just the life of the party? Sorry."

Jake was trying to stop being flummoxed by Gwen, but it wasn't easy. How was all this turbulent personal analysis affecting Sara? He had to say something.

"No. No, that's the most fascinating bit of personal history I've ever heard, but, no, anyway." He raised his eyebrows. "So yeah, it really does seem like there's plenty that's arbitrary in life and we're all products of social engineering, or unnatural selection, to some extent, aren't we? We've been pretty far removed from the wilds of nature for a long time, haven't we? I mean, most humans live in towns and cities as soon as we can, right?"

Gwen raised her head slowly and managed a wan smile directly at him. "Yeah, unnatural selection. Wow, I think I used that phrase in my paper."

Jake didn't join Gwen's chortling. "Who better than you? Look at the results." He felt it escape before he could finesse it. It was too literal minded, too enthusiastic considering how torn-up Gwen's past was.

Gwen scrunched her face and smiled at him affectionately, saying, "A few times at school chapel we sang the song, 'We've Got the Whole World in Our Hands'. Right? Know that song? It used to be on kids' shows on TV. I'm not sure if it still is." She aimed at him, then looked to Sara who was almost the color and rigidity of celery. Sara only blinked.

Gwen continued, "Well, so, I remember finding out a few years later, in college, those words were reversed from the old gospel song, 'He's Got the Whole World in His Hands'. The original song was stating we humans didn't have the whole world in our hands. God had the whole world in God's hands."

Jake leered, saying, "Now even chapel's telling you we've got the whole damned existential nightmare in our hands. The whole toxic mess crumbling through our fingers."

"Exactly!" Gwen locked faces with Jake as both of them grunted laughs. Half a dozen seconds of that and she pulled away and grimaced theatrically at Sara, who was barely smiling, shyly watching them.

Gwen switched to a lower register and slowed down. "Anyway, we can only do our best with the cards we're dealt. I was unlucky, then I got lucky, I guess is what I'm saying."

"Yeah. Good," Sara said, some blood back in her face.

Gwen moved her chair closer to the table, saying, "Sara, you said you like French Impressionism. Want to go to those galleries next? When we're finished eating?"

* * * * *

Sara got on the internet as soon as she got back from the museum. That Bardon School looked so gorgeous and so sophisticated in some very adequate way. It was worth gazing at its website for an hour.

The rest of Saturday night Sara spun around the whole experience of being with Gwen Minot at the museum. She didn't say anything to her father. Hell, it was obvious he was in love with Gwen Minot just like Gwen Minot was in love with him. Sara wanted to laugh the whole time she was in the National Gallery, with them both poring their eyes all over each other instead of the paintings. Then, when Gwen talked about her past, Sara was rapt but not half as rapt as her father. He looked like he was going to lunge over the table to wrap his arms around Gwen.

The thought of Gwen Minot and her father getting married or something sent a major shot of adrenaline through Sara. Meanwhile, Gwen was a big-time architect who made lots of money and collected art. She probably had a bunch of wealthy friends who collected art, who could bring in work for Sara's father.

Sara knew it was all too good to be true, but even some part of it happening would be way more than adequate.

She did a bit of homework and watched some Instagram and listened to some music, all the while spinning around thoughts of how her father, poor or not, was quite the catch and that Gwen was, without a doubt, the coolest, most brilliant, beautiful woman ever, anywhere. Gwen was married so she'd have to get divorced and that was too bad. But people get divorced.

CHAPTER SIX

September 10, Sunday

G wen was awake in the middle of the night, her mind rushing to solve problems, any and all problems. Old Alexandria was never going to amount to a lot in her life, or in Larny's as far as she could guess. After spending a year in Ghana helping set-up a Quaker school with Larny, after they were both finished with graduate school, and after them spending a month in Tokyo right after they got married, and one summer traveling in Nigeria, and places in Britain and New England and California on extended vacations, it was going to be hard to find any one place all that stimulating. It was just the house she lived in now, that she put so much into and, so far, got so much back from, that Gwen saw as her place in the world. It could almost be anywhere. Almost.

Getting out of bed, she didn't seem to stir Larny. She carried her thin dark blue robe downstairs and put it on, sidling quietly to the living room. It was verging on three-thirty in the morning as she sat in her favorite window seat with the crimson velvet cushion. Some distant streetlights discharged through the large Georgian windows of her end of the large room making an artificial dawn shift away and gradually disappear in the far corners. The lower antique shutters next to her blocked half of outside.

She turned sideways into the window seat, slippers off, feet up, just fitting, tucked into her one-woman enclave. She had questions. Why did Larny, driving home from Aaron and Joe's, suggest she buy a second house somewhere? He knew better than to suggest she was professionally bored. That argument was in the past, a few years in the past -- him saying she should start her own firm and hire people, or work in some established architectural firm. She got the logic of big clients and big money. She just didn't want to. She wanted the flexibility of working on her own, finding her own projects, free of office politics. She had good projects and made plenty of money on her own. Larny was just more gregarious than she was.

He'd suggested buying a second home before but at dinner with Aaron and Joe her groggy inability to converse must have made him worry she was bored. Driving home he kept saying she had options. Vermont? Up-State, New York, or Chesapeake Bay?

Finally, he got her laughing over the absurd fact that too many choices were an on-going curse for the rich.

The fact was, she laughed nervously at Larny's teasing because she was still groggy from spending the day before at the museum spilling her guts to two strangers. Jake and Sara didn't seem to have many choices, being locked into some gorgeous life together -- a wholesome codependency. But locked into it they appeared to be. Gwen didn't have to remind herself she was lucky to be rich. It gave her lots and lots of those options most other people only dreamed about. So what flipped her out at the museum? Jake and Sara were so supremely polite and attractive and unpretentious that her brain erupted? What was it? They had the one thing she didn't? All Gwen had to do was give Larny the nod. He told her emphatically a few times he wanted to have kids, if she did. And she only had to remind him, very occasionally, about her fears on that score. Her background made her strong and independent and it even made her a good lover and companion, she hoped. But she got the shakes when she thought about bringing little ones into the world.

She didn't inherit good examples of parenting.

God, she got the shakes thinking about parenting.

And God, that Sara was so adorable, both times. Maybe she could adopt her and her adorable, adorable, Goddamned adorable father. And some miserable wreck of a mother abandoned Sara? The ominous heartlessness of that background story made Gwen's shoulders stiffen and twitch now. Her intestines twisted and she groaned with a vengeful, hopeless anger.

Gwen stood and, barefoot, paced across the room, watching one floorboard at a time.

She halted and stayed fixed to one spot as she controlled her air intake, making an effort to think about Jake and Sara being the exception in her life. That was obvious. They were the exception that proved some rule. What was it? There were so many rules they proved. She loved Larny, the one and only person she teamed up with and built so much with for so many amazing years. Jake and Sara were so white and so established middle-class. They fascinated her for that reason. That was it.

Walking while facing the floorboards continued. A few minutes of traveling that route she sat down again to steady herself, steady her brain and heart. An affair was not possible for millions of reasons. She wasn't an eighteenth-century French aristocrat. And Jake was so attractive by being so well founded, taking care of his daughter, the true-blue, non-slimy-cheating kind. Jesus, that was so attractive.

Sex with Jake was too much to even dream up. Anyway, what was she dreaming up, scheming up? Divorce? Hell no! Never! Not from Larny!

Meanwhile, she'd just met Jake.

She walked into the kitchen and got a glass of water. The overhead LED lights were too bright because the dimmer wasn't working. She'd have to call the electrician. She retreated to her spot in the living room, glass of water in hand. She didn't sit, afraid she might think about having some sort of French aristocratic affair with Jake. That stupid thought had to be exorcised. That was it! She put the glass of water on the sixteenth century French coffee table/chest. That was what she was doing in the museum -- she was exorcising them from her life! Did it work? Were they repulsed by her? She wanted them to be, didn't she? She had to stop them goggling at her, as if she were the coolest person alive. Did she shock that out of them?

No, they all – including her -- seemed even more captivated as they left the museum restaurant and toured the nineteenth century galleries. The day seemed to end with them all more bonded. Hopeless. It felt so good. And it was the weirdest sensation she'd ever had, maybe similar to being a crazed teenager, being attracted to some nice, stylish boy in some extremely romantic way. She never had that problem since marrying Larny. Some flirtations, but not that. Was it something about Jake's artistic style? His easy elegance that only people in the arts seem to have? That was it. There was Robbie Chrysler in high school. She always stared at Robbie, marveling over his gentle manners, his smooth, young male polish. He was the first luxuriously nice, polite, seriously good-looking, simply cool person Gwen had ever known, up to that point, and he was an art student. Of course, he scared the hell out of her, and they just smiled at each other from safe distances.

Gwen shook her head. What the hell was wrong with her? High school!?

And she wasn't trying to exorcise Jake and Sara. She knew spilling her personal history would unite them all emotionally.

*   *   *   *   *

The shower head spouted onto his upper torso. It was Monday and, same as ever, Gwen was on his mind, that much more ingrained after the museum trip. She had a way of moving when she spoke to him, slightly swaying, head bent. And he actually grunted a couple of times at the museum when she stared back into his eyes. He almost grabbed her but stopped himself each time and shouted inside that she was *married!* He also reminded himself Sara was there. There were other people there too.

He neglected Sara in the museum. He made that jaundiced remark at lunch about the toxic world crumbling between our fingers. He was in a Gwen trance, and of course, her start in life was a nightmare and he and Sara were knocked sideways by that. But he just couldn't forget his daughter, his responsibility. Gwen was as great an inspiration for Sara as possible and it was going so well until he piled on his own stark picture of the world.

He wanted Sara to grow up her own way, not get pushed and pulled by cynical adults. He wanted her to have hope.

Meanwhile, Gwen was so great with Sara and that drove him up into another sphere at the museum, and now. He had to get a grip. More warm water pouring over him, he slowly slowed down, telling himself he just wanted to kiss Gwen. He wasn't expecting more. He wanted to kiss her and then just quietly, honestly explain to her how he felt -- that he never felt so intimately connected to a person. He never felt so completely attracted. He wanted to tell her how excited she made him at the museum when she connected so well with Sara. That did it for Jake. He thought Gwen was gorgeous before he saw her with Sara, but after introducing them, Gwen soared in his estimation, and his imagination – Gwen and him making babies.

He couldn't get enough oxygen. He had to stop panting.

The fact was it was only another impoverished Monday, and he was standing, slowly remembering his work search for that day, staring at his shower head, feeling its beads of water hit his chest. No longer pretending, at least for now, he had to try to wash away a sticky layer of gloom, knowing it was the day he and Simon were going to try to scrounge up some work for Jake and maybe some for Simon, who didn't need any more work. A shower and shave and crisply washed blue broad cloth shirt, fresh jeans, organic cereal and coffee and definitely not even a glance at news items on his phone, and his gloom might be almost thirty percent gone.

Jake always leaned on the galleries in Georgetown, but today he and Simon would venture farther over to Dupont Circle. Simon drove, the whole effort being a favor to Jake, and it took fifteen minutes to find parking.

Simon often let Jake know galleries were snake pits where only Jake, the art conservator, had some clout. So walking up Twenty-First Street Jake opened up briefly, even if it had all been said between them before.

"There are only a few big, fancy, reputable galleries in the whole damned country, mostly in New York or LA. These little DC galleries all have a hell of a lot to prove. They're jeered at by the actually cool people in museums because museums are absolutely pure and non-profit, and it's absolutely assumed curators are absolutely the best and the brightest. So, yeah, that means these galleries are pathetic money grubbers and extremely replaceable."

"What about us? We're not non-profit."

"Yup. It's just, you know, screw them. These galleries. Right?"

Simon jerked his head back, expressionless. "Great start to the day."

Jake grumbled a laugh as they entered the Mikael Mondale Gallery, a medium sized white box space on the second floor. It was a wall of glass onto the street in front and then, about fifty feet back, another wall of glass facing the alley behind. Inside, the one thousand square foot room was defined by dark gray rectangular stone slab flooring and upright white canvas covered partitions. There was an exhibition of ten of the blown-up photographs by Soni Zuma that were on opposite walls and a partition. Then other partitions here and there had smaller works by contemporary artists like a few small, amazingly beautiful pastels of individual birds by Boston artist, Janice Updike. Walking to the receptionist, Jake noticed Simon standing back. It was Jake's show.

She smiled slightly with a minimal nod at him, still listening to her phone, offering a few words into the phone about insuring a shipment. An address in Sewickley, Pennsylvania was recited in a Japanese accent. She was very young and slight, dressed in a black cotton shirt with a very narrow collar and jeans. Her name, Kasume, was printed on cardstock, held by a glass holder on her glass desk -- all seeming tenuous.

She soundlessly clicked off, facing him. "I am sorry. Can I help you?"

"Yes, hi. I'm Jake Holtz and this..." Jake turned to reluctant Simon ten feet back..."is Simon Leary from Arthouse Framers. In Georgetown. I'm the paper conservator at the M Street Art Conservation Studio. We wanted to see Mikael for just a second."

"Oh, sorry. Mikael is busy this morning. You can leave your information. I will be sure they get it."

Jake stepped closer, not too close, not sure how formal and Japanese she was.

"Actually. Yeah, sorry, we usually make an appointment with Mikael. We were just wondering if there were any connection between you and a collector we've been helping."

"Ah. Who is the collector?"

"Gwen Minot?" Jake knew his bait was too obvious.

"Ah. I don't know that name." She was tapping at her elegant little glass and light gray plastic computer searching for Gwen Minot. "Ah, yes I see her name here."

Jake wanted to laugh because he was pretty sure Gwen didn't buy her art from them. "Yeah, well she's been bringing us a lot of works for conservation and matting and framing and we didn't want to ask her where she collects. But she said she liked the way things were exhibited somewhere. I can't remember where."

"What artists does she collect?"

"William T. Williams. Yeah, was one."

Kasume sat still. Her condensed dark eyes said it all. She had stupid petty challenges like Jake and Simon daily and would probably quit the stupid little job any day now.

"Yes of course, William T. Williams. But we don't represent him. Most of our artists are more current."

"Newer, right." Jake wanted to make a joke about expiration dates, but didn't, because it was so weak and so old. "Well, anyway. It must have been another gallery, sorry. She does collect other artists."

Kasume's eyes looked toward his, stopping a mile short. Obviously, she knew his desperate little game, but it was her job to pretend she was receiving anyone who might have even the remotest potential. She texted her hideous boss, keeping it short, probably in some code.

"Mikael will be right out."

"Thanks."

Jake and Simon were back to waiting, hands behind their backs, pretending to look at things on walls, brochures on tables. Jake glanced around and spotted the security cameras in the ceiling, hating the possibility Mikael Mondale was looking back.

A prolonged ten minutes later the gallery produced a wholly different visage from Kasume, an overtly hostile one, dislodged from a back office, shuffling and sashaying, dragging his leather and wood sandals on the floor and looking for all the world like an aged, overweight WWF wrestler. His short, jagged hair ran straight back and was bright gold. He displayed a sixty something pocked gray complexion and displayed large, fleshy arms and legs in pale green shorts with a matching short sleeve shirt.

His Facebook page and website let anyone out there know he was related to the Mondale construction dynasty that built everywhere in the Mid-Atlantic, but mostly New Jersey, where Mikael spent his first twenty-plus years. Then it was Brooklyn before the presumably easier prey of Washington attracted him. He met with Jake three times in the past fourteen years, but never remembered and would make sure he didn't again.

Stopped and standing after not shaking their hands, glaring at the two men, Mikael waited. Kasume already gave him the short pitch in her text but there had to be more, or they wouldn't have wasted his time. There wasn't more. Yeah, he knew Gwen Minot but, no, he didn't have any Williams in his gallery. It must have been another gallery. What did they charge?

Jake was so filled with self-disgust at that point, he just handed over his brochure and client list and said nothing.

Mikael barely glanced. "Yeah, well, I hope you give galleries a discount. We usually do business with Stanley Framers."

"Framing's Simon's business."

Like it or not, Simon had to step forward and hand Mikael his brochure and price sheet. Barely glancing again, Mikael sneered, "Yeah, Stanley Framers gives us much better prices. You two won't get much gallery business with those prices." He was sashaying away.

They both moaned thank you at Mikael's green, gold and gray back and took one long step at a time away.

They evaded each other, standing fixed on the nearest shady spot on the sidewalk, glancing around.

Jake knew half a minute of that was enough. "That was a given."

"Then why even try with these galleries? I never work for them anymore. Mikael Mondale uses Stanley Framers? For now. When that framer figures out they're losing money, they'll stop and Mikael will move onto the next sucker."

"I know. I have to get any work I can at this point. Why don't we just go to one more and call it a day. Sorry. I appreciate this, really."

They visited four more galleries, two more in Dupont Circle and two out on 77th Street. The other gallery staff in Dupont Circle were less corrosive than old Mikael, but still treated Jake and Simon like they were interruptions.

Receptionists or volunteers took their information. On 77th Street the galleries were kinder and spoke to them in full paragraphs and asked them questions and actually looked over Simon's price list and Jake's brochure. In fact, at the Faulkner Gallery, one of the oldest in the area, the owner, Toby Zuckerman, remembered Jake and apologized for not getting back to him. He actually had some large contemporary prints that needed flattening. How much would Jake charge? Jake looked at them, mulled it over and left with three works wrapped around a four-foot-long cardboard tube. And Toby wanted Simon to frame them if they could be delivered. He was very bad at getting to things and hated arranging all these details. Thank God they appeared that day, Toby said. He was around their age and gay, referring to his husband a lot.

Jake mentioned it on the car ride home.

"Yup. He thought we were a twosome." Simon's voice was end-of-the-journey fatigued. The sun was low enough to mean buildings blocked it and sunglasses could come off. Simon stretched, then looked at Jake. "By the way, are you chasing after Gwen Minot?"

"What?" Jake knew it was just a matter of time before he'd have to explain himself.

Simon leaned his head to the side incredulously.

Jake said, "I know. I'm an idiot. There's no hope."

"Is there?"

"No idea. She's married. I can't really talk about it." Jake just shrugged, short of breath, and once again that day gloom engulfed him.

*　*　*　*　*

Tuesday meant Jake had to get to the bit of work he had. He knew what he was doing when he had something to do. Twenty-three years of experience, eight at the DC Art Conservation Center and fifteen on his own, gave him that assurance at least. There was no point sinking down into self-pity, obsessing that he might have done more in the past to make money. He always hated the idea of doing something in an office or in sales. It wasn't like he wanted to be a dentist or a doctor or a TV weather forecaster. He wanted art conservation since he bumped into it in a documentary online one day when he was a junior in college. It was fine while he made enough money to stay afloat, even coast along, but there was more competition for fewer collectors now. And Sara was dependent on him -- forever forsaken Sara.

CHAPTER SEVEN

Sara was born after the divorce. Jake and Emma were married for a bit less than a year when Jake suggested they separate, when he suggested they had nothing in common. Emma seemed more insulted than sad but even her anger seemed to dissipate within a couple of weeks of them living apart. Two months later Emma found out she was pregnant. Jake was just settling into Simon's apartment above the frame shop and well into building the studio and painting the kitchen and bedrooms. All the excitement - new prospects, new life - became biologically fused to his pregnant ex-wife.

His memory was of a blunt, compulsive delirium, the afternoon they had sex. He was visiting Emma to get her to sign some divorce papers. She was dressed in a red and green tartan flannel shirt, nothing else. He tried not to look as she bent over, signing the papers.

The bit of paperwork done, she stood facing him looking both enthralled and withdrawn. She murmured, "Want to have sex?"

Their official divorced state had just taken over his psyche, so he was staggered by the question.

"Why?" he asked vacuously.

Emma knew why. "It feels good," murmured in an even quieter, even more aroused, shaky voice. Yeah, he knew why too. The thrills had already started. It was deeply implanted – limitless thrills – until it's over.

Her IUD didn't work.

Emma genuinely seemed surprised, but as he thought about it, she had always said she didn't want to have more than one kid. And there were so many ways Emma's life made her into a twenty-first century fatalist.

Anger and all kinds of loathing in Jake regenerated into a single animate life force when tiny Sara was in his arms. It was true love, unselfish love and, in a flash, Jake felt a fervent resolve to be her father, through and through. Emma continued to maintain some sort of low yield equilibrium, appearing happy buying a house, getting a new car, fine with sending emails to Jake twice a week, happy enough arranging for him to pick up Sara for weekends.

It was The Bent Elbow in Columbia Heights where he met Emma that first time. They left and slept together, and both liked it more than enough to want more. His condoms worked as gift wrapping for feral sex exchanges in bed -- exchange, exchange, exchange. After a few months of all that, Emma got her IUD and they shared an apartment in Bethesda, the southern section, close to DC.

With very little forbidden fruit left, it might have been convenience, staying together as a couple. Jake hesitated talking with Emma about it. Was it opposites groping each other? He thought that was it but knew he'd never get the right moment to say that. Any verbal, non-sexual exchange got nothing back but a disgruntled shrug from her. She told him a couple of times –*she lived life. She didn't analyze life.*

Emma grew up in Richmond Virginia, with one older sister who stayed in Richmond and even went to university there. It was the local regional public schools and then American University in DC for Emma. Her parents were divorced, and she barely knew her father. He was a dentist who moved to the other side of Richmond when she was ten. He started another family. Her mother was a pharmacist who remarried after Emma left for college.

After the divorce Jake needed someone to explain it all to and that was his rediscovered friend, Simon. After getting their first beers, sitting at in a booth at Grub and Libations on Wisconsin Avenue, Jake found himself wanting to sum it up -- "Emma and I got on like a house on fire, caught in a flood, rushing downstream." There was the right amount of laughter from Simon, laughter and sympathy. Jake wasn't sure Simon really cared to grasp the rest of the long story, but poor Simon had to listen to Jake rumble on and on, sorting and questioning.

"Why did I marry Emma? Was it all that sex? Partly. But I just turned thirty and panicked, feeling old and feeling like my chances of meeting anyone really great were less and less. She wasn't exactly the girl next door, or maybe she was just a slightly traumatized girl next door. Anyway, there was no next door anymore for me, living in the city. Right?"

Simon perked up. He said he had very little to do with his neighbors in the suburbs.

Jake needed that kind of needling. He rumbled on, "So, I was in a shambolic hurry to rescue Emma and me from the eternal present. Emma didn't see any difference between being married and just living with someone. That's what she repeated many, many times in as few words as possible. Yup, the proof was inescapable after living with her for a year and being married to her for a few months. It alienated the hell out of me. I mean, not only did I not love her, she didn't care if I did or didn't. There was no way to build anything with her, no future. Now, we're divorced and having a baby...together I guess."

Simon's next job as a good friend was to listen to Jake repeat all that, with a bit of variation, for hours. Leaving Grub and Libations, Simon patted Jake on the back. "Endure the present and get to the not-so-distant future as soon as possible."

He left Jake at the brick warehouse, very soon to include a functioning art conservation studio, and said goodnight. That was followed by once-a-week trips to Grub and Libations and echoes of the first time, for months, until Sara was born.

Fifteen years later Simon was much too busy for Jake's second act with Emma and Sara. Simon was running his business and being a husband and father to two kids and didn't scrutinize the intimate complications of non-family members. So Jake had no Simon to consult last May, when Emma told him she wanted to move to LA. Jake should have been surprised by Emma telling him that but wasn't. He'd lived in fear of her moving for years. Emma worked for a social media agency and Jake had to withstand her ongoing complaints for years about not making enough money. He hoped it was the standard griping that just about everyone did, including him. What he had to seriously worry about was Emma moving somewhere some day and him losing Sara. He never half learned to live with that fear.

And then late last May the day came when Jake sat down in his studio, just like Emma asked, him knowing something dangerous was about to happen because it was a first. Emma never asked to meet with him in his apartment. She was fidgety but got herself onto the matching old steel stool.

"I've been offered a position of Manager of Media Accounts at Altmax in LA."

If she saw his panic, it was her own that took her over. "I can't take Sara. I can't!"

Jake had to try to grasp a strain of thought. It was hard to believe what was being said.

She was sitting with her arms folded tightly. She was dressed conservatively for Emma, in jeans and a long sleeved, button-down, dark maroon shirt.

"You're moving to LA?" He tried to keep his voice steady.

"Yeah. I've taken the job."

Jake looked away from her, knowing that so much was at stake he was better off saying nothing until she revealed more, and she wouldn't reveal anything if he said anything critical or negative.

He sat still, not too still, trying to convey calmness. "Okay."

"Sara's almost finished with school for the year. I told her and she was upset, but she settled down pretty soon and said she wants to live here. She wants to go to high school in town here. I can't afford to take care of her and do this. LA's too expensive. I have to do this, Jake. I have to. I took care of Sara all these years. You helped, but I did most of it. And this is the career job I've been waiting for."

"Uh-huh." It was contempt he had to hide, and that fear of losing Sara. He wanted Emma to go and go that far away. What he wanted and only occasionally let himself dream of, was Sara living with him full-time. This move by Emma would mean he'd be able to raise Sara by himself?

Emma stood up. "There's no one in my life. I hate living in the burbs and having no life."

"Okay. Do it. I'm not giving you a hard time. Sara's okay? When did you tell her?"

"Last night after dinner. She's good with it. She wants to live here. You have enough room."

Sara was good with it? Jake suppressed any reaction to that convenient summation. "Yup. Plenty of room." Because he damned well made sure there was a nice bedroom for Sara fifteen years before. "You're selling your house?"

"I sold it myself to a woman at work. I saved real estate fees. But after paying off the mortgage and after what I bought in LA, I'm broke. It's in Culver City right in the middle of LA. It's just a one-bedroom condo but cities are so damned expensive. You know that."

He saw it in her bloodless face, behind her done deal eyes. Guilt. Gulping while trying not to, he said, "Yup, so you're all set." He didn't add anything.

Emma didn't have an addendum and sat staring down at her thick white Nikes. Her mauve lips tightened to a narrow crevice.

He wanted to finally blot her out, her sitting there looking like an incensed teenager in detention. He wanted to tell her she was a lying cypher, that he'd turned down more than a few opportunities over the years for jobs in other cities. He had no social life largely because he devoted every weekend and most holidays to Sara. Emma had lots of weekends and a series of lovers. Dylan, the sports equipment sales rep, who lifted weights for fun and wore shirts and shorts so tight they only existed to expose his bulges, lived with Emma and Sara for over a year. Jake was as nice to Dylan as he'd ever been to any jerk in his life, hoping stupid old Dylan would get bored or Emma would. And someone finally did. Jake never asked. He never asked about anything but Sara. And, after so many years of living with that fear of losing Sara, this. His elation had to be tamped down, down, down.

Emma was still closed across from him, in her compressed emotion mode, still in detention.

He just wanted her to go. Something abrasive would definitely skewer things if he had to talk to her much longer.

"When do you leave?"

"In three weeks. I'll help Sara move."

Three weeks! He was speechless and she watched. It was where she might show some remorse but didn't. Her face drooped. "I'll be in touch all the time. We'll Zoom and talk on the phone, Sara and I will, and you too. There'll be vacations."

"Vacations," Jake repeated, then played with the word in his mind. Yup, she was vacating like her father did, and what was elation for Jake would have to be rejection and pain for Sara. But that had to be dealt with after Emma got the hell out of the way.

The extenuated shifting toward exiting was hell for her too, no doubt. He just had to let her wane, so he never, during that encounter or the next few, looked or sounded excited or happy or angry or sad, he didn't think. He never mentioned custody rights or any legal arrangements. Those rights and arrangements should become less and less Emma's as time and distance established themselves. Days shifted along and he loitered from a safe, he hoped, distance. His assumption was she wouldn't change her plans to move for her new job, but she might soften and get motherly and beg Sara to move with her. But she didn't. It had taken Jake years to realize he and Sara were the limit for Emma. She was finished with her Richmond family years before and now she was finished with children and husbands.

The three weeks were the longest of Jake's life, but Emma did it. She moved far, far away and he and Sara were free to try to build a future together.

*　*　*　*　*

It was the end of the week, four days after gallery begging with Simon. Sitting in his room after a full day of work plus dinner with his daughter, Jake was alone stewing in a more self-assertive mood than he'd experienced for many months. He was tired of worrying about work and money and he was tired of playing passive-defensive in general. What about an online dating service? No dating because he was fantasizing about Gwen from an impossible distance? What a grotesque joke.

There were bad memories, though. The two times he tried online dating sites in the past were not fun. Jake, who prided himself in general verbal skills, couldn't get anything back either time. Those women looked like any discussion beyond food, the weather, or jobs was either too intellectual or too intimate. Both times he felt like he was piercing into them with his eyes, two headlights into their deer eyes -- especially when he told them about Sara. It was on the form, he was a father, but he saw that fear on their faces and second dates were no option for him.

Was that what happened to Gwen? Her whole disposition changed when he told her he had a daughter one room away. The museum trip was her idea, but then that was where she got so graphically intense about her past. Gwen was no deer in the headlights. He was sure she was made of much sterner stuff than that. He had no idea what happened to her at the museum because he barely knew Gwen. He just knew she eclipsed all other women, and he wasn't sure exactly how or why, because, for him, she eclipsed all reason and sense. He hadn't dated her or even spent a lot of time with her. She was married, spending all her dating time with her handsome, accomplished husband.

So much for being so enticed by the easy way Gwen connected with Sara. Jake scorned that illusion now.

He'd try to read himself to sleep, telling himself to retreat when the sun retreats, in late fall.

*   *   *   *   *

The third week of September was a new week forming. Gwen was coming in. When he emailed her to say the Williams works were flat and dry, he added that the French drawings weren't quite dry, but she emailed back that she had a few things to do in Georgetown and had a few watercolors needing work. Jake didn't discourage her. He cleaned his kitchen, bathroom and studio, took a shower and put on clean tan khakis and a light blue cotton shirt. Something about the shirt looked good, he thought. Probably the quality of the material. It wasn't cheap. He was ready, but for what?

Gwen opened another portfolio, this time with seven English watercolors, all by the same woman, Mary Woodall, all signed and dated on the back. They were painted during the nineteen thirties and forties on thick watercolor paper, and were small, about seven by ten inches. They were all slightly abstract, beautiful views of luscious rolling, green and gold English countryside.

"I got them in a London gallery, years ago."

Jake just nodded. They were Turner influenced, he thought, but didn't say that and sound off. He waited for her to say what she wanted.

"I couldn't resist them, and the price was right, but that was years ago, ten years ago, and I haven't done anything with them. They have that tape around them."

Jake nodded again. He'd seen this before, too many times. There was an old brown paper tape around the outside edges of most of the watercolors. Some of the paper tape had come off and there was a glue residue left behind, although not much.

Gwen added, "I love these things and I'd like to mat them so the whole paper shows. I've seen watercolors in museum exhibitions matted that way. It makes a difference."

"Yeah. No, it does. I've noticed that over the years, that if the mat covers the edges of the paper the image comes out at you, not the paper."

"Right." Gwen gazed at Jake for a second, thinking. "Yeah, these are watercolor sketches, but so if you see the image only..." She stopped and Jake knew where she was heading.

"You want to see it less finished than that, so actually see the edges of the paper."

"Exactly." She looked pleased, her face shining like he had just helped her complete a thought.

Jake felt himself sinking into her eyes, so he turned away and settled on the small watercolors. "But, yeah, these things are great. Anyway, I can try to get most of the glue out, or off."

Her face faded, losing some luster. That didn't jive with what he'd just said, so they were both halted for a few seconds.

He stepped back and she said, "So, yeah, I want to apologize for getting so crazy at the museum the other day. I don't know what got into me. Sara must think I'm nuts."

His head snapped back. "No. The opposite. Sara thinks you're the coolest person she's ever met."

Gwen looked down, burbling, "Oh, well, that's sweet. Sara's the cool one."

"But really, Sara needs, you know, to meet dynamic people who've put a lot together."

Gwen's face flushed. "Well, anyway. Thanks. So I saw on your website you grew up in Frederick, Maryland?"

Gwen was trying to steady herself, so Jake became a storyteller. "Yup. My parents did too. Population of around seventy thousand with a miniature cityscape downtown and miniature historic district and miniature suburban sprawl. My parents both went to the University of Maryland, not far away...at different times and met at a small bank in Frederick...engaged at a Christmas party, her a twenty-four-year-old assistant manager, and him a twenty-eight-year-old branch manager. Apparently, they were destined to have three kids and live in the blandest tan vinyl four bedroom mini-McMansion in the mini-burbs."

"Nothing wrong with a bit of stability when you're a kid."

"I know. I know. I know that now. Yeah, I was a spineless punk. At least as a teenager. Umm, it was a wasteland, and I was vanquished and complained like a starving Banshee." He wondered if he was saying too much, but it felt like he was following her direction.

She hadn't lost her concentrated stare now for a few minutes. "You have two siblings?"

It hit him that he was revealing he grew up with so much of what she didn't have as a kid. But they were the basic facts of his story.

"Monica is five years older. Lives in Portland Maine and Sean, the middle child, lives in Colorado Springs. My parents moved to Albuquerque a few years ago, largely for the dry air. My mother has asthma."

"Oh. Wow, everyone's so far apart."

"Yeah. Yup. We lost hold of the erstwhile American dream, that wayward way, I guess."

Both of them still standing a few feet apart, were somehow silenced. Gwen still kept her eyes on him.

Jake felt obliged to amplify. "Well, see, Monica was enticed by Maine when she went to Colby college there.

And Sean went to Denison in suburban Ohio but fell in love with Colorado and the Rocky Mountains during a trip there after graduation. But, yeah, it means we only see each other physically-in-person during Christmas and that means Albuquerque because our parents are in an assisted living condo and no longer travel."

"Wow."

"Wow?" He laughed, but she didn't.

"So that's how you developed so well and raised such a great daughter." She immediately looked away -- probably afraid she'd just revealed all her cards. He was the one staring now, seriously complimented and so aroused. Gwen liked him as a father?

Glancing, then looking at her elegant sandals, she interrupted his stare. "A bit of stability mixed with a bit of wanting more. I mean, we need a certain amount of stability in life in order to grow as kids. Hell, it's awful enough for adults who struggle to survive with little or no security."

His Gwen trance got interrupted with her words reaching into him, because he was trying to raise Sara with no money. But, it might be Jake's chance to expand on the life of Sara and him. "Uh, do you want to sit down? Do you have any time?"

"Yeah. I did what I had to do before I came here."

"Want some tea or coffee? I just made some coffee."

She said coffee sounded great and he was off, straddling the kitchen, getting cups, spoons, milk, feeling like a whirligig caught in the wind.

Heading back into the studio, Jake handed Gwen her coffee. She gave him a wary smile. "Uh, if you don't mind, could you turn off the camera? I trust you and you can trust me."

Jake obliged without a word, heart pounding. They sat on the wood and steel stools several feet apart, careful as ever, but him wanting more intimacy, saying, "Let me tell you something."

"Okay."

He took a sip of coffee. "I invested a fair amount of time and money to do this, be an art conservator. It was clearly never going to actually make much money, but I wanted the excitement and stimulation of messing around with art objects all day long. Preserving our heritage, right? But more and more, serious people are trying to shed themselves of too many material objects and sometimes I feel like a fool playing in a trash heap, pretending everything called art is precious. Right?"

"Too much art. Yeah, I guess that's a possibility." Gwen drew inward, thinking.

"It feels like an infinite amount. I know it can't be, but it does feel like it…more and more all the time." He rubbed the back of his neck.

Gwen said, "So we get buried as we phase out."

He rotated his head and grimaced.

Gwen tilted her body. "But there's still always going to be great art that we need, new and old. How can we learn from the past if we don't preserve our heritage?"

"Yeah, you just said what I concluded a long time ago."

She erupted into that full-faced smile he loved so much.

He raised his shoulders and grinned, trying, one more time, not to grab her. "Anyway, what I'm trying to say is, Sara came into my life after I already committed myself to indulging in the noble-noble, holy-holy cause of preserving things. Sara offered a whole other level of living, human connection and any self-delusions I had blew away. Raising her, being there for her even when, at times, she appeared to not need me, actually offered me real stability." He sipped coffee, looking at the windows, then back at her. "More than anything I wanted to give her some stability back and I think it worked." He looked at Gwen. "Now I'm not so sure."

He sat still, looked at his coffee cup, then up at her. Gwen was the person he wanted to say these things to. She was zeroed-in on his face. Jake added, "Clearly, she's a great person and fairly formed by now, but she's not an adult yet. It takes humans a long time to be strong and independent."

"Um, in a world rupturing apart." She grinned at him.

"Um. Sorry, I was in a melodramatic mood the day I said that."

"Nope." Gwen expression was dour now. She wrinkled her forehead, saying, "Well, but however it happened you turned out. You know, you got yourself here. It seems like Sara's very sound without being boring or insecure."

"Yeah, you're right. I'm obviously biased, but she does seem that way. She's so great. She is going through something nasty with her mother though. That's not good."

Saying nothing, Gwen's face tightened, still pointed at him.

He grumbled, "I hate talking about it. I can't say anything objective."

"She moved to LA."

"Yup. Better job and exciting LA instead of North Bethesda. Not enough money or something for Sara too."

"Ugh! Sorry," Gwen grunted, leaning forward, her arms folded.

"You know what though?" he added. "She was physically there, available, so I think Sara had that stability for her childhood, until now."

Gwen clearly wasn't buying any exoneration. She stood up, scowling, muttering, "Until puberty, when it gets tricky."

It looked like she was heading for him, but veered a few steps to his side and, looking agitated, shimmied over to look at the watercolors. More than a bit confused, he joined her, keeping a safe two feet away, but noting her still stiff body and deflecting downward stare.

It was going so well. What happened? Something about Emma? He sorely wanted more emotional connection but was forced back to business and quickly tied the strings to her portfolio, then put her Mary Woodall watercolors in acid-free folders and put the folders into his wide, flat metal flat filling cabinet.

Some sort of tension filled the room. He had the sensation she was wrestling with wanting sex and romance right there and then, and he had to stand back because he was sure she wanted him to. Her ambivalence was as strong as any attraction they both felt. He wasn't ambivalent. After that conversation about Sara, Jake craved Gwen. He and Sara needed Gwen. He just had to stand back for a while. They were new to each other. He had to try very hard to not make a mess of things in any way that could end things.

If she brought in more work he'd have more time to engage.

Downstairs, with the outside door open and sunlight filling the cement stairwell cavity, she turned to him, blinking. "Thanks. I'll bring in more. And, Jake? Sara's like any kid. She needs some adult bonding and adult structure in her life... not too much, but definitely some. No doubt about it, you're a truly great version of what she needs."

Blood rose, his shoulders lifted unconsciously, and his words of thanks and goodbye got lost in car sounds and splotches of light, with her walking away.

CHAPTER EIGHT

W alking down any hallway at school was potentially humiliating but Sara really hated the hallway to the cafeteria. Maybe it was because the cafeteria scene was almost always so hostile -- from the bad food to the screaming voices, to the rank smells hitting you when you weren't ready.

Sara postponed linking herself with anyone for days in the beginning, but she had to be polite to avoid conflicts, and she knew she'd need allies. Walking to the cafeteria with anyone though linked you with that person and that person would be linked to other people. It shouldn't matter, in an ideal world, but Sara wanted to survive the real world. She didn't want murky sadasses clinging to her any more than she wanted pissy psychos bullying her.

She sat next to Natalie the second day. Natalie was fine. She took in carbs like a fiend and would weigh a ton in the future but could talk about more than clothes and media stars. Jason was cute and gay and funny, and she sat next to him the fifth day.

There were a couple of other kids who started hanging around Natalie and Jason, which meant they were linked to Sara.

It got explosive suddenly on Wednesday, a few weeks into her ninth-grade escapade. Walking toward the cafeteria Sara realized she was in a group. There were five of them. It attracted attention. The worst attention was from older boys, the ones who didn't give a damn about the school social scene anymore and who declared themselves top of the pile, based on some undeniable primal killer instincts.

Three such unfriends looked at the five ninth graders. The unfriends were standing still, probably wondering if they should bolt the school for lunch, unofficially, or gag on some salmonella bile in the cafeteria. Sara came up with all the terms a week into ninth grade and Jason and Natalie were very amused.

"Hey, look at the little oinkers going to suck in more fat." The smallest of the three unfriends shouted that. The other two looked and laughed, but then, another group of older kids yelled something too. A bunch of girls started yelling at the unfriends who sneered and yelled back telling them to fuck-off. All Sara heard at that point, cantering as invisibly as she could, was the unfriends yelling something about, "fucking oinker school" and a distant teacher trying to yell something threatening at all of them.

Sara and her friends got into the cafeteria and Sara turned her head quickly to catch a glimpse of the unfriends at the doorway shouting at some other neurotically over-muscled boys, all of them laughing. They came in and one of the unfriends gave Sara the finger as the swarm of predators moved along to the far end of the huge cafeteria. It might not have been Sara he was aiming at, but she felt threatened. She hated feeling that way, but what could she do?

*　*　*　*　*

Jake was at Sara's doorway asking Sara when she wanted to eat dinner. They settled on six-thirty.

"I saw a free old movie online last night. After your homework, I'd recommend it. Really, for insight into the past try a silent movie. Buster Keaton and Charlie Chaplin. Or nineteen-thirties and forties movies like *His Girl Friday* or *The Lady Vanishes.*"

"Told me that before Dad."

"Okay. Be respectful."

She flinched, turning around quickly to look at her father.

"I am being respectful. I will watch those old movies. I just haven't had the time."

"Okay. So how does a salad with avocado sound, in an hour?"

"Great. I'll cut the vegetables."

"Great."

Jake headed back to his studio, stopped in the center of the room. He knew Sara, most of the time, was open to him passing on information, even just subjective fragments of information, about the past. It wasn't that he knew so much himself, it was more that he could introduce a connection or two, maybe. She very seldom saw her grandparents on either side and so there weren't family stories being passed down. Sara's world was transparently shallow in that way. How aware of that was she?

He had to get back to work.

An hour and a half later and it was tomato, avocado, carrots, zucchini, celery, onions, broccoli and lettuce all cut up by him while Sara made the dressing of olive oil and balsamic vinegar. She crushed some walnuts to sprinkle on top. Once again, the kitchen was too stuffy to sit in, so they took their plates of food into her room and ate on the fold-out table they'd been using most of the summer.

"If you can't stand the heat, stay out of the kitchen. Know who said that?" he asked.

She dulled her eyes sarcastically with a mouth full of salad, no longer chewing.

He said, "A hint. It wasn't Jamie Oliver."

She chewed, then said, "Benjamin Franklin."

"Nope. Harry Truman."

Again, she dulled her eyes at him sarcastically.

"President at the end of the Second World War."

"I know who Harry Truman was, sort of. Why was he saying that? Something about dropping the atomic bomb?"

Jake choked. "Oh my God! No. No, no. Jesus!" He tucked his chin in and arched his neck, completely disturbed and knocked off course for a minute. Sara ate some more, reddened, her perverse smile stuck to her face.

He had to finish what he started. "It was probably him saying he could handle the pressure of the job. If others couldn't, they should get out of the way. Something like that."

Sara went on eating and so did Jake. He'd wait to ask her about school or some other parental, checking-in question that he relied on at least a few times a week to keep tabs on things. He noticed a sudden somber look about her though and decided to give her some room. Then she stopped eating. He watched and waited.

Tears flowed down her face.

He stood up. "What? What's wrong?"

She shook her head, looking down, shoulders stiff.

Jake went to her, putting his hand on her back. "What?"

She shook her head, sniffling, tears still flowing. He had to wait and wonder. Something to do with school? Friends? Her mother? Her mother getting out of the heat of the kitchen?

The longer he waited, the worse he felt. He sat on the edge of the bed, several feet away.

"Okay?"

Gurgling and sniffling, Sara got out, "I don't know why I'm crying. I'm sorry."

He stood and put one arm over her shoulders and squeezed, feeling a powerful push against his heart as he did. He kissed the top of her head. "Don't be sorry." After a minute, he stepped away, back to his seat across from her. She fingered hair away from her wet and multicolored face and blew her nose in the paper napkin from her lap.

"Sorry, I really don't know why."

"Something wrong at school?"

"No. Not school. It's boring and stupid but, I don't know. I hate it that I have to deal with a crazy mother going three thousand miles away from me when I'm in the middle of all this shit with starting high school. Fuck."

"Yeah, I'm sorry she did that."

"Nothing you can do…about her."

"Um."

"I don't even want to hear from her," Sara snarled at the wall. Looking back at her father, she said, "She sent me an email last week, Jesus, saying how much she missed me and then saying she loved her job and California and wanted me to visit and maybe I could go to college out there. Fuck!" She blew her nose again. "Pisses me off so much that she thinks she can have it both ways."

Jake knew he couldn't say anything for a minute. If he agreed, aloud, that Emma was a selfish jerk, he'd be a jerk. He wanted to spew his anger, but he couldn't, for Sara's sake. Emma was Sara's mother, no matter what. It might take years for Sara to work out something with Emma. It might be a total break, or it might be some sort of reconciliation. Jake had to keep his hands off what he could only mangle even more than it was already mangled.

Sara looked at her plate of food and sputtered, "I know, I shouldn't use disrespectful words."

Jesus. Now he wanted to cry. He caught his breath after a few seconds. "Sara. I can't get between you and your mother, but it might be a good idea for you to talk to someone else. You know you can talk to me about anything but then, maybe not this always very effectively. Right?"

She slowly shrugged.

"I'm worried that's not good. I mean, it can't be easy for you...what happened."

Tears flowed down Sara's cheeks again and Jake was up putting his arm around her, wishing he hadn't said anything, knowing he had to say something.

She stopped crying after a minute. He sat down again, stuck like a knot in an old stump.

"Maybe you could talk to Gwen."

Sara frowned. "No. What the hell?"

"Fine. But think about it."

"Talk to her about what? She doesn't know me. I don't know her. She has better things to do than listen to me."

"Okay. Just an idea. She's older and has been around and knows a lot and likes you a lot. She was filled with praises."

Sara coughed and blew her nose again. "She comes here to see you, not me."

Jake said nothing to that. "Can you eat?"

"Um. A little. It's really good. Sorry."

"Nope." Again, his whole insides were swelling with love and affection and remorse for Sara and then Goddamned fury at anyone who would hurt her.

They ate. The spare words they used were about the weather, about waiting a few weeks to take the air conditioners out of the two bedroom windows.

*   *   *   *   *

Perfectly providential Gwen sent him a text a couple of hours after dinner.

Hi Jake. Sorry if I seemed abrupt or weird the other day. I just hate it when kids get abandoned by adults. Personal history and all that. I really am an emotionally stable person! You have to believe me!

Gwen – I absolutely believe you. In fact, it was seriously helpful to share any of this with you.

Well, share anytime Jake.

Sitting in his old red leather armchair, Jake was halted. He wanted to text something right back but had to take it easy. He walked in circles in the studio for five minutes. He didn't want to wait too long. Okay, he'd take one step forward.

Gwen – It is great talking with you about Sara, but if you ever want to talk to Sara alone, that would be great too. If you ever have twenty minutes? Sorry if that's asking too much given your busy schedule.

He sat anxiously.

I'd love to get together with Sara. Anytime. I could take her to The Haunt for a cup of coffee or tea. Or would that seem like too much to her?

No, actually, I think that would be great. The excuse could be her fifteenth birthday. It's this Sunday but you could go anytime.

Sunday wouldn't work for me. Do you think Friday afternoon would?

I'm sure it would. Ask her if you like. Thanks. She will think we're scheming behind her back – the way we are.

Yeah, it's tough being a kid.

Thank you very much Gwen

☺

Of course, Sara becoming more attached to Gwen would mean his daughter would be more attached to not moving. Jake wrestled with that a few minutes after drooling over Gwen's texts. But he knew Gwen offered Sara serious depth. He also knew, pathetic or not, he didn't want to move away from Gwen.

*   *   *   *   *

A day after Sara's pissy, inadequate weeping, whining, dining scene, Gwen emailed saying she wanted to give Sara a birthday present and didn't know what to buy. *So, how about coffee at The Haunt?* Sara had to go along, half dreading it, half fascinated by this so-cool woman who was in love with her father.

She wondered what to wear and looked up The Haunt online -- good jeans and that expensive dark blue silk shirt she had, that she found on sale after Christmas last year.

It was Friday after school. Sara had the jitters entering The Haunt. The place was a big boost up in adequate vibrations from Starbucks or whatever. It was on the other end of M Street and Sara walked by it all the time, glancing in. Of course, going in was extra exciting, because she was with Gwen. There was a wait staff in white aprons and there were stone walls and light blue tablecloths and antique booths. Gwen asked Sara to choose and the booth near the window was it. Good thing she was in jeans and a long sleeve shirt because the air conditioning was a bit intense. Gwen said the booth might keep them warm -- something about very old churches having booth-like pews for that reason and for privacy. Gwen was a freaking genius, obviously.

Weird, forced conversation was finally interrupted by their coffees and organic, low sugar carrot cakes arriving.

Sara moaned, then blushed. "Sorry. It's just so good, the coffee and the cake. Not too sweet."

"Who needs sugar?"

"I know."

"I think they did add coconut or something."

"I know. The carrot bits are probably the only thing actually good for us."

Gwen just smirked slightly and shrugged.

Sara continued digging into the cake, telling Gwen about Natalie at school who ate junk food all the time and

was overweight. Gwen asked how school was going, and Sara
was surprised when it was enough saying, "It's fine."

After settling into the comfort of the old, beamed
tearoom, tucked into the antique booth with one, low wattage
lamp on the table and the incredibly delicious cake and coffee,
Sara was ready to talk.

"Thank you very much for doing this, but, like, should I
call you Ms. Minot?"

"No, that's okay. Please call me Gwen."

"Okay. Well, thank you for bringing me here. This place
is so nice." She looked around the room, then looked down
at her mostly eaten cake. "Anyway, I think my father's afraid
I'm going to have a nervous breakdown or something without
female contact or something. I'm really all right."

"Good. You certainly seem all right."

"Thanks. Yeah. You know about my mother moving to
California. So, but I just don't want to be all damaged and,
you know…"

"Um. Yeah, I think I actually do know, Sara. I lived
with that issue when I was your age. I made my high school
promise not to tell any of the teachers or students that my
father was killed, and my mother died as an addict. I only told
one friend, Lady. Yeah, believe it or not, that was her name.
Her nickname. Anyway, Lady grew up rich in Toronto and was
very well mannered, refined, even shy. So her nickname was
an affectionate joke I came up with. Lady was as dark skinned
as me and that was one reason we became best friends and
talked about everything. So, I told her. She promised not to
tell anyone, but you know what, Sara?"

"What?" Lulled, Sara was in a happy astounded state.

"I don't think Lady ever really got why not telling people
about my past meant so much to me."

That hit Sara like a laser. Gwen told her and her father about her past. Wow! This astounding woman sitting across from her, who just got Sara's angle on things so well, got rescued by that boarding school when she was Sara's age. So, Gwen might actually identify with her. Wow.

Sara indulged in some mutual appreciation. "So maybe I'll be a deeper person, like you. Filled with character instead of marshmallow."

"Marshmallow!" Gwen pulled her head back and laughed with her whole body. They finished their cake and drank some more coffee.

That was all she said on the topic. The longer Gwen didn't add anything, didn't shovel on the adult advice, the more Sara enjoyed herself. They talked about books and music and movies and TV shows they liked.

Later, back a few steps in her Georgetown home, Sara wondered if she thanked Gwen enough. It was after dinner, after her father sheepishly didn't ask her about her coffee and cake experience with Gwen. Sara was sure he wanted to ask. There was no way his not asking made sense any other way. He wanted to ask for a million reasons but wanted to allow her to have her own relationship with Gwen.

Sara sat at her desk facing her computer screen thinking and not looking. She wanted Gwen to be her mother. Sara was jolted back in her chair. She had been living with that desire for a few days but announcing it in sentence form was quite a shock. Nothing more occurred for a while as Sara stayed very still.

She found herself lying on the floor. It was a thing she liked to do, lie there and really see everything around her. Now though, thoughts were bubbling deep inside. It took ten minutes for her to stand up again. Needing a mother replacement was such an obvious psycho mind state she wanted to laugh.

She patted herself on the head. "Get real Sara."

She had a brain flash and tumbled back to her computer. Already knowing Gwen's husband's name because she'd already done some snooping, she did some more snooping. It didn't take long. She gazed at pictures and read articles about him and by him. She sat back. Okay, he was solid middle-class, black and probably a great guy, but the point was he was middle-class like Sara and her father. He might be rich now, but he went to public schools and grew up in the suburbs of Albany, New York.

And, he and Gwen didn't have any kids. Did Gwen want kids? Sara wasn't a kid, but she still needed something Gwen offered. What was it? Guidance? Adult information? God, it was an ego boost for Sara to have all that to offer. Adults love being needed.

Sara chewed on her pen, then tapped it against her knee. If Gwen wanted her father, it had to be partly because he was cool and lived in Georgetown in a place he designed and was an art conservator and Gwen was cool and an architect. So why would she just go for money, for the rich husband? Hell, Gwen made her own money and Gwen collected art and Sara's father took care of Gwen's art. And he had a nice, smart, complete daughter, if she could say so herself.

Sara found herself practically hyperventilating. Okay, she had to steady herself. She had to stop projecting. If there was one thing her father taught her, it was that wishful thinking could result in puffing up yourself until reality exploded you into pieces.

She got back on the floor, lying down, staring straight up. She didn't know if her father and Gwen got together in the physical way, yet. It was a disturbing thing to even begin to contemplate, and she immediately stopped. She chewed on her lips, slowly, top, then bottom. She didn't know a lot about what was likely to happen, but she had a very strong sense where to basically aim -- more involvement. Yeah, somehow, she had to get more emotionally connected with Gwen, without glomming onto her like a hot mess. Sara stayed there, lying still for a few minutes.

Back up, she walked to her computer where she did a search for a Buster Keaton silent movie. It was fun, but only for ten minutes. She sat in her armchair and read a few more pages of "War and Peace". It was taking her forever -- two months and only ninety-eight pages -- but she hoped she'd get into it at some point. Obviously, Gwen read it, probably in high school, along with tons of other major books, like kids do who go to private schools.

CHAPTER NINE

September 24, Sunday

Happy Birthday. Only five more and you're out of the teenage paradox of -- too old to be coddled, too young to be on your own. Picnic at two? On your floor?

That was your birthday card message to me?

Yup.

Sounds good. Two o'clock.

Jake gave Sara online subscriptions to the Economist and The New England Journal of Medicine.

She said she was 'happy, really happy' with that and the party. He baked a cake and they picnicked on her floor.

*   *   *   *   *

Larny looked over at Gwen, his phone in one hand and a cup of coffee in the other. "Someone shot on M Street late yesterday."

Jesus. Larny saying that jammed her heart. "I know. I just read that. They killed a store clerk." She wondered if she should text Jake or Sara, but Larny was a few feet across from her in their kitchen.

He raised his eyebrows. "Good thing we moved out of that hellhole."

He smiled as she lowered her head, feigning indignation, growling, "The hellhole that was our first actual house together." It was the best she could do.

Larny countered with a mock frown and drank some coffee. "You miss it?" He held onto his coffee cup and leaned back against the large down chartreuse damask pillow between him and the antique maple back of the breakfast booth.

"Uhh, yes and no. I missed the house until this place was done. This place is a lot bigger, and I think better for us."

"Yeah, I think so. I think you've gotten even better at interior design. You were already an ace at exterior design. Maybe landscape design's next? Work on our backyard?"

Gwen raised her head. "No, I don't think so. I think I'll just get someone to design the garden. There's only so much I want to take on."

"No, I get that. Neither of us has the time or inclination, I guess, to tend to a garden. It has grass and the row of evergreens in the back look great. There's room to run around a bit."

Gwen balked. Why was he talking about running around in the yard? The two of them running around? Not likely. Kids run around in yards, and pets do. Larny didn't want a dog. He made that very clear many times. It was the second time that morning she didn't say what was on her mind.

She might text Jake later.

She finished her breakfast and took her dishes to the sink. Larny was standing, sideways to her in the middle of the kitchen, facing the doorway to the dining room, that led to the living room. "Want to lounge on our new downy sofas? Sink into more big downy pillows?"

She really did want to move on, sink into something tangibly comfortable, and said so by nodding and moaning. Walking, moving, might help her replace the awful unease that seized her insides when she read about the shooting in Georgetown, and the unease when she wanted to surreptitiously text Jake, right across from Larny. Why couldn't she just tell Larny about Jake and Sara?

"God, that little family...the father who's the art conservator and his daughter, Sara? They live across the street from that store."

"Yeah? You feeling protective? You said you got a charge out of taking that Sara to the museum."

"Protective?"

"Yup. I know you...you and all those girls you help at Bardon."

Gwen's racing nerves attacked her brain. "I guess. I'm sure she's safe. I'll relax. It's my day off."

She had to grab her computer and coffee, just like Larny was doing, heading to the living room. It was becoming their Sunday morning reading ritual. He sat on his dark mustard velvet sofa, across from Gwen on her satin slip covered black geometric-on-a-light-gray-background sofa. The sixteenth century French hope chest between them had coasters for their coffee cups.

"What are you reading?" Gwen asked the obvious to keep steady.

"The Post. You?"

"New York Times."

Larny reached for his coffee. "Read any good books lately?"

"Uhh, fiction? No. I'm reading that Colin Powell biography you gave me for Christmas. I'm actually liking it. No big surprise."

"Yeah? I thought you might like it, just because it's such a rare bird story. Really, the guy's one of a kind and came along at a particular time. Yeah, it's crazy how he did what he did and then, it's not crazy at all. Know what I mean?"

"Umm. I think I do."

Larny fixed his eyes on her. "You okay? You seem sort of bugged."

"Really? I'm just tired."

He sat back, eyes on her, calmly receding into the sofa.

"Are you bored? Not enough stimulation?" There was no irony in his voice or face.

She glowered. "You can have too much stimulation."

"Yeah, I know that now. Instagram taught me that when I looked at it that one time."

Gwen put her head back with a satisfied chuckle. She gave him a knowing smile. "No, I really am having a true blast with this house and I'm not a jaded jackass. And I am thinking about buying a summer house for us.

"Jaded jackass." He grumbled his appreciation for her using his old expression. "No, you're not. God, if you were, that would make me Mr. Jaded Jackass."

"Mm, sorry, it would." She wasn't able to enjoy much in the way of quipping, especially since it felt like Larny was compensating for her in some way.

He sat still and she tried to think of something to say.

He interrupted her blankness. "So where are you thinking?"

"Uh, maybe Vermont. It's far enough away and different but still not so hard to get to. Fly to Albany and drive an hour over the border, right?"

"Fly to Albany without telling my parents?"

"Not every time, I guess. Your parents are a part of our social contract though."

"Social contract?"

"Yup. I said it and I'm sticking with it. Instagram is the opposite of a social contract. Marriage…now, marriage is a social contract."

Her tangy phrasing and peculiar declaration of principle certainly seemed to please Larny. He grinned and stuck out his chest and wrinkled his brow at her. "Wow. Say that again, please. That made me incredibly hot for you."

She shook her head, snipping, "I refuse. The moment's passed."

"Yeah, okay. But I want to hear that social contract talk again sometime soon. Please."

Gwen beamed, very heated up too, wanting to go to bed right then, but after years of experience with Larny, knew it would be better in a few hours, probably much better -- midafternoon, when the lazy brain gets so easily overpowered by the libido.

He seemed to be remembering that too. His voice was husky and tight. "Anyway, Vermont's different all right. Could be fun."

"Yup, I'll let you see things when I've actually come up with some options. And, yeah, owning instead of renting will mean headaches, but I'll be able to buy something that I restore and sell, or we like enough to keep."

Larny just nodded. She was stating what had already passed between them a few times recently. She summed up, "But I'm taking my time, enjoying looking on that real estate site I showed you."

"Um, good. Yeah, I'm ordering myself to rest. Nothing to do for one whole day." He leaned forward and took off his shoes, beautiful Italian leather in the style of nineteenth century British rugby shoes. He leaned his head back at one end, with his summer thin light gray, alpaca stocking feet over the other end of the sofa. "Great article about the Japanese situation in the Post."

"I liked the article on California in that issue."

Larny mumbled, "Okay. That'll be next."

Okay, he was being extra overtly accommodating. Why? She wasn't imagining it. She knew him. He was polite and even formal almost all the time. It was a major trait that drew her to him on an on-going basis. But she could also tell when his effort was forced. She'd think about it later, after they stripped and joined together naked in bed, after they rose up and over the top of the top together.

Meanwhile, nothing was more titillating than teasing each other, putting it off. For now, they both receded into their own screens. That lasted five minutes for her.

The predicable ideological rigor of the New York Times only frustrated her, and she told Larny the long stone bathtub was whispering to her and headed upstairs to their ensuite. It was only the second time she'd used the new salmon with wiggly white stripes, marble bathtub – a perfectly carved out oval hunk of luscious sensual potential sitting alone on the right side of the twenty-five by eleven-foot bathroom. A row of windows extended the long wall in front of the tub to the view of a row of seven tall junipers, seventy-five feet back. The evergreens were there for backyard privacy year-round, but Gwen loved the look of them. She wasn't sure why. Because of the rows of junipers around the campus at Bardon, probably.

Larny hadn't used the tub yet. She slid in and sighed. She'd take an extra-long soak, her head back. The hot water in the mildly cool air-conditioned room startled her senses and, with her eyes closed, she started to think. It was Sara's birthday. Jake was with her having some sort of gorgeous little private celebration. That thought was about to lead Gwen to some sort of passionate reverie, and she splashed some water and redirected herself, opening and closing her eyes again to concentrate on buying a house in Vermont. Her mind slid collaterally to having coffee and cake with Sara. That get together was even more fun than she'd expected. With the kids she helped at Bardon she often felt hopelessly distant. Her role was just to raise scholarship money, sit on committees, and interview scholarship candidates. Gwen pushed back her wet hair. Sara seemed much more mature than some of the nervous, extremely distrustful poor kids Gwen interviewed. Why was that so intriguing, that more trusting calmness of Sara? Gwen always imagined Larny being like that. She gathered all the scattered particles of information she could over the years, from his family's photo albums and videos, and from Larny's stories. He matured like a young person ideally should, one stage at a time, growing and stretching and growing, like a healthy, strong, slow growing tree. The comparison with her was obvious. She always felt Bardon allowed her to rise out of her ashes like a phoenix. Larny's background was more gradual. He had to put a lot together himself to get into Colgate and then Yale, and then build a very successful business on his own. But his roots were already pretty firm and deep.

Gwen knew she'd never have that deep, firm support. She was already well into puberty when Bardon got her. She shifted in the water, lying flatter, wanting to laugh at herself being a wet phoenix, looking at the flat white ceiling, her hair submerged. She sat up more and squeezed some water out of her hair.

She didn't ever quite get middle-class people. Lower class people she got. Upper-class people she usually got. Larny seemed to get every class of people, but most of the middle-class types Gwen came across seemed to cling for dear life to the petty bit of power and comfort they owned in their own middling world. Larny was the exception that proved that rule, but then she met Jake and Sara. They were exceptions too. They were so perfect.

She sat up and got out of the tub. The thick, pale green terry cloth towels got her dry quickly. With the soft white, terry cloth robe wrapped around her, she sat on the rock maple contemporary interpretation of a Windsor chair.

Gwen was going to have to get more information on Emma, the woman who walked away from her only daughter. She'd already looked up her Facebook page. That was as vain and stale as most Facebook pages. The pictures only told her Emma was attractive, in a sullen sort of way. She might be able to ask Jake a few questions someday.

There was the problem of running out of art to take to Jake. What would she do to see him and his daughter?

*　*　*　*　*

Late Tuesday morning, clouds mercifully blocking the sun, Jake stopped working, turned off the air conditioner in the studio and opened the windows, all five of them. He had to climb on top of his soapstone counter, shoes off, to grapple with the old black steel frames, wiping away four months of cobwebs, soot and dead insects. Walking across his counter to rinse out his dishrag in the stainless-steel sink was precarious in his socks, so he took them off. He left the top windows down, feeling the air push in. He got down and opened the studio door. More air came in the row of windows. It was air mixed with muted street sounds, near and far and it was air that was still fairly muggy, but it was a freakish cool spell. At least, for now, Georgetown wasn't overcooking out there.

He opened the door to his bedroom and walked to the distant windows facing M Street. As expected, the pull of back to front air through screened windows energized his indoor atmosphere right away. He'd learn, like he had all his adult life, to adjust to the inflow of city noise and slightly noxious city air. Soon enough, it would be mid fall, then late fall and the windows in his apartment would get lowered more and more as the outside began to freeze. He had to move on by then or stay. But how could he stay?

He went back to the studio, put on his socks and shoes, pulled open one wide steel drawer and, with two hands beneath the acid-free folders, lifted the Mary Woodall watercolors to the soapstone surface. The watercolors, Gwen's watercolors, had come out almost perfectly and Jake only had to dab a tiny amount of solvent with cotton swabs to get them looking like there never were any tape stains along their edges. He phoned Gwen and left a message.

Apparently, she didn't answer her phone very often. Maybe it didn't matter. He was going to be desperate soon if he didn't get more work. Rent, utility bills, food -- what was he going to do? He saw that ad two nights before and it lived large in his brain. The New England Art Conservation Center, NEACC, in Newburyport, Massachusetts had a job listed. It was for a paper conservator with at least five years professional experience. The pay was eighty thousand with benefits and a raise after two years of successful results or performance. He didn't remember how they worded that. The money sounded so damned good to him, and the health insurance and the location looked unbelievably good. It was ideal. Jake had never been to Newburyport, but some people gushed over it online, so Jake assumed the job would get filled fast.

The problem was, would Sara want to move there?. That job began at the end of his time limit pledge of late fall, but he'd have to apply now. Was that rushing things for Sara?

Or was he holding back because of Gwen? Was he that lost in love with her, lost in the studio encounters with her that danced around and through him minute by minute, day by day, making him crazy with just wanting her to come in and be in the same room? Yeah, he was that nuts about Gwen, but he was more and more desperate for money.

He placed his computer on the counter and looked at the web page for the town of Newburyport. It didn't seem possible anything could be that attractive. Maybe it was just the pictures and the pitches of the Chamber of Commerce and the Center. Eighteen thousand people lived almost entirely in beautiful antique houses next to the estuary of the Merrimack River meeting the Atlantic. The public high school was in the center of the town and looked gorgeous and not too large -- seven hundred and eighty students, grades nine through twelve, so less than half the size of her current high school. The reviews of the Newburyport high school were mostly raves.

What if he got that job in Newburyport? Would that lure in Gwen? Could he use it as leverage by asking her to move there with Sara and him -- divorce her husband and marry him, or at least live with Sara and him? Jake's chest heaved as he leaned against his work counter, knowing he'd just planted a seed inside his psyche.

*   *   *   *   *

Gwen did come in, after calling him back later that day, flowing in her dark blue cotton skirt, white shirt and narrow sandals. And Jake was fomented. He turned on the camera before she got there and now was asking himself, why? He'd never touch her. She'd never touch him.

She did a slow turn, scanning the studio. "Maybe I should have gone into art conservation, just to have a place like this to work in every day." She grinned at him, shaking her uneven lustrous black curls for emphasis.

Jake surprised himself as he suddenly grew steady enough to utter his prepared pitch. "Yeah, it's hard to make a living though."

"Really?" Her posture hardened.

He stopped any movement, aiming at her. "No, I'm not saying I wouldn't do it over again, but it's so seductive." He paced himself. "I don't know if you've ever seen the set-up for the art conservation graduate program at the University of Delaware. It's actually at Winterthur…the Du Pont Estate?"

"Oh, really? Oh, that's right. That's where the University of Delaware art conservation program is. Yeah, I've gone to the museum there a few times. Wow, yeah, so, that's where you studied." She was walking back to him.

"Yeah."

"Um, lucky you. All those acres of gardens on the rolling hills and those gorgeous buildings the DuPonts built."

They stopped speaking for a second and nodded in agreement. He had to complete what he started.

"Anyway. I think the arts look so good when you're young, but I'll have to admit I'm tired of having to chase after work. See, I was going to ask you today if you know any other collectors who need conservation work."

"Oh, right. No, I'm sure I do. Let me think." Gwen became still now, her mouth opened slightly, the tip of her tongue touching a couple of top teeth, thinking. A few seconds of that led to her compressing her eyes, hands squeezing her hips, as she looked up at his ceiling. "Aaron and Joe, might have a couple of things. Uhh, sorry." She looked at him. "Let me think. I'll think about it. I'm sure I know someone."

They were very far from encouraging words for Jake. He felt severely frustrated. How could she have some big solution to his sad lack of work? He needed too much work. "Yeah, just…yeah, if you manage to bump into someone."

She tilted her head. "No, I'll think of someone. And, Jake, please don't hesitate about these things. It's just business. I don't mind at all."

Jake did mind because he had to mind. Words squeezed out, through his tightened jaw, "Anyway. You have a portfolio?"

"Yes. I have a group of documents, Civil War letters and medical reports and discharge papers from the Civil War."

"Okay."

"My husband collects Civil War documents." She blushed and looked down at the portfolio on the counter.

It hurt Jake slowly, the way suppressed bad news hurts, twisting the knife already deep inside. She hadn't mentioned her husband since one of their first conversations. Of course, she had a husband so he would be mentioned.

Jake had to assume this was the end of Gwen coming in, bringing in work for him. He sucked in his stomach, tightened his jaw again, knowing Newburyport was the subject for dinner with Sara that night.

While they quietly studied the assortment of letters and their original envelopes and the half dozen official documents, Jake was pretending normalcy, his guts knotted, but his face and torso forcibly loosened. He focused hard just to get through the ordeal. Most of the husband's twenty-seven letters and six documents were in very good condition except for a few tears. At a glance it looked like about half of the items would need work. Gwen asked Jake if there were any methods of boxing the letters he'd recommend, and he said he'd look into it and get back to her. He'd keep all the items for now. He wrote her an estimate as she walked around his studio, silently. He handed it to her, and she began to read it, stopped herself and just signed.

"I'll put narrow, thin shredded strips of Japanese paper on the tears with wheat starch paste. With any luck you won't see them. And I'll get back to you about the archival storage albums and boxes or whatever." He'd already said that and his voice clattered around the room.

"Great. Thanks." Nothing to add, they began to head out, her first, carrying her now vacant portfolio. She stopped at his studio door. "Oh, I forgot to give you my check. For the work you did on the Mary Woodall watercolors."

She fumbled in her bag, a small cotton bag that had bright abstract geometric designs on it. Her check was in an envelope. Her checks were always in plain white envelopes, always folded and wrapped in small, unmarked sheets of paper. Architects, Jake was aware, tended to love human imposed order in shapes, sizes and materials.

He had to accept her offering, enough to pay one third of one month's rent. She turned to walk away, and he knew he saw pity on her face. Downstairs at the back door, she said thank you and disappeared.

Jake stormed, groaning, coursing through his apartment. He wanted to get away from his rage, but Gwen seemed so damned blasé just then. Jake stopped coursing by hitting his fist against the closet door in his bedroom. He turned and leaned back against the same door, groaning, rubbing his sore hand. He needed money to survive. He needed it to be a father to Sara.

The Newburyport job started in December. Jake hobbled to his studio counter, sat with his computer placed waist high and began the application process. Finally, after years of hesitating, he was applying for a job away from the bogs of Washington, the luscious, sultry, Gwen bogs.

He spent the rest of the day lecturing himself, rubbing his hand. He had to stand on his own firm ground. If Newburyport lived up to its online looks and cools, at least he might be able to do some of that Gwen luring. It was all he had.

CHAPTER TEN

September 27, Wednesday

A t least now dinner was over and Sara was alone in her room. God, finally, she could breathe. What a nightmare. Fuck, she hated the idea of moving to that stupid Newburyport place her father was talking about and showing pictures of as she was trying to gulp down dinner. First, he sat her down in the studio and gave her the dire fact that they had to move for a job. She knew he was struggling to get collectors and all that, but she didn't know it was all that damned dire. He couldn't pay the bills? What a nightmare!

She barely said anything to him. Nothing could be said to talk him down, talk him back in off the ledge. That seemed obvious. And she knew he wasn't actually excited about moving to that stupid place. He loved Washington, the place he'd come to for college and came back to after graduate school. He loved his fantastic apartment as much as she did. He just kept talking up stupid Newburyport at dinner and she stared at the pictures on his computer, hating the place more and more. Very old, snug seaside smug. Eighteen thousand people? And some small hick school that he was talking up because of its size? Jesus H. Christ! A little New England school filled with hicks. And nasty freezing winters. She was living in the middle of Washington, in Georgetown, and her father had to move them to inadequate Hickville for a job?

It took Sara less than half an hour of panicking to grasp her only hope. She had to think it through by lying on her floor and staring at the ceiling, and she did turn it around in her brain a few times but, she was sure. She had to call Gwen Minot. Getting closer to Gwen was always her plan, anyway. She just had to speed things up, fast.

First, she'd email her. Sara sat at her desk. It was twenty to eight and Wednesday night so was it a good time to catch someone's attention?

> *Dear Gwen,*
>
> *I was wondering if I could talk to you on the phone at some point. Something dire is happening that I'd rather not try to explain in this email. Any time that suits you. Thank you very much.*
>
> *Sara Holtz*

She added her phone number and then sent it. It was almost seven-thirty. Sara figured Gwen might have to work out a time to talk during the next few days. Fine, as long as it didn't take too long. Her father already sent his job application to that center. She stood up and got her Spanish book to read and sat on her bed. Wading through homework was torture sometimes. At some point, about eight o'clock, she checked her phone and there was an email from Gwen. Good thing she checked.

Hi Sara. Nice to hear from you. Hope you're ok.
I can talk now. Good time?

Sara looked, heart galloping. Gwen sent the email about ten minutes before.

Hi, yeah, now is fine for me. I just read your
reply.

Sara waited. Five mangy minutes of nothing at all and her phone made its imitation old phone ringing sound, lights glowing. Sara walked to the far corner of her room as she answered, super consciously focused. There were the on-going night street scenes out the window, but she stopped seeing.

"Hi."

"Hi Sara. How are you?"

"Fine."

"You wanted to talk about something?"

"I did. Thanks for calling. Uh, I don't know if you've heard my father's applying for a job in Massachusetts. It's an art conservation center north of Boston?"

A slight pause, then Gwen grumbled, "No, I haven't heard that."

"Um, well he wouldn't want me talking to people about it probably. I just wondered if you knew any collectors who could bring him work. That's the reason he's wanting to do this. He says he's done all the work there is around here. Other than your art. Is that true? Sorry, I just would so much rather stay here. I really like it here. I don't know. Sorry to bother you." Sara wanted to control her emotions and thoughts more and just stopped yakking.

"No. No, Sara. I'm glad you told me." Gwen's voice wavered. "No, I had no idea he was applying for jobs."

"Yeah."

"Mm, well he asked me earlier today when I was dropping off some work, if I knew any collectors. Yeah, I'll work on it. I will."

Sara didn't respond right away. It sounded to her like Gwen was bothered and needed to work some things out. Sara needed to pull back and not push her away. More talk might make Gwen feel like Sara was annoying. That was the last thing Sara wanted Gwen to think or feel.

"Anyway, thanks," Sara said.

"North of Boston?"

"Umm, Newburyport. Yeah."

"Oh, Newburyport. Right." Gwen coughed. Then, back with a deeper, more reflective voice, she said, "Really gorgeous place. Yeah." A pause. "Uh, Sara, any other jobs he's applying for, that you know of? I'm just wondering."

"Not that I know of. He just mentioned that one job. He did say there aren't many jobs in art conservation. But I'm afraid he'll have to apply for other jobs, other places until he gets one. Right?" Sara had the feeling the bait might be working now.

"Um, well thank you, Sara. Thanks for telling me. I'll see if I can do anything. Your father's work is too good for us to lose. I mean, for us around here in the District to lose. Mm, so how do you feel about it? Moving to Newburyport?"

"Not good. Not good at all. I really like it here. I don't want to give my father a hard time."

"No. Not at all. Of course. You like Georgetown, and the whole District, right? I'm sure he understands that. You have your own gorgeous place in the center of things." Gwen's voice was still grumbly, halting.

"Anyway, I just wanted you to know."

"Thanks. Good."

Sara steered toward a polite ending, thanking Gwen again with as few words as possible. Gwen thanked Sara back again and they said good-bye.

Sara put her phone on her desk and walked over to her other window. Even if things were potentially awful, Sara liked that conversation. It made her feel more emotionally connected to Gwen but Sara kept it short enough for Gwen to feel the loss, the empty loss of losing them. And Sara wanted her father to find out about that conversation. She just did not want to move out of Georgetown. She stared out the window, a lump in her throat. It was so beautiful and felt like home to her, those cool nineteenth century buildings all around. So many of them were painted great colors, some just bright white. She leaned her face close to the glass to see more laterally. There was that dark green painted brick building she liked with the small Italian restaurant on the ground floor and probably an apartment above and then one more apartment above that? Or was it all one apartment? Probably one per floor. The shades were pulled halfway down in the top floor apartment and Sara could see the top of a table and a sofa or something in there. People lived in mysterious ways inside those condos or apartments. They probably thought that when they looked at Sara's windows. Maybe they saw her sitting at her desk in front of one window, or looking out the second one, like now.

She had to be careful. She knew that. She stepped back and sat on her bed. DC was just so intriguing. There were so many places she remembered as a little kid, seeing things on weekends only, then back to nothing anywhere all around her in the suburbs. She was just starting to finally make DC all hers.

*   *   *   *   *

Gwen went back upstairs to Larny who was now naked in bed under the sheets, his hard, erotic outline just visible, his muscular chest and arms on full view, all of it enough to incite a sex riot. The phone call only took five minutes and she'd try to get her mind off the pent-up emotion she was feeling, because there was Larny smiling at her, expectant and looking his beguiling, alluring, burly self. He always took her mind off troubles in the past. She turned off her bedside light.

Sometimes there's a payoff for waiting. Instead of having sex constantly, as in the first few years, they then began to savor it, saving it for weekends, then some weekends. Now it had been over two weeks. They owed this to each other, to all those quintessential times in the past that were so easy to summon up.

"Everything all right?" He began to gently stroke her arms, shoulder, neck.

"Keep doing that and it is." A cold wave of guilt and anxiety washed over her. She had to push through it. She couldn't fail Larny. It wasn't that often he initiated sex. She started things most of the time and he always said he was aroused by being on-call, willing and able. Once or twice, to get a laugh, he stood at attention and saluted when he said that -- always with some clothes on.

Gwen had to get into the Larny and Gwen zone, but also had to admit to something, a bit of something.

"I think I'm losing that art conservator I've been using. He's moving out of town." The words were garbled at the end as Larny kissed her neck. Something, everything, was heightening her reaction to their bodies pressing together and Larny whispering in her ear.

"I really liked the way you looked in that skirt earlier."

"Yeah?"

"Umm…those smooth, soft legs. You have the most beautiful legs in the world."

And they were off. Larny was murmuring sexual things and feeling so hard and smelling so good, Gwen knew what to do to rise to the occasion with him. They'd do it together, very, very much together. Except, Gwen had thoughts of Jake getting hard looking at her legs…her getting less and less capable of censoring anything.

TWO

CHAPTER ELEVEN

SEPTEMBER 30, Saturday

Earphones in during the flight, Sara only responded with single words while they knocked around getting their bags and getting a rental car before driving thirty-five miles north out of Boston on Route 95. Jake asked her to ditch the earphones during the drive. Yes, she would glower out the window and yes, it was as if the sour mood made the landscape around them calcify, but he did have to raise her to have some standards, even if, for Sara, the standards might seem to only revolve around behavior.

Unfortunately, the hotel was indistinguishable from the little drab strip next to it, so Jake's fatigue was heralded by Sara flopping down on her bed next to the window with a look of disgust. He knew she liked having a window next to her, just like on the plane, so to placate her a tiny bit he let her choose, neither of them saying anything. She sat, then slowly reclined, moaning.

Jake put their two bags on the chair next to the desk, before he did his more reserved version of sitting and reclining. He closed his eyes for a minute or two, then sat up, checking his phone. He didn't want to think about Gwen, and he was starting down that path when he closed his eyes.

"It's going on two. Want to sleep for a bit and then head into Newburyport and eat? We never got any lunch."

She sat up slowly. "I'm fine with going now."

A laconic, pallid Sara shuffled to the bathroom. She emerged and it was his turn, urinating, washing his hands and face, checking for his wallet, car keys, room key cards and cap. They made their way down the hallway past orange and blue striped wallpaper and over dark blue carpeting with small white stars, then down the reflective black-steel elevator, through the shaded glassed-in lobby, out into the sun blinding parking lot to the dark gray Toyota Camry and got in. The metal composite shell immediately grilled them, enough to make him open all the windows and turn the air conditioning all the way up, which howled through the vents as he drove quickly, hoping the movement would push the hot air out. It did after a minute, and he turned the fan down to a less histrionic level, closing the windows.

Trying to cruise along, Jake mumbled to himself about parking as close to the center of the town as possible to avoid tourists. "Although, it's well after Labor Day so tourists might not be a problem."

"Tourists?"

Jake didn't respond to his daughter's contempt. The drive was almost attractive -- an old New England local highway dividing occasional worn-out houses and small, anemic shopping centers, and a fallow field with a barn claiming it sold granite and marble slabs. The slabs were barely visible, mostly covered in tall weeds. They got to Route 1 and turned right.

He offered a small apology. "Honky-tonk, old New England style."

Sara shrugged, looking straight ahead. "Ugly, inadequate style."

Jake kept positive. "Famous Route 1. It's an early American highway. And look at all the gorgeous wetlands behind the buildings."

"Um."

Jake laughed. "Stop. This will get us to Route 1a, which is the stunning one. I was on it once years ago coming up here to Plum Island. I never got as far as Newburyport."

The strip on both sides of them was standard stuff but he'd expected something better. They started over a bridge that arched over the Merrimack River where it almost met the ocean and everything suddenly glistened. There was deep blue water slowly bobbing white boats everywhere, next to a classic heirloom by the sea, townscape. White church spires off to the left and new brick townhouses with huge balconies to the right, all faced the water. Driving to the Newburyport side of the wide estuary they exited and turned left under the bridge and headed into the center of town. Jake's pulse increased with every dazzling block. It was an effort to not point at the boatyards and seaside restaurants or the antique brick townhouses in a row, all with window boxes jammed with flowers. It got better and better. The center of town curved to the right around Market Square, where Jake moaned. He couldn't help it.

He glanced at Sara who was turning her head to look out the side windows. He said, "It's Federal. I've never seen so many connected Federal buildings."

Sara said nothing.

When he pledged to himself to try to keep a lid on any enthusiasm, to not look like he was trying to sway Sara, he didn't know it would be even more beautiful than the pictures online.

"Let's drive around a bit and then park."

"What's Federal?" Sara asked.

"Simon's warehouse is. Uh, basically, big multipaned sash windows, a door in the middle, a flat front, all symmetrical and classical. It's sort of British Georgian architecture made American right after the American Revolution. That's all I know."

They drove up a gentle, steady incline for a few more blocks of three-story brick buildings, most of them still connected. There were restaurants and cafes everywhere, with clothing stores interspersed. They passed an obvious landmark, a gorgeous brick library with a sign in front saying something Jake could only half read as he drove; something about George Washington and General Lafayette meeting there.

"Look at that." He still muffled his real excitement, his jaw tight, pointing to the left at a Victorian Italianate bank. The elaborate cocoa colored sandstone was accented with large curved original windows and with a spectacular Italianate door in the center. It was the best-looking bank he'd ever seen.

At the top end of the gentle hill, perpendicular to them, was High Street. Jake took a left. On both sides were large eighteenth and nineteenth century houses, all more gorgeous than the last one.

"Damn. I can't believe it. Sorry. Now, this is Route 1a."

She just shrugged. "It's very nice looking. Any non-billionaires live here?"

"Yeah. Yeah, it's probably cheaper than Georgetown."

"But Georgetown's part of a city, a major city. This is just a place for yachts and stuff...antiques."

He said nothing. Sara's alienation was bound to be intractable, but he had to push forward and there was far from anything wrong with what he was seeing.

High Street continued and while Jake glanced down leafy residential side streets with two- and three-hundred-year-old houses all tucked in tightly - that all looked gorgeous too - he knew he should turn around and get to a restaurant. He would in a minute. Most of the houses on High Street were early nineteenth century mansions and a number of them, on the right as they drove, were up a slope, hundreds of feet away from the street. Jake kept his thoughts to himself. There was clearly a ton of money in the town way back and, apparently, still.

After making a U-turn, they headed back along High Street toward the center of the town. On second review, the houses looked even more gorgeous, one after another, after another, for a few miles. Jake had to snap out of it. He pulled down a side street and turned around. Halfway back, he turned right and found himself looking at signs saying, Bartlett Mall. It was a very old-fashioned *mall* -- a few plain grassy acres with a pond in the middle. Jake parked, telling Sara it was only a few blocks to the commercial center.

They walked the gravel pathway around the duck and geese pond. The air was cloudless, bright and dry and floating somewhere in the mid-seventies. Jake could feel sunrays filling the pores on his face and hands as they passed between occasional trees. There was a fountain spurting water in the center of the large pond.

"Cute," Sara said, only willing to trivialize. No response from him might underscore the hollowness of her doing that.

At the end of their path, they came to a stately brick building with its back to them.

"Bulfinch? Really?" Jake poked his face closer to a bronze plaque on the building. It was an old courthouse, Federal styled.

Sara looked away as he read the plaque aloud, an inscription about the famous early American architect, Charles Bulfinch who designed the perfect brick courthouse in 1805 with its back to the pond, facing the center of the town below and the earlier, seventeenth century harbor beyond. They crossed High Street.

They walked down sloping Green Street toward the harbor. Jake ignored Sara's lumbering form next to him as they passed Federal mansions converted into law offices and an old Inn and a late nineteenth century Mission styled church turned into a restaurant. Jake suggested they head to the street they drove up earlier, but as they walked, Sara said she liked the look of a restaurant on Pleasant Street. The menu looked good to Jake and not overly expensive. Plus, they had crab cakes on offer.

Jake nodded and Sara looked bloodlessly at him. "I'm starving."

*　*　*　*　*

A bit before seven the next morning, Jake roused himself to move out of his bed, shave and shower as stealthily as possible, and write Sara a note on a pad of hotel note paper.

I'll be in the lounge at the end of this floor. Text me when you're up and ready for breakfast. Xxoo Dad

Sunday morning meant most people were still asleep. He rounded-up oatmeal, toast and coffee in the main lobby's breakfast room and carried it up the elevator to a small lounge area he'd noticed the day before. Each floor must have had one. Apart from offering him some privacy, it had a large corner window facing out from the side of the building with a view of a local road, a wooded area and, off in the distance, some modestly attractive detached houses of mixed periods. He sat on a sepia toned fake leather chair and leaned over to eat his cereal. Stuffy lack of fresh air or not, he was prepared to contemplate.

Why didn't he and Emma come into Newburyport during that trip to Boston? They did drive up to Plum Island, two miles south of Newburyport. It was part of their honeymoon concept -- not much of a concept because they didn't have much money. They spent three days in Boston and a week on Plum Island. Sadly, Jake's main memory was how stultifying the effort became. The bits of romping in bed were weak tremors after all those eruptions at home, before they got married.

For years since, Jake remembered feeling guilty about looking at Emma and seeing a boring, alien creature during the trip. It was their honeymoon, but he kept questioning, in his mind, her choice of clothes, like the red dress she wore out for dinner the first night in Boston. It wasn't just the shininess of the red, it was the cheap shininess of it and tight fit. She had a lot of clothes, all cheap. Then there was the fake leather jacket she wore around town.

She drank too much and laughed too loudly, all more extravagantly than anything he thought he'd seen from her before. He began to hate Boston. He complained to her about how haughty and conservative it was in style, living up to its image of being so politically progressive and so socially repressive. He made a speech to her at dinner one night, early in the trip, about the place no longer being the WASP enclave depicted in old movies or books. It was actually entirely dominated by colleges and universities. "There are tons of them in and around the city, way more than any other city anywhere. Adolescence everywhere you turn, all wrapped up in the latest damned social and political dogma. The actual adult world is sealed off."

He knew he didn't really know Boston. Jake also knew he was making Emma more and more unhappy. He had a creeping sensation that almost everything about him made Emma feel bad about herself. There was no way Emma wanted to explore historic, beautiful Newburyport. She said she didn't even like the beach. It was too cold to swim. By the fourth or fifth day sitting or walking while looking out to sea, him giving his tormented speech a few more times, letting it leech out of him in some form, he began to shut down. Emma seemed to have permanently hunched shoulders, her skin increasingly sallow, even at the famously beautiful beaches of Plum Island, next to the famously beautiful Newburyport they never visited.

*   *   *   *   *

Sara was as close to dire mode as she'd ever been in her life. The pull of Newburyport for her father was obvious. If she said she didn't like the supergloricous town she'd sound like a supreme brat. What could she say to her father who needed a job, who was desperate for money, especially now that his damaged little daughter was living with him? She couldn't tell him how much she hated leaving Gwen behind, leaving DC behind, leaving her cool Georgetown bedroom behind. He didn't want to leave DC behind, did he? Gwen? Did he want to leave her behind?

His message was he didn't have a choice. Sara got that.

Torrents gushed through her head for hours while her father slept. Now that he was finally out of the room eating breakfast or something, she sat up, went to the bathroom, got a drink of water and grabbed her computer.

She sat on her bed with her back against the fake headboard. At least in Georgetown she had a real bed, a beautiful antique one. Straight into it, she typed, *Bardon School*. She'd already looked at the astoundingly beautiful pictures and videos of the school but that was a few weeks before and right now she didn't have time to pretend-indulge. She clicked on, *Admissions*, her stomach empty, feeding off bitter remnants of itself.

Okay, there were the requirements listed -- applicants needed to take the SSAT exam, send previous grades, letters of recommendation, examples of written work and write a personal statement. Hell, just that exam alone sounded scary. The deadline for applying for next year was months away, but she was in a big hurry and would let Gwen and her father know that. Bardon recommended a school visit and tour, with an interview. Wow, a lot of weird stuff that would involve Gwen and her father. Sara wiggled in fear thinking about Gwen. She'd be shocked Sara wanted to apply to her special, big deal high school, but would she just think Sara was being a stupid brat?

Sara sat upright. Gwen would think there was no chance in hell of Sara getting in, all paid for by them, the Bardon School, but the point was Gwen and her father would see Sara's Bardon scheme as an SOS – Gwen had to rescue Sara and her father had to help. They had to see that Sara desperately needed both her father and Gwen in her life.

At least that long pissy application process would involve Gwen in her life, and in her father's life, for six more months.

Of course, if Gwen just married her father anytime soon, they'd have plenty of money to just all live in Georgetown. Why wasn't Gwen just divorcing her stupid husband? There was no way her husband was as cool as Sara's father. The guy might be rich and handsome, but Sara knew Gwen was in love with her father and Sara knew Gwen was making big money of her own.

Sara was sweating, her whole body wrenched stiff. Apply to Bardon? She glanced at the pictures of the very, very adequate old stone buildings with ivy on them and the campus quadrangle and the playing fields. The library was the most gorgeous thing she'd ever seen. Her heart was pounding. God, it was the best high school in America.

She closed her computer. She needed a shower to clean off her dripping anxiety and to think more calmly.

Hot water streaming over her, eyes closed, she schemed. She had to wait to say anything to her father. She had to start slowly and build a case with him. She had to play him very carefully, and talking to Gwen was where to start.

CHAPTER TWELVE

OCTOBER 2

Ew job day arrived and, as soon as he was awake, Jake had to lecture himself to stop thinking about Gwen. His cravings had to be squelched. Still, seeing the beautiful town out there, he knew it would be easier to suggest she move-in with Sara and him. Maybe Newburyport would be the ticket. She'd love it. It was time to tell her how he felt about her and ask her to divorce her husband -- politely request she divorce her husband?

He had too much on his mind -- too much. He had to concentrate on one thing at a time. Now, it was getting a job. And there was nothing guaranteed about that. Jake showered, shaved, got dressed, ate and got out.

He talked Sara into hanging around town instead of the hotel as he went for his interview. She looked a bit forlorn as he dropped her off, but he was confident she'd like the cafe they'd tried the day before. She could eat there and wander off to the big, old bookstore in town, or the library or some shops. There was every chance in the world the town would charm the bejesus out of her.

He drove to what he assumed locals only endearingly named, *The Industrial Center*. He and Sara drove there the day before. It only amounted to around thirty industrial buildings a couple of miles from the town center. Most of the buildings were mid-sized warehouses, but some were small manufacturing companies that managed to look architecturally designed. The New England Art Conservation Center was in its own small building right on the main road. NEACC was laser cut through a large rectangular sheet of black steel over the front door. The single-story building was made of dark red painted cinder block with a pitched gray metal roof and Jake noticed the skylights between the solar panels on the pitched roof.

He was ten minutes early and sat reviewing. They could see from his resume that he met all the educational standards, plus, he had all the experience and letters of recommendation. His stellar letters of recommendation from the DC Art Conservation Center might be his most powerful appeal. What else? His experience was on the full range of issues, working in a major city. He'd tell them about the conferences and lectures he'd gone to in the last ten years and, if he could, he'd mention some of the articles he'd written too. But Jake knew it was compatibility and professionalism that usually landed the job. Okay, he had to just go in and hope for the best. He wanted that job.

Not exactly emboldened, but determined, he pushed the doorbell, aware of the camera on him, and five seconds later he was buzzed inside.

A woman sitting on a stool twenty feet away, behind a long metal table with what looked like a very large old map on it, said hello to him. He walked to her and introduced himself.

"Oh, hi. Yeah, I'm Beth Sanchez. Uhm…" She turned to someone sitting at a bench against the wall, ten feet to the side. "Is Mary still on the phone?"

The young woman nodded, her head down facing the map. "I think so."

"Well let me tell you a few things until she's free. Mary Brooks is our Chief Conservator. I don't know what you know about us. Mary and Cathy Redmond started the Center about, let's see now, about eighteen years ago. Cathy no longer works here. She's a paintings conservator and works in New York, in Brooklyn. Uhh, so we serve the New England area, mostly the northern region, so lots of public and private collections in Massachusetts, New Hampshire, Maine and Vermont. Some things come from far and wide. We did a Tucker Margeson oil painting for a collector in Knoxville, Tennessee two months ago. Uhh, anyway, here, I'll show you around."

Beth waved her hand for him to walk around the fifteen-foot-long metal table with Upson board on top. She was possibly his age or older with gray hair to her chin and no makeup. She had on a light blue cotton shirt over another shirt -- something Jake had seen conservators do before. It protected their clothes from the, *rare smattering of splattering*, as one of Jake's graduate school professors liked to say. Art conservators were notoriously careful and physically conservative as a species, so that professor knew she had to emphasize how rare it was that anything messy should occur.

Beth had on very sensible, albeit nerdo, white nursing shoes and baggy flannels. Jake was glad he didn't wear his sports jacket and tie.

He got the tour of the place, and it was almost exactly what he pictured ahead of time -- a few large stainless-steel sinks, lots of flat surfaces for benchwork, easels in the paintings section, lots of tall vertical shelving and lots of metal, sliding drawers. There was a loading dock with an electric metal door on the parking lot side of the building. It took Jake back to the eight-plus years he put into the DC Art Conservaton Center, right out of his graduate program.

Beth asked him about the weather in Washington while she walked him through and introduced him to the two paintings conservators, Carla Levy and Hope Jefferies, who barely looked up from their easels. Hope was the young woman sitting near Beth in front earlier. She was really looking young to Jake and, while Carla Levy was middle-aged, Hope's brief, slightly askance looks at him made him feel like maybe he was looking too old to her or too male. There were no men to be seen.

Hope was the only person with any style so far. It might have been her being in her twenties that made her care, but her hair was a perfect Afro. Her over-shirt was a beautiful dark blue, slightly wrinkled beautiful cotton. And her jeans fit. And her dark brown leather flats were elegant. And she stood up, did an about face and walked away.

Mary was off the phone and waving him into her office just as he was beginning to tell Beth about his time at the DC Center. He was just starting to ease into constructive, positive descriptions, but excused himself and opened the small office glass door. Damned if Mary didn't look like Beth. Maybe it was the other way around. Mary had a bonier face but the same hair and clothes. He reached across the desk and shook her hand, as she stayed seated. He was no longer in open workspace filled with natural light from all the skylights. The only office in the place had the coldest coating of LED whiteness possible, and that was just from one light fixture in the ceiling. Mary sat behind a small wooden desk, dominated by a wide screened computer forcing him to stretch a bit to see her from his chair.

She quickly ran through the same things Beth had about the history of NEACC and the facilities. She then asked him about his time at the DC Center. This time he had a chance to describe his responsibilities at a center similar to the one they were sitting in. A few minutes into it he wound to an end and waited for her to ask him questions, waiting for his moment to proclaim his success in the last twelve years and his reason for wanting to move and change jobs and work at the NEACC.

It never came. The ten minutes of sitting and chatting ended with Mary standing up and thanking him for coming. Stunned, he followed as she walked him out of her office to the front door talking about the nice temperature outside. His brain began to frazzle. What was happening? He was getting the bum's rush?

He stood still, one hand on the front doorknob, trying to think. "You have my contact information? Is there anything else you'd like to know?"

"No. We do have all your information and we got your recommendations. All set. If we have any questions, we'll get in touch. Thanks for coming."

He walked to his insipid, bland rental car, got in and sat for a few seconds, fumbling ineptly with the car key. Somehow the car was on and he drove away, not seeing. They already had someone for the job? Why didn't they tell him that before he went to so much trouble? All the damned trouble and expense. She didn't even ask him if he had any questions, and the interview and Beth's tour took less than twenty minutes? He flew up from Washington for that?

*　*　*　*　*

Sara never asked him about the interview, and it was pretty deadly schlepping back to Georgetown with her that same night knowing how little chance he had of getting hired back in Newburyport and how much was at stake. Would he even want to work in what appeared to be a hostile, cult-like place? The simple answer was, he'd have to take the damned job if they somehow offered it to him.

With the gorgeous seaside town fading away, *no more than two more months of hanging around DC,* whirred in his ears during the trip home. October had begun.

Torn between wanting to see Gwen and desperately needing work from anyone, including her, he managed to get to her husband's Civil War documents. Nothing like rote work in a crisis to make you feel like you're driving in deep dry sand. And yet, mysteriously, it only took him a day and a half to mend the tears with Japanese strips and wheat starch paste. It was the Thursday morning after the trip, at nine in the morning, with Sara at school, when he sent Gwen a text saying the documents were done. It was pure mercy when she texted right back. It was arranged. She'd be there sometime after two that day and she always paid right away.

He was surprised she was so available and responsive. Maybe she had as much romantic need for him as he had for her. Maybe he could lean on her for connections, lean more than he already had. He rehearsed his appeal while he put things away and wiped down the counter in the studio, and then the kitchen, in case she'd stay for coffee. He mopped the floors in the studio, kitchen and hallway. He cleaned an apple and grabbed some walnuts and almonds and ate.

Meeting Gwen at the backdoor after she texted him always felt especially personal and confidential. They'd arranged that a few meetings before, avoiding the frame shop, when Jake knew things had moved beyond initiation, into the full disclosure stage in their relationship. He hoped, now, they were both ready for more than conversational disclosure.

Gwen said she wanted coffee walking up the stairs, before Jake mentioned the possibility. She walked into his studio, put her handbag on the wooden stool and turned to him.

"Sara told me you're applying for a job, in Newburyport."

He felt his backbone go rigid. "Yeah. When did she tell you?"

"She texted me last week and then we talked on the phone. Sorry. I got the feeling she wanted to keep the conversation private, but I knew she was telling me something important, beyond just her and me. I should have texted you or something."

He was too off kilter to know how to try to stay on any planned course. "No, it's fine. I know she hates the idea of moving anywhere right now. I just don't have a choice."

"I know. I get it. I have a possible way to get you more work here, though. I mean, I'm sure I could get collectors I know to bring in their things. I just don't want to, you know, make empty promises when I can't really guarantee how much work there would be. I know how much rides on this."

"Um." Instinct told him to stand back and not lean on Gwen at that moment. He looked at the floor, listing to the side, arms folded, wanting to be a birch bending just enough in the wind.

Gwen said, "I already have two collectors, maybe three, who have as much as I've brought into you."

He straightened up. "Thanks. Uhh, really the thing is, the Center in Newburyport wasn't exactly offering me a job."

"Really? Why?" Her voice faded away. "They'll what, get back to you?"

"Yeah." He shrugged and walked to the counter, leaning against it. "I think they want a younger person or different sort of person maybe."

"No." She perked up. "Oh, are you overqualified? I looked it up. I mean, yeah, it's in a stunning town. I went there once to visit a friend who lives there. But, and I can't ask you what they pay, but I've worked in the field long enough.

Damn, Jake, with your training and experience and expertise
wouldn't you intimidate the heck out of the provincials?"

Jake spluttered and grunted a laugh, lowering his head.
"Wow. No, but I'll coast in that alternative universe for a
minute. Thank you." He was too embarrassed, along with
stimulated and in love, to function. He just stood, eyes blindly
cast to the side, feeling her eyes on him. Neither of them
spoke, and instead of that growing more and more awkward,
it becalmed him as they stayed in place, momentarily moored.

Finally, he shrugged in slow motion. "Anyway. So, let me
show you the documents."

"Okay. Actually, uh, can that wait? You did promise me
some of that great coffee you make and then show me the
documents."

That roused him even more. The way he made coffee
entertained her once before and he needed the time with her
now. First there was the brief floating with her to the kitchen.
She stood watching as he poured boiling water, cooled a bit,
into a stainless-steel French plunger for five minutes. Then
he approximated cafe au lait with microwaved milk. The trick
was to use good coffee and lots of it. The hell with not really
being able to afford it.

She moaned, exclaiming how good it was and they went
back into the studio, sitting a polite five feet apart and he
delved in.

"I worked for the DC Art Conservation Center right out
of graduate school. It was great training in a bunch of ways."

"Then you just wanted to be on your own."

"Um. I did. You want that too, right?"

Her face set on him, her eyes steady. "Oh my God, that's
for sure. I worked in offices when I was in college just because
I had to. I interned at an architectural firm later. Spending a
lifetime entwined in workplace interaction is not for me and

it's nothing to do with masks and diseases." She widened her eyes and laughed. "God, I do love my fellow human beings. I do."

Jake laughed too. "No, I'm with you. Look at my life."

"Meetings? Ever had to go to meetings?"

"I did. I went to them at the DC Art Conservation Center for eight years. We had meetings at least once a week for an hour. Yeah, the more neurotic a person was, the more they had to say."

She laughed her deep laugh, frowning at him, shaking her head in disbelief. "God, I'm so ridiculously lucky. I'm so damned unrestrained, independent."

That sidelined them for half a minute. They chuckled and readjusted themselves on their stools, sipping coffee, him wondering where to go with that comment, especially since she left it at that. Was she independent of her husband?

He wanted to keep things rolling in the moment and remembered he wanted to divulge more. The coffee drinking social occasion underscored his mood. "So okay, I'll tell you my opinion about art conservation, but I have to ask you to never repeat it. I'd be attacked all over social media or something. Crazed mobs of art conservators would burn down this building, maybe the whole town."

She laughed. "I promise."

"See, it's never going to be easy to know all the things you need to know to take care of such a wide range of materials and artists' traditions, artists' intentions. Who's going to know enough about say, a Rembrandt etching, the intentions of the artist and then know about the paper and inks of that time and place? And then there's a Japanese print and then a twentieth century American watercolor by Fairfield Porter in front of you. Then there's a French eighteenth-century charcoal drawing and then a twenty-first century piece of machine-made paper from China with some Brazilian acrylics all over it."

Gwen watched him.

He summed up. "You have multiple centuries of different cultures' art history to learn, along with fairly complicated paper and ink and paint chemistry and you know what else?"

She shook her head.

Right hand raised, he slowly rubbed his fingertips together. "You have to not be ham fisted."

"It's like surgery."

He laughed, his head back, then faced her groaning, "Um. Well, I mean, lives aren't at stake. I don't want to sound berserk."

Gwen laughed, head down, and he watched smiling.

She sipped some coffee. "That's actually why you should want to work in groups? To share expertise?"

"Jesus, no matter what the subject is, you get the whole thing right away, every time, don't you?"

She blushed so deeply, he had to move along. "Yup. No one person has all the skills and information. But it's just that, big surprise, there are groups and there are groups. People might assume large, wealthy art museums would get the best groups together and they do sometimes. Then some independent regional centers can be great. Or not."

"The D.C. Center wasn't so good?"

"It was great. Then the person in charge retired and her replacement was not so good. I left. That replacement is still there and I can't go back because she thinks I'm part of the old regime. But I have very good letters of recommendation from their head paper conservator and from my graduate school and some major collectors. I didn't ask you, yet"

Gwen suddenly seemed distraught. She down shifted, almost growling, "God, I really don't want you to go." Her perfect eyes flashed from him to somewhere on the floor. "I'd miss you and Sara too much."

Jake almost shook with the sudden agitation rising in him. All the self-discipline he relied on, all the warnings he held onto so tightly to keep from veering over that line, the intimacy line, could vanish in a second. Should he let it all vanish and tell Gwen how he felt about her?

She spoke first. "Look, I'm really trying to put together a group of collectors who will bring you work. I'm sorry I didn't think of it sooner. I didn't come in here until about five weeks ago. But anyway, I really think it will work. And I'd benefit too, Jake. I need to get back to some serious design work and stop just building my own places. So I'm appealing to my contacts from school and college and the local collectors and the museum people I know. I'm telling them I need work. See, I want good projects, not just someone's fancy kitchen or new sunroom. I want bigger, more challenging work and it's out there, Jake, and I think if I get it, there'll be art conservation involved. I do. Meanwhile, I'll also just tell collectors I know about you."

So, now what -- now that he was fixated on her goals? He and Sara did have a choice? They could stay in DC, with a new life for him and for Sara including Gwen in that way?

He had to say something and not just glare at her, feeling his face redden and eyes swell. "Well, yeah. I'd love that. Thank you. The thing is, I just had to look for a steady income for me and for Sara. Right? And Newburyport looked really good and gentle and quiet. I mean, the high school didn't just look great but seems to have a great reputation. Yeah, and it's in the middle of town. Sara could walk to it, safely, probably very safely...if we could find a condo we could afford. Here, I don't know. It's a city and I know I probably shouldn't, but I worry like hell about Sara."

He stopped himself. Gwen was looking ash gray, like nothing he'd ever seen from her. He wondered why he just vanquished what she was trying to do, unite them, bring them together. His inner conflicts had him in knots. He closed his eyes for a second. "Sorry, sorry." Eyes open, he said, "I can't tell you how much I'd like to stay here and work with collectors you send and all that. It sounds great."

She drew her head back. "I know. You need a steady income for Sara." She cleared her throat. "So that high school in Newburyport looked good? Sara walks to school here?"

"Yeah, it looked really good. But, yeah, she takes a city bus now, and walks some days and she'll walk less often when the weather gets nasty."

"She told me she likes the school here."

"Yeah, mainly, I think, because she gets to live in Georgetown. I hope she likes the school. She tells me it's fine. And she can try to get into that nearby Charter School next year, if we're still living here."

Looking deflated Gwen stood up, saying, "I have to get going. I have a bunch of things to do." She had a way of abruptly ending conversations, then telling him why another time.

He stood up watching and wanting another hour's interaction at least.

Instead, polite, perfunctory remarks from Gwen followed as she barely looked at her husband's Civil War documents and handed him an envelope with a check in it. That was it. Gwen didn't leave any work for him.

*   *   *   *   *

Gwen hit the steering wheel of her car with one palm. Fortunately, her car stayed in its lane. That was it? That was her day with Jake? What was she going to do when she got home?

The idea was to sit around with Jake and devise schemes for a joint future. It was supposed to last hours. Gwen hit the steering wheel again.

She had to calm down, and hope no one saw her. That was her pitch to Jake? Well, it didn't go well. It didn't go anywhere. She was out of art for him, and she was telling him she'd get other collectors into his place? That was it?

There was no way he wasn't a prime candidate for that damned Newburyport job. His humility only made her doubt his sincerity on that topic. Too old? Most of the art conservators Gwen knew looked decrepit. Jake was as far from that as possible. Gwen knew the art conservation field. She worked alongside conservators in major art museums, and she took things to private conservators and to that stupid DC Center, for years. Jake was way cooler than your average art conservator. He had the best resume that stupid Center in Newburyport would ever see. He not only had the skills, he had the professional manners of Barack Obama. Of course, they'd offer him the job, and whatever the salary was, he'd take it because he had to.

Okay, she had to apply more pressure, she told herself with her heartbeat in over-drive as she pulled into her driveway, then around back into her two-car garage, deciding she'd text Sara. It was after four so Sara would be home from school.

After looking around her, checking for any thugs loitering, she thumb tapped away, still in her car, the garage door closing behind her.

Sara, please call me when you get a chance. I'd love to know how the Newburyport trip went.

Love, Gwen

145

Gwen's phone jingled three minutes later as she was walking into her kitchen. Sara's name showed.

"Hi Sara. That was fast. So how was it? Newburyport's gorgeous, isn't it?"

"Um."

"You don't sound enthusiastic."

"It was heaven on earth."

Gwen couldn't help chortling. She needed that teen drollness from Sara.

Sara added, "I still hate the idea of moving there, of living there."

"Your father doesn't think he'll get the job."

"No? He will. He just says things like that. He doesn't like to boast."

Gwen was heading for her living room, aiming for her favorite crimson velvet window seat, seeking comfort to deaden her fear of losing Jake and Sara.

Sara interrupted that foreboding, saying, "Can I ask you something?"

"Sure." Gwen loved Sara's sweet young voice.

"I've been thinking about it. I keep coming up with something I want to do that I think will make all the difference here."

"Okay."

Sara took a couple of seconds. "Well, please don't think I'm being a brat or that I'm over my head here. But I want to apply to Bardon. I mean, I know it's very, very hard to get in and we don't have the money, but I'd like to apply for financial aid. If I don't get in or I don't get the aid, fine. I just want to try. And the reason I'm saying this right now is because if I went there and my father and I moved to Newburyport, well, see, you and I and my father would still be in touch that way."

Gwen was jarred. Losing Sara and her father sounded like misery itself, but Sara wanting to go to Bardon? That came at her from nowhere and felt slightly brazen on Sara's part. Gwen didn't want to take too long to respond. "Hmm. Wow! Okay, I'm sort of surprised. Do you know much about Bardon though, Sara?"

"Well, I've been researching it online. I've been thinking about it for a month now. I mean, I know they say you should go and get a tour and talk to them and get an interview."

"No, I'm just surprised. I mean, of course you can apply, if your father wants it too."

"I haven't said a thing about it to him. I have to wait. He won't want it, not at first. Me even saying I might live away from him? But…"

"Yeah, I can't imagine, Sara."

"But, Gwen, if we move up to Newburyport, that's it. We'll never see you again."

Sara sounded like she might be crying. Gwen completely choked up. "God, Sara. No, I'd hate that."

They needed time to regain their voices. Gwen also needed to get the idea straightened out in her head.

Sara sneezed, then said, "Please know I want to go to Bardon all on its own. I mean, yes, I know it would bind you and me and my father together, but I decided I wanted Bardon before moving to Newburyport was even mentioned. You said such interesting things about it, and I looked it up and, wow, it just started to get under my skin. And, again, I know it's extremely hard to get in and I'd be a crazy long shot, you know, kind of applicant."

Gwen was astounded by the wiles of fifteen-year-old Sara. The girl was blatantly contriving some way of binding them all together. A thrill ran up and down Gwen's spine. It was bold, impetuous youth magic, what this Sara was proposing. Gwen knew that's what it was and that she should stand back from it. Silence seemed like her only-defense.

Sara waited.

Ten adulterated seconds of that and Gwen felt herself partially surrendering to Sara's blatant contriving. "All I can say is, you should talk it over with your father, Sara. I can't even describe the endless complications of even just applying. Anyway, I don't want to influence you or discourage you, but I also don't want to discuss something as big as this behind your father's back. You can understand that, right?"

"Yes. Oh sure. Okay, I just wanted to mention it as a possibility. I will mention it to my father. Can I mention it to him first?"

"Oh, of course. I won't say anything. Uh, tell me when you have said something, okay? Please?"

"Absolutely. I actually have to go because I have a lot of homework to do tonight."

Gwen agreed, knowing she had to think, and catch her breath, away from Sara – catalytic Sara. They said good-bye.

Gwen spent the next hour almost motionless, sitting, standing, mumbling to herself, and then occasionally rolling her head in circles. Sara's audacity was one thing. The kid didn't shy away from what she wanted. But Sara's vulnerability was another thing. The kid was just rejected by her mother and her father was worried about financial solvency and he was trying to move her away from Washington, away from Gwen. That's when Gwen's thinking would come around to Sara wanting to bind them all together. It was so damned potent and compelling; Gwen couldn't get it out of her brain.

Gwen sighed at how easy it was to convince herself that Sara should just apply to Bardon as an exercise, and to see what might happen. She wondered though, how Jake would ever go along with such a thing. She had to try to put it out of her mind. Sara applying to Bardon might be fun and games, but Sara would have a hell of a hard time getting in and Gwen just plain couldn't help at all. Sara was not a poor, minority kid.

* * * * *

Sara bit her nails, not something she encouraged herself to do, except she was zeroing in. Ever since saying good-bye to Gwen, Sara knew some force of nature had been let loose. She opened her window a few inches to take in some new air. She looked around wondering how she ended up sitting on the floor earlier, legs crisscrossed while she talked to Gwen. She knew she was going to say all those things to her, eventually. It was just that the text came, and Gwen asked her about the trip to Newburyport and Sara just let loose.

How the hell did it go?

She kept biting her nails, desperately hoping she hadn't put off Gwen -- blown any chance for Gwen to come around again, at least some coffee at The Haunt.? Did Gwen get that Sara was just trying to alert her to the situation – Gwen had to do something, or they were going to split apart?

One thing was for sure. When she said the Bardon plan would bind them all together, Gwen reacted. Sara could practically hear Gwen gasp. So, was it a good gasp or not?

Sara just wanted to get off the phone after she unveiled the Bardon idea. There wasn't much more to say or do. If Gwen didn't get that Sara was trying to grab hold of things before her father moved away, then there wasn't much Sara could hope for.

They didn't have a lot of time. Sure, applications to Bardon weren't due for months, but her father moving could happen any time. Sara had to talk to him and put him on proper alert.

CHAPTER THIRTEEN

October 9, Monday

Jake – How's everything with Sara? I send her emails and texts and she almost never sends anything back. I know she's angry at me, but I can't have her act that way or things will just get hopeless. I need your help with this. I always said good things about you to her. I just hope you're doing that for me now.

Please try to get her to stay in touch with me.

Emma

The text hit Jake's phone just before ten on Monday night. He expected that complaint from her, that he wasn't saying enough about just how wonderful Emma was, now that Emma was looking so uncaring and self-serving.

There it was. Did he have to answer her? Was he supposed to worry about engaging her scorn if he said nothing, or said the wrong thing? Should he tell her to screw off? Ten minutes after getting Emma's text, he groveled the least amount he could.

Emma – Sara's fine. I'll tell her to answer you. I didn't know she wasn't.

Jake

Sara was still awake in her room. He heard her go into the kitchen a few minutes before the damned text from Emma. He texted her

Sara -are you busy?

No. Busy?

Can we talk for a minute?

Talk now? Ok.

He made his way to the hallway, determined to keep it short. Sara opened her door and leaned against the jamb.

"Uh, I just got a short text from your mother asking me to encourage you to answer her when she emails or texts."

"Oh, God. I do. Just not every time. Why does she do that, lean on people emotionally all the time? It's so…." Sara didn't show any sign of wanting to finish her analysis.

"Okay, but, yeah, just try, please."

"Try what? By the way, she doesn't even send that many emails or texts. She's just, I don't know. What did she say, that I'm not staying in touch?"

"No, just that, well, yes, she thinks you're not answering her."

Sara's facial muscles tightened, and her eyes narrowed. She stared at the door for a few seconds.

"Dad, can we talk? Sit down somewhere? The studio for a minute?"

"Sure, okay." Slightly surprised, he turned and made his way a few steps down the hallway, and she followed. He pulled a stool to the middle of the floor for his daughter and then one for himself. It was all a bit formal, and Jake's curiosity was mounting as he let her set the stage.

She was as perched five feet away. He waited.

"I'm going to make a suggestion and I think you might not like it, but I want to ask you to just think about it. Please?"

He nodded warily.

"It's something I've been thinking about for a while; for weeks in some ways. Mom sending that text to you just nailed it, I think. See, I think we're doing really well, you and I, here. Except, of course, we don't have enough money. I know Mom's one hundred percent gone and I know I'll have to come to grips with that in some way at some point. But, Dad, it's already done, basically. She can't change that. She's gone. She did it, left. Plus, I am getting older, and I have to figure out a few angles for my future. Just like you have to. You have to make enough money to pay the bills and I have to do well enough in high school to get into college and get financial aid. That's the big deal. The rest of it, like me having friends and a social life in high school are big deals too. But Mom leaving and you being here and struggling and having to get a job up in Newburyport, that just tells me I have to do what I can do for myself. Please don't get insulted by that. Please. You're the best person in the world."

Tears flowed down Sara's cheeks and Jake began to tear up. He was swept up with Sara's homily and emote at the end. It wasn't the end. She was holding her hand forward, palm facing him. She blew her nose on some tissues he grabbed from his desk, and he sat back down.

"I need an angle, Dad. We all do, but I'm fifteen. I really do."

"Okay." Now he wanted to laugh but stifled it. He was still waiting.

"Okay, now please just listen, please. Don't freak out." She licked her dry lips. "I want to apply to Bardon. I've researched it for weeks and thought about it and thought about it. I even talked to Gwen about it. I know it sounds crazy. How could I even get in and there's the crazy cost of it and all that and living at a boarding school. But just hear me out."

Jake felt his head tremble and all his insides turn cold.

"Really, Dad, hear me out, please. Whatever job you get, wherever you have to move, I'd have that as a base, Bardon. I need a base, Dad. It's, from what I'm reading, two hours from here. But here's the thing…if it's even half as good academically as it claims, and Gwen claims, I'd get an amazing, amazing education. There's no comparison with what I'd get here or even in Newburyport. Plus, plus, I read about this on the Bardon site, but also a bunch of other sites online, that financial aid kids at high schools like Bardon have a much better chance of continuing to get that financial aid in college. Weird but true. The colleges know those hotshot poor kids are sure things. Hell, schools like Bardon just get kids into better colleges, anyway. They educate better and then they get you in with aid and they do it all for you. I mean, I know I'd have to do my bit, but…"

"And they work the hell out of you," Jake blurted. "What is it, five hours of homework a night?"

"Nope. They brag about having all sorts of academic and non-academic kids and only two hours of homework most of the time."

"Sara, I think it's murder to get into schools like that, especially Bardon, and you'd have get it all paid for. And no, come-on, I want you here. You just moved in with me." He was halted, fully aware of his compromised position with

Sara now that he brought up moving away from DC. Sara was waiting, letting him vent.

He altered his route. "You're too young." He leaned forward being melodramatic to emphasize his feelings. "It'll be hard enough for you to go to college, hard for me watching you go away then." All interaction stalled for a moment. Jake hunched over, sinking into the elemental fear that he couldn't afford to send her to college. And she was thinking Bardon would erase that problem? She wouldn't get in and he and Sara didn't need complicated farfetched illusions added to their problems.

He sat up and tried to reason it out, feeling desperate. "But, seriously Sara, what makes you think Bardon would accept you and pay your way?"

"I know it's a very long shot. I just have to try."

Jake had nothing to say.

Sara said, "I know it sounds nuts. I've spent hours and hours thinking about all the stuff involved with applying. Think of it as practice for applying to college."

He stretched his back. "My God. So, you've been researching the hell out of this, haven't you?"

She wrinkled her forehead. "I have."

"And you talked to Gwen about it? When?"

"Just a couple of days ago. I asked her a couple of questions on the phone. By the way, if you go to Newburyport and I go to Bardon, at least we'd stay connected to Gwen. I hate the idea of losing touch with her, Dad. She means so much to me."

He knew when he was outmaneuvered. Sara did have a genius social IQ. He sputtered, "If I went to Newburyport, as you say, and you were way off in Delaware, living on some campus, I'd never see you."

"There's a train to Boston and then to Newburyport. Plus, plenty of kids from New England go to Bardon. I could get rides and be with you practically what, a third of the year?"

"Sara, sorry, but it's such an impossible, crazy idea. Sorry, but it is. I'm sorry we don't know where we'll be living a few months from now, but we will know."

"I need a base Dad. I need Gwen, Dad. I need her in my life along with you."

He froze.

She said, "All I'm asking for is a visit. We can go and look at it and see what we think."

He was stymied. Like it or not, Jake was being asked to march in Sara's cavalcade of outrageous prospects. He stood up, just to end his torment. "Let's talk about it some other time. You've just worn me out. I'm an emotional wreck." It was him pretending to remain neutral, positive, kicking the can down the road.

Sara, emitting an air of partial triumph, rose, kissed him on his cheek and said good night. And Jake had to twist and turn in the grotesque chasm between Sara's unreal ambitions and his all too real lack of prospects for hours, whether he wanted to sleep or not.

*   *   *   *   *

Tuesday morning's mortification lasted until he decided what to do next. At eleven-thirty Jake texted Gwen asking if she could talk. He guessed she knew why, because she immediately texted back.

Yes. I'll call you.

He didn't have to wait long for his phone to buzz.

155

"Hi Gwen. How are you?"

"Fine. How are you?"

"Sara mentioned her idea to you?"

"Bardon? Yeah."

"It has me feeling nuts. I've dealt with Sara having far flung ambitions in the past. It's usually been great, one of her best traits. But applying to Bardon? Me, barely able to pay rent?"

"I know. Sorry."

"It's not your fault, Gwen."

"Well, yeah, I guess. I did try to pour some cold water on it, but I knew I had to be careful, or she'd get her back up. I remember adults trying to dismiss my teen age schemes."

"Exactly. That's it. But, Gwen, can we safely get across to her how little chance she'd have of getting in and getting it all paid for?"

"Yeah, I've been thinking about that. Uhh, does she know it's really unlikely? She might. I mean, I'm assuming this is a non-starter for you, that you wouldn't even want her to go."

"No, sorry. God, I absolutely wouldn't.

Nothing was said for a few seconds.

He grumbled, "Problem is, I know Sara has her heart set on applying." He cleared his throat. "I know she does, at least for now. I mean, Gwen, she's been doing research like crazy for weeks on it."

"God, I know. And, so, she probably knows more about getting into Bardon than she's letting on. She's saying she just wants to apply, right?"

"Um. That's what she said to me. She wants to visit first."

"Sorry, but Sara might even know the demographic game. She really might not be expecting to get in. Right?"

"Right. That occurred to me, too."

"Anyway, so, Jake, meanwhile, just so you know, they'd ask both you and your ex-wife to contribute. Sorry, but that's what Bardon would ask for on their applications for financial aid."

"Well, apparently Sara's mother's spent her savings on her condo and car and makes, from what she says, just enough for food and electricity."

"Okay, hmm. You have to tell me about her sometime. But obviously you realize Bardon would probably not be impressed by that. They'd ask for tax return info and, you know, proof about what you and she can afford, not just what she claims she can afford. Just like colleges, they want the parents to contribute something."

"I hate to say this Gwen, but we are dealing with a fifteen-year-old who might think Bardon's so well-endowed they dish out money left and right."

"Exactly, and yeah, sorry, but they don't. Bardon has over three billion dollars in endowment. It's a really wealthy school. But, I mean, Sara, I hate to tell you Jake, is pretty much a middle-class kid technically. You know what I mean? Demographically. The school loves to boost the same kids universities like."

"Right. Sure." Jake hated the idea of Sara getting rejected by Bardon or any damned institution. He stood still in his studio with an inner conflict no words could truly express.

"And Jake I couldn't do much at all to help Sara. I mean, if you even wanted me to. That's one of the things that bothered me so much after Sara brought it up. It's a non-starter for me, too. I'm all about getting poor, talented minority kids in. That's my mission there. Right?"

"Oh, sure. No, of course. Well, so look, I read online only fourteen percent of their applicants get in. What the hell? Maybe we can gently communicate that stat to Sara."

"Um, if she doesn't already know."

"Yeah."

"Again, sorry for sounding officious, but tell me this. What are Sara's grades like?"

"Pretty much straight A's in middle school. She got a C in history last year."

"Extracurricular stuff? Violin? Basketball?"

He was surprised by her hardened voice.

"She played the harp for a year. The school's music teacher had one in the room. Yeah, she loves joking about that. Mediocre at sports so far but writes. She started, and then was editor, of the middle school literary magazine and wrote most of the poems and short stories. She had to because no one else cared. She likes that joke too. I know jokes don't get you in."

"Oh, God, I love her." Gwen's tone warmed up again. "No, Jake, she's so wonderful. Jake?"

"Yeah?"

"I have to keep some distance from this, but I hate the idea of dismissing Sara in any way. I just have to tell you that because I can't tell her. We'll have to soften her disappointment together, I guess."

Jake's whole being reeled. He said nothing while shaking his head in disgust.

"Jake? You still there?"

"Yeah…sorry, I just have to grasp what we're saying. We're trying to steer Sara's white-water raft to hit the rocky beach as gently as possible. Yeah, and I think I've been swimming upstream emotionally so long trying to raise Sara I'm worried I'm too tired to do anything but stop and let the current take me. It's not easy stuff."

His ad hoc poetry seemed to stop Gwen. He thought he could hear her breathe in and out.

Now he had to ask for a response. "Gwen?"

"It's awful." She groaned. "And all I can do is bear witness from a distance. God! Sorry, but again, Sara has to fit the latest exacting admissions algorithm. Right?"

"Right. Seriously, I absolutely get that. No, Gwen, please don't worry about it. Sara has to deal with that kind of reality. We all live inside someone else's quota system."

He shocked himself with that sour judgement. And Gwen didn't say anything. He sat down in his bedroom chair, frayed. And he couldn't even bother to add, once more, that he didn't want Sara to go to Bardon, anyway. He rolled his head and held the phone away for a second.

They were both stalled, unable to find any words to sort out the impossible situation. Jake remained silent while Gwen slowly filled in with a few more regrets. He resorted to asking questions about Bardon and they talked for another ten minutes. The school was good for all sorts of kids when Gwen went there. All sorts of kids excelled academically and socially. They became a tightly knit group with very few stragglers. And, yup, Bardon very conveniently shared the same curriculum and definition of political and social standards with almost all universities, so Bardon kids did very well after graduation.

It was when he was off the phone that Jake began to get a poisonous dread in his guts. He was out the door, walking the streets of Georgetown. He saw nothing and heard nothing. He'd lose Sara. The pull of Bardon meant he'd lose her. For one thing, he'd lose Sara's confidence. He just got her into his life, finally, after so many years of watching from twenty miles away. He walked faster. The idea of him not being able to protect her from disappointments was bad enough. All parents had to deal with that. But, even if Sara weren't serious about Bardon, her groping for it made Jake feel truly desperate for the two of them.

If he could just get enough work to stay in Georgetown Sara could apply to those alternative public schools. A big if, almost entirely dependent on Gwen, who was already the out of reach love of his life even without all this added disruption.

*　*　*　*　*

It grew inside her for the rest of the day. Gwen hadn't expected to feel so irrationally conflicted and found herself uttering stupid praises for Bardon on the phone with Jake as if she were rubbing it in. She might as well have been squealing with delight at how happy she was at their lousy lot in life.

She had to help them the only way she could. There was the list. Sitting at her desk Wednesday at two in the afternoon, Gwen reread the names of twenty-one collectors she could try to nab. The cover letter was complete. She'd print it twenty-five times and go to UPS that afternoon. Her resume, with Jake's added, should appeal to the people she picked. Six of them went to Bardon -- two the same year as Gwen. It was pushy, but professional. And, hell, she was only sending it out to wealthy people with big houses and substantial enough art collections. She was doing those people a favor.

CHAPTER FOURTEEN

October 14, Saturday

A Saturday drive took the shape of Jake and Sara in a rental car aiming for Delaware, straight north on I-95. They cruised along in the metallic blue Subaru and Jake liked the looks of the car, telling himself he was nuts to have a wayward opinion like that. But Jake asked himself if he were nuts every five minutes all morning. And meanwhile Saturdays were important days for him to meet with whatever few potential clients he might have. He didn't have any, so that concern was well short of moot.

Sara looked preoccupied, not saying much, then chattering. She was dressed in clothes she bought on sale after Christmas the year before with money she got from her grandparents and money she earned babysitting. The clothes were formal and elegant for Sara -- forest green cords, black leather ankle boots, a pale gray turtle-necked sweater. Then, her naturally thick wavy dark hair was brushed as flat as she could get it. Jake often heard her complain that her hair was, *impossible to control.*

Her chatter was about the music her new friend, Ryan listened to.

"It's like he has no clue and so I said, 'There are decades of great music. You don't have to listen to what your friends listen to.' Jesus, he's such a conformist."

Abnormally disengaged Jake looked blankly at the highway. His mind shifted to his own clothes, him sticking with his summer work kit – khakis with his favorite pale blue cotton buttoned down shirt. No reason to go to much dress-up trouble.

Sure enough, almost two hours into no pertinent communication, they drove down Hollows Mill Road the way the GPS commanded and there on the right, about fifty feet back, on the edge of tall pine woods, was the name carved in a large oblong tan granite boulder -- *Bardon School, Established 1764.* The deeply incised letters and numbers were painted dark burgundy. Jake drove up a slightly inclined road with woods on either side, still mostly tall pines and, after about half a mile, meadows and buildings appeared on the left. Two young girls and a boy were jogging in the same direction Jake was driving. There were soccer and football fields and stone walls in the distance, bordering woods. They passed over a small fieldstone bridge with a creek bubbling below. A couple of hundred acres were cleared out of the middle of the eight hundred the school owned.

They followed the wooden signs, painted white with carved, burgundy colored lettering, to, *Admissions, Visitor Parking.* The parking lot was almost filled.

They were fifteen minutes early but maybe they could hang around inside until one o'clock. They wandered where the signs pointed them, between some pines, Jake aware he was on Gwen's property, half wanting to be an idiot and swoon. Maybe the sweet terpene smell of pine sap was drugging him as he felt the soft give underfoot from the thin bed of pine needles over granular red clay serving as a path to the door of the admissions building.

They passed under the white clapboard portico and entered a large room with a receptionist straight ahead. There were people milling around -- two Bardon students talking to two parents and a young girl, and five groups of parents in various combinations of sitting and standing. Some of them seemed to be speaking German. Jake, starting to feel sensory overload, vaguely took in the heavy, white-washed beams everywhere and the fact that the eighteenth-century thick plaster and beamed ceiling was fairly low but luscious. They walked up to a dark gray paneled wooden counter.

Jake introduced Sara and himself. The fifty-something receptionist smiled facing her iPad. She was a small, bony woman, natural beautiful gray hair to her shoulders and very little make-up.

Responding to Jake introducing himself and Sara, the woman said, "Hi, yes, good to see you. How are you, Sara?"

"Fine."

Jake wanted to hug Sara.

"Your tours will begin in a few minutes. If you could have a seat, then we'll get two sets of students to take you both on separate tours. Okay?"

He wasn't going with Sara? He decided not to ask and just sit, both first using the bathroom.

That done they sat in a corner on an empty antique bench with padding tied at both ends and with the coffee table strewn with magazines and a Bardon School Prospectus. The framed pictures on the walls, some paintings, some drawings, were mostly colorful abstractions by students, not what Jake expected. He expected old pictures of the campus in different stages of development from as far back as the school's mid eighteenth-century British colonial founding.

Jake and Sara sat back as much as the right-angled bench allowed.

"How are you doing?" He looked at Sara.

"Fine." All pinched, she was looking down at her boots.

He concentrated on his shoes. A few students entered the building and passed, creaking loudly on the long floorboards toward the receptionist. Ten seconds later they were in front of their father and daughter prospects.

"Hi." A girl and a boy both said that, and another two girls stayed back a few steps. They were all in the same thin cotton burgundy turtlenecks with Bardon embroidered in small black letters. Jake hadn't seen school clothes on any of the other kids out there and never online, except at graduation.

"My name is Martha Bernoni and this is Leon Fields. We're your student guides for the tour."

Jake and Sara stood. Martha was aimed at him. Nadia and Shelly something shook Sara's hand.

Martha announced, "So let's get started and please ask questions along the way."

In the middle of a group shuffle, Jake and Sara followed the guides outside into an overcast sky gleaming through pines. They all followed the admission building's scrunching pine needle path. It was getting windy and damp. The sun might reappear but without it, there was a hint of autumn –the deadline. They were out in the more open *Bardon Common* when Shelly and Nadia began to lead Sara along a brick pathway off to the right, fronting a row of stone buildings. Martha turned, walking backwards facing him.

"We'll go a different route, so we don't bump into them." She had a bit of a New York accent.

They went left on the curved brick pathway passing a few of the hunky impressive old stone buildings around the grassy Common in the center of the campus.

"We'll show you a house first. This is Barnaby House, a girl's residence."

Inside Martha yelled, "Visitors present!" Sure enough a couple of solid old doors closed, thudding loudly somewhere as Jake followed his two guides upstairs to see a girls' double. Martha knocked at Room 17 and five seconds later just opened the door. It had the predictable bunk bed, two small closets, two desks, and two chests of drawers. The two girls seemed less than excited about being on view, both standing dead center, mumbling hello, glancing away. It was approximately twelve by eighteen feet, not counting the closet and small bathroom. The room was a bit messy, nothing unwholesome, but with some clothes piled on the beds and the two girls were in sweatshirts and jeans with morning teenager disheveled faces, not completely ready for the day. There was a golden Sisal carpet on the floor and rippling white plaster walls, and a big twelve over nine white wooden framed window that looked new, solid and beautiful.

Martha thanked them in her slow, throaty, gravely nasal way. Calm, raven-haired, sharp featured Martha was in charge of her own space and was not your ordinary, insecure and angry about it, sixteen-year-old. She closed the door and escorted Jake and Leon back outside. She walked at a steady pace, not exactly quickly, but methodically, with an almost weightless scrapping of her green rubber boots. Her blue jeans were nothing special, but they fit well, and she had the sleeves of her Bardon sweater pushed up to her elbows.

When they got back outside to the middle the Common Martha explained that most of the original eighteenth-century buildings circling around them were now houses, meaning dorms. Then there was the next grouping of buildings that fanned out around the eighteenth-century buildings. They were mostly nineteenth century classrooms, and then some twentieth and twenty-first century buildings fanned out beyond that.

Jake said, "The buildings just keep growing over time?"

Martha smiled politely. "I guess. Although, the number of students remains pretty much the same."

She and Jake faced each other and then away. Jake glanced at Leon, who just about smiled tolerantly.

"So, the library?" Martha apparently knew from the form Jake filled out online, that he chose to see the library and the art museum.

Jake nodded. He was getting a headache and wished he'd eaten more that morning. He needed to drink some water and would if he saw a chance. He started to wonder who this confident young Martha was. She did have a pimple on one cheek and her long hair had a showered but barely brushed lack of concern. But he began to feel that Leon was more and more left out. Leon was only a first year and said nothing so far. He was black and young looking even for his age, so Jake wanted to include him. Jake asked him what subjects he liked.

Leon was walking next to Jake with Martha ahead, who half turned to listen.

"Uh, Spanish is good and Introduction to Art's good."

"Yeah? What do you do in art?" Jake noticed Leon perked up.

"Draw. We sketch compositions and then we paint. Next term it's printmaking and then ceramics."

"All first years take that course," Martha said, walking next to them now.

"How much homework do you have?" Jake planned to ask this. They were at the steps of the library, and he stopped and looked at Leon.

"Two hours a day, I guess," Leon said.

Martha added, "It depends. First year is a little less, then it increases. Third year there's the most, then it relaxes again." She steadied her eyes on him.

"Okay." Jake was distracted for a second by the scene around them. There were very few students before, but now there were groups heading to the dining hall. He wondered where Sara was and how she was doing.

The sidewalk for the next group of buildings curved in front of Jake. There was a petit, very cute Classical Revival building with stone columns, a couple of Federal styled rectangular brick boxes, a brick Victorian building of dormers and gables and then, right before them, the heavy Romanesque styled H.H. Richardson designed library, with large, thick, rough-faced stones and long, low arches. His doubts about the school and this tour were, sure enough, getting nudged by the design feast around him They walked up the steps, under one of those long dark gray stone arches, through large medieval styled oak doors, through a vestibule to a series of extremely bulky, dark, double oak doors, all open. To the right and left a hallway curved along the periphery of the building. They walked straight ahead into the main room of the library. It was brain-rushing beautiful. There were heavy old oak tables in a series of ten long, curved rows, backing away from a dark oak counter facing them from the far wall. Small lamps with green glass shades accented the tables. Students were everywhere. Jake's eyes automatically moved up. The tall ceiling was covered in sky-blue tiles, each spotted with a single gold circle in the middle. A mezzanine with a dark oak railing ran around the entire space.

Jake wanted to gape but turned away, forcing himself to not ask any questions. Meanwhile there was Leon, saying nothing, looking like some stellar world had hit him between the eyes. A bunch of younger kids had that look.

Outside and away they went, Martha leading, to the nineteenth century neoclassical gray granite museum. The Bardon School's, *Rowley Art Museum*, was known for its American art, although it recently began adding art from the rest of the world. They simply walked through with Jake agreeing with Martha that he could come back later. The museum also made him think of Gwen. Did she spend any time there nowadays? As a student twenty years ago?

Since Jake chose the museum and library, the humanities building and art studio and student gallery complex had to be skipped. That moved them beyond the second ring in the school's evolution to the new sports complex, the auditorium and the math and science buildings. They were all tucked in one or two story, elegant, horizontal structures in various materials – stone, glass, brick, concrete, wood, done at different periods after the Second World War, all by interesting architects, apparently.

He walked on. It all had the appearance of a small, elite private college. Jake avoided country colleges when he was eighteen and aimed at larger urban universities. Gorgeous as everything around them was, the elite high school did feel remote and stuck away to him.

At the end, back at the stone and clapboard Colonial, sylvan, verdant, bucolic hunk called the Admissions Office, Sara was just arriving. There were thanks and handshakes and Jake and Sara sat down on a bench against a far wall. He asked Sara how she had done, noticing her slightly swollen face and her eyes flitting around the room.

She whispered, "Fine. It was amazing. I can't believe it, how great it is."

"Good."

Jake sat back with his heart wrenching, knowing enough to say nothing because he had almost nothing positive to say. He'd hold his breath a little while longer.

They sat and stared at other tormented parents and kids now milling around them. There were very few smiles and much phone staring. People walked by in groups, all getting tours. Jean Smot from admissions texted Sara for an interview upstairs, and Sara was off leaving Jake sitting, watching the video on a tv screen mounted on the wall. Students were filmed explaining the tolerant culture and high standards of the school. The same pitch was on the website. He read through the news on his phone out of desperation. Avoiding the faces of the people around him who were avoiding him, he checked his watch and checked it again impatiently. Sara was only gone for twenty minutes but reappeared, looking even more bloated around the eyes.

It was Jake's turn. He looked back at Sara seated in his place.

"Like going to the dentist?"

She stared blankly at him.

He followed signs upstairs, then to Jean Smot's office. It was about ten by twenty feet and rimmed with beams on the white plaster ceiling and running down the corners. He looked around as he nestled into a large, ornate, antique Windsor chair across from her desk. She smiled mildly, sitting in a low, fifties modern leather chair. Jake almost told her how much he liked the chairs.

"Well, Sara's really wonderful. She asked all sorts of great questions and I hope I answered them and now, please ask any you might have." Her short, unnaturally red hair didn't quite match the naturally faded freckles of her middle-aged skin.

Jake wasn't leaning forward, ready to bolt. He sat back, telling himself to be polite and ask a few questions.

"Well, the tour was great. Uh, I guess my main question is about the schedule and homework. I mean, Martha...I don't remember her last name...."

"Bernoni. Yes, Martha's wonderful."

"Yeah, more sure than your average sixteen-year-old. I'll have to admit I'm wondering about the lifestyles of the students. Do they have any time on their own?"

"Uh, actually I think that's a question you really should ask. No, they do. They learn to manage their time. See, they're here all day and all night." She took a second and then said, "I saw on the information form that you and Sara's mother didn't attend independent schools. I didn't. I went to a large, not always very productive, public school in suburban Pittsburgh. I got through but barely and I don't think it was until graduate school that I knew how to read and write in anything like an organized, effective way."

Jake leaned his head back. "Sounds familiar."

"Yeah. And, after a few years of practice here we just do know how to show them how to manage their time well, and a big part of that is getting work done and then having time to just read a book or watch a TV show, throw a ball around with friends or stare out a window alone or go for a long run with a friend." Again, she paused. She was a pro. "Leon. Leon comes from a very poor background but is bright and wonderful. In a few years he'll be able to do the work and we hope manage an extra-curricular or two. We pride ourselves in offering this opportunity to great, deserving young people."

Jake nodded, feeling absurdly seduced. "No, I can certainly see it's fantastic."

Jean Smot stared at him, her routine smile gone. "I have to add that students at Bardon aren't treated like helpless children who get their hands held by adults. Our students are encouraged to think for themselves and take care of themselves. We do seem to instill confidence in our individual students to go out and tackle the world."

"Right. Great." He managed to just about smile, aching to leave.

"The secret to our success is simple -- students feel it's theirs because they chose it. With boarding, young people get to have their own private worlds for those awkward years when they might need that. This is very much their own world."

Jake's knew it was the best social engineering money could buy. So should he yield to some parental competitive instinct and beg this woman – *please, please, let my daughter in?!*

Jean Smot spoke about Sara making sure she took the SSAT's and arranged for letters of recommendation. The fifteen minutes ended with a smile and a handshake and Jake was downstairs walking out the door onto the bed of red gravel and pine needles, with Sara next to him. He got to the car, dazed and confused. Sara sat in silence as they drove out, down the school's roadway heading to Hollows Mill Road, then toward I-95. Jake asked Sara again how she liked her tour, and she grunted through her rigid jaw that it was *great*. The school was *amazing*. That was all that was said for the next fifteen minutes until Jake had to say whatever he could say.

"Sara, just remember, it's very, very hard to get in. Sorry, but I have to remind you."

"You want me to apply?!" Sara's astonished glower came from weeks of pent-up anxiety of some kind.

It hit him. He hadn't actually said she could apply. He was petrified but he knew, he had to confirm that, yes she could apply if she wanted to.

Sara added, "I won't be disappointed if I don't get in. I mean, I won't get in, but, like, it's just so great, I just want to try."

He didn't know what else to say or do at that moment, because they were now driving away from the land of Bardon, where the world's most righteous standards were bred into the world's most deserving. He had to think about tactics alone at home to pull Sara away from the brink – the brink of being labeled a loser who wasn't accepted.

Sara became animated, not slouching anymore. Maybe her father needed to understand how incredibly cool Bardon was and slowly at first, then more emphatically, she spun the tale of the fabulous institution she had just seen. Jake got in a few cautions along the way, but they got no more than a blink and a nod from preoccupied Sara.

CHAPTER FIFTEEN

One compelling enough question remained and Jake emailed Gwen asking for a one-to-one conference. There were no more artworks from her, but they had enough interaction to sort through with the Sara Bardon issue. Anyway, his jangled nerves would feed on themselves if he didn't talk to Gwen.

She arrived the next morning at ten-thirty. Jake's special made coffee in hand, they sat in the studio facing each other, his camera on out of habit.

"Again, I'm sorry, Jake. I had no idea Sara would want to apply to Bardon until a couple of weeks ago."

He shook his head slowly. "Not your fault at all. She looks up to you and you happened to go to the perfect place. But Sara came up with wanting to go through this application ordeal on her own."

"But is she moving beyond just applying for fun to being sold on it?"

"Probably. I hope not, but probably. I mean, Jesus, Gwen. Really? And, I mean, it's not even too beautiful. You know, Bardon manages to feel understated in all its stony-woodsy-perfection. It makes Georgetown or Newburyport feel crass and gilded. Unfortunately, it's impossible to resist, Gwen."

"Ugh, God. I'm so sorry. I know. Bardon does that to everyone."

"Yeah. They've perfected aura." Jake leaned back, needing to know something. "Apart from all of us dancing around Sara not being qualified for getting in, I have a question. Is she saying anything to you about applying to any other schools?"

Gwen grimaced at him. "Not to me."

"And not to me." Jake raised his eyebrows. "She was going to apply to some alternative public schools around here. But I'm planning to move us, so that's dead in the water."

Gwen sat upright. "Oh, right. It's just Bardon."

Jake just groaned, "She's probably possessed since the tour."

At that they sat quietly frowning.

Gwen stopped frowning and looked tentatively at him, her eyes watery, "Umm, yeah, I'm fairly possessed too, by Sara. But, Jake? Sorry, but I mean, you can't troupe off to Newburyport in the middle of all this, can you? Sorry, but what if I can actually promise you there will be plenty of work for you here?"

Jake waited, speechless. Gwen was moving past Sara's rejection issues to another paranoid topic? She was promising enough work for him?

Gwen wasn't speechless. "I just hate the thought of you and Sara moving to Newburyport. I hate it."

Jake leaned down harder on his wooden stool, facing Gwen. He measured his words, words considered again and again for weeks.

"I hate it, too. I want you in my life and Sara wants you in her life and that's what got her started on this Bardon thing. I still can't ditch the Newburyport plan, though Gwen. I mean, the high school there might be a fairly good consolation prize for her…and anyway, so if I get that job you'll have to move there too." His chest was puffed up and pounding, and he knew the Newburyport job was really unlikely. He just felt compelled to apply whatever momentary leverage he had with Gwen.

Gwen's unsmiling face solidified on top of her long unbending neck, making her head seem to jut out, a very unusual, ungainly posture for her.

She muttered, "Well, anyway, yeah, Newburyport is beautiful, but I need more of a metropolis for architecture projects." Her painfully thin smile pained him too. She added, "Jake, please hold on for a few weeks. I think we'll get some conservation projects for you."

She said nothing more and he finished his coffee, then she did. At least for now, he had to stop himself from painting the whole picture, where she'd live with Sara and him after divorcing her husband. But at least they were endorsing the triad plan. Apparently, they were all entwined, Sara, Gwen and him. But the lack of any mention of a husband was unambiguous, Jake hoped. Jake was not including the husband in the conversation and she wasn't.

Gwen stood saying she was sorry but had to go. So Jake stood facing her, wanting to tell her how bored he was as a single man, how being with her was what he looked forward to all week. He didn't say that.

More togetherness would have to wait. When she arrived, Gwen said she couldn't stay long. Sure enough, they were saying goodbye, both promising to set up another meeting, both agreeing another museum trip would be good. Both, it seemed to him, straining on their leashes.

*   *   *   *   *

Jake levitated the rest of the day as far up as his leash allowed. Gwen was now directly included in his life. All the contorted Bardon interactions, plus her trying to include him in her architectural practice, amounted to a lot of interaction potential. He ate lunch, alone as usual, managing not to worry about his lack of work. Maybe he could stay put and wait for events to define them -- the triad.

Jake had to hold on. He read some news items online and then watched a free mindless TV series on YouTube.

Computer off, he cleaned the studio. He scrubbed his large stainless-steel sink, still levitating on high from thoughts and feelings about Gwen, and waited for the indefinite hours to end when Sara came home.

* * * * *

Sara was spending her afternoon free period in her high school library doing an extra credit paper for English. She glanced around, cautious to not see too much, to not get engaged. Big enough room, she thought, but definitely not enough books and too much bland space devoted to bottomless computers and idle frolicking. There were always tables filled with frolickers, just like now. If she looked at them, they'd look back in anger. She hated being mean and she was determined not to turn into a snob, but how the hell was she supposed to function on any level when there was no place to concentrate, no place to avoid the noise? The ceiling was low and there was no charm, no warmth, no beginning, middle or end to the public space. It was as barren and uninviting as the library at Bardon was world class beautiful and serene and inspiring. She was altered now. She didn't say anything to anyone about Bardon. There was no reason to and no way to. Her pulse slowed.

The library she was sitting in was dull but, God, the cafeteria was bleak. She hated spending time there. *Blobs eating globs.* Sara didn't say that to Natalie or Jason or anyone.

It wasn't funny so she suppressed it when it reoccurred to her one day recently. She came up with, *blobs eating globs* a year before in North Bethesda, one day in the middle school cafeteria. There were so many kids eating so much bad food there. She almost said it as a joke but knew better that time too.

Anyway, she had to pay attention. Her inadequate, long-shot efforts of applying to Bardon meant she didn't have to care about any of the people around her at school except the teachers but, somehow, for some murky reason, it meant she had to nail her tests and homework assignments. Gwen would hate it if Sara flopped totally in her application.

Other than Gwen, who should she get to write the letters of recommendation? Simon still seemed good. And the middle school principal, Ms. Martinez, who adored Sara, would be good. She'd write a good letter.

Sara had to straighten her back and try to focus on reality. She shouldn't overthink the stuff she had to do, like the personal statement she had to write, or the examples of past writing she had to provide. She could just forward copies of Juggernaut, the literary magazine Sara started in eighth grade. The writing was inadequate, but Ms. Martinez loved it. But Sara shouldn't think about all those things because she had to nail some top grades now. It was just almost impossible to forget how funny the name Juggernaut was for that puny, cheap, miserably designed middle school attempt at a literary journal. God, how embarrassing -- the weird mix of fonts and the confusing layout and the fact that most of the stories were written by the editor, her. Sara laughed about it in the past with her friends and her father. Not now. It seemed stupidly inadequate now that she thought about it. But it was all she had, so she did send it to Gwen, hoping like hell Gwen would think some of them were good enough to use for her application to Bardon. That was last night. It was all she had. She added, in that email last night, that she could write something better now.

Sara looked around again, quickly. No one she knew was anywhere in sight. That was the way she wanted it. The friends and the unfriends had to fade into the background and they seemed to be doing just that. She could concentrate for half an hour.

* * * * *

Wednesday afternoon, two days after verbal intercourse in the studio with Jake, more fluttering bat wings occupied Gwen as she read Sara's middle school short stories. She read things by kids Sara's age before, but Gwen felt so attached to Sara and couldn't even try to be objective. Were the stories signs of talent, or was Gwen just haunted? All that night Gwen fluttered inside wanting greater and greater connection to Sara and Jake. The searingly obvious problem of her not being able to even influence Sara getting into Bardon, pointed Gwen right at getting work for Sara's father. Then, next year she could help Sara aim for some charter school or something.

She had to tell Larny she had work to do after dinner and head for her office. She didn't want to explain her shaky, brooding mood. But, sitting at her desk, it was impossible to come up with the appropriate email response to Sara. And stewing didn't help. She went to bed a couple of hours before Larny and let her stewing drift into fantasizing about Jake.

She answered Sara's email the next morning.

Sara,

I read some of your middle school short stories and some of your literature essays. They're very good. I'd certainly recommend you send a few of them to Bardon; like the last two stories and maybe not that history essay on World War Two. History can be a divisive topic. But, Sara, please don't worry about things, please. Do your best in school now and let the future present itself.

Love,
Gwen

After so many hours of inner debate on whether she should wean Sara off Bardon more emphatically, that was it? But, any words of caution, any warnings or doubts just smacked of harsh put-downs. Gwen just raised her shoulders in defiance of endless analysis and sent the email.

What was very exciting for Gwen was the enormous kick of being so involved in Sara's life. As for that father, same thing. She'd already received some positive answers to the letters she sent with Jake's resume and hers.

CHAPTER SIXTEEN

October 20, Friday

J ake woke up, rubbed both eyes slowly in the leaden gray light and wrestled with his left arm caught in the twisted sheet. It took a minute to see his watch -- ten after four and he was not going back to sleep. He leaned on one elbow whispering, "Maintain the status quo. Don't make any rash decisions about Newburyport or Gwen and work coming in, or anything at all about Sara, yet." Head back on the pillow he remembered warning himself before going to sleep, there was always potential breakage. Fissures too fine to see could somehow threaten the sudden reinforcement in his life with Sara and with Gwen. Now, at four-twenty in the morning, the term fissures seemed ridiculously understated.

At four-thirty he just got up so he could go for a quick walk before Sara was up at six. Getting winded was the goal as he walked quickly in the gorgeous gray Georgetown dawning cool mist, telling himself to wait to hear from that NEACC, but obviously to not count on that job. But, normally, he'd expect them to ask him for some follow-up materials or a second interview on Zoom.

He had to wait to see if Gwen could deliver on her plans to gather up work for both of them. He wanted to stay in place for everyone's sake, but not lose consciousness in the process.

He had to have a time limit on hanging around and somehow communicate that more effectively to Gwen. She seemed too relaxed when she talked about getting them both more work. Did she have any real sense how much work he needed?

His walks hadn't been exactly tranquil since bankruptcy began to rumble beneath his steps.

Back home he grumbled, "Bemoan the fissures or don't bemoan the fissures; just get Sara off to school and mop the floors." There were a few more times throughout the morning when he grumbled to himself as he cleaned, listening to Porcupine Tree or Shostakovich coming out of the old CD player.

He used to like cleaning his specially designed apartment, but not anymore with two thousand dollars due for rent and him having a bit over three thousand in the bank. The rent was almost three weeks late. The rent was low, very low, for what Jake and Sara were getting in Georgetown. Simon never upped it. Seven years before, Jake told him the rent had to be higher and made Simon raise it from seventeen hundred to two thousand. Simon didn't complain once when, in the last two years, Jake was late. Jake was late four times.

He didn't tell Sara much about their precariousness. The gap between their fiscal reality and her sudden life ambitions was impossible for Jake to comprehend, and he could never expect Sara to reckon with it. Sara just knew Bardon would pretty much guarantee her enormous amounts of current and future security and she was willing to play that stupid lottery.

The next few days were self-conscious, lone processions of thinking and sitting and walking around his apartment, mumbling to himself. He forced himself to phone a few galleries and even a few collectors from the past. No work. He forced himself to try to not think about money, not for a while. He'd wait a week, then maybe comb the internet for conservation jobs. He'd still hope Gwen would come through.

He got food and cooked a few organic frozen entrees at night for Sara and him -- adding a fresh salad. The days of the week scraped by as the outside heat hung onto his windows, a gummy, dull late October humidity that felt like nothing forever. At least the students were a bit quieter, even on weekends so Jake could tell himself to look forward to November when exams would mean students would sit in dorm rooms and libraries and be shut-up for a while.

He scrubbed everything clean every morning and the empty afternoons degenerated into a prolonged atrophy. Money and bills strangled most of his bouts of longing for Gwen, and he was just very irritated most of the day. At night, Sara was preoccupied with homework, so dinners were just standard procedure and fast because they both needed that.

On Monday night, hating to even try to read or watch anything on his computer, he ran in place with Abbey Road playing, him borrowing some of the music's energy. It was hard accepting the sharp lull when he finished running and turned off the music. It was dark and he finally put some lights on in his bedroom and ate a bowl of the cereal he bought with Sara at the new organic store on Wisconsin Avenue as he checked his phone for texts. Startled, he saw there was a new text from Gwen.

Jake,

Hope you and Sara are well. I just wanted to pass on that a collector I know wants to take some things into you. Abby Malingus. She's the nicest – in her eighties - person in the world and has an important collection. There will be more collectors soon. I've just received seven very positive responses to letters I sent out for design work and art conservation!

Best wishes,
Gwen

He waited, panting for five minutes, to not seem like he was rampagingly desperate for work or Gwen's attention. Then he sent a text back.

Gwen,

Thank you very much. You're the best. I'll look forward to that.

Jake.

Maybe he'd stay in place and he and Gwen and Sara would do a Georgetown version of family fun.

Two hours later he went to bed and to sleep, flat out fatigued by the long, drawn-out effort of grasping at gifts from strangers. The next day was Tuesday.

After breakfast Jake's phone buzzed and jingled. It was Abby Malingus. She had some works of art on paper that needed to be conserved. Yes, he could see her that day at one. Twenty minutes later someone named John Forester called wanting to bring in twenty-nine works. Jake's mood swung from brittle to supple in twenty-four hours, not something he was used to.

*   *   *   *   *

Ten Daumier lithographs from Abby Maingus were one thing, but a whole archival box of early twentieth century collages and other works on paper by Picasso and Braque and Leger and Max Ernst and Jean Arp? There were twenty-nine pieces all in need of some work. John Forester brought those in late Saturday afternoon. He was on the board at Bardon and was thinking of leaving the works to the school. As for Gwen, John told Jake that Bardon wanted her to design an addition to the school library. If Gwen agreed, there would be a group of large Audubon prints to hang there that needed Jake's handiwork. He described to Jake how Bardon's museum had a small budget of ten thousand dollars a year for conservation. They no longer employed a part time conservator at the museum.

It was heart-recovering news because earlier that day Jake got an email. The NEACC thanked him for his application, but they had chosen another candidate for the position. It was a bit over three silent weeks since his trip to Newburyport. The rejection felt as paranormal and occult as the interview.

*   *   *   *   *

Sara lay on her floor facing her beautiful tall ceiling. Her mind revisited her maybe, possible, dreamlike future. Bardon was like a college, in looks – an extremely cool, small college. Nothing wrong with going there and then off to an extremely cool college afterwards. She'd already explored online and scrutinized the idea of going there, of living there and becoming a part of Bardon, enough to have some real sense of what being there represented, she thought. She knew not to take the videos and pictures and even the tour too literally. Of course, all major boarding schools and universities gave pitches. Ethos was a word Sara had to look up. Just living on a campus on your own at age sixteen was such a big deal that it was going to help you grow up, become an adult.

Sure, overall, it was Jean Smot and Gwen who preached the ethos thing to Sara, but there was so much logic to it and it was what she felt when she was there. Meanwhile, just like Gwen, Jean Smot was a really impressive person -- well beyond adequate. The only other impressive older person Sara had ever known was her father. Her mother? God, no. Her mother reminded her of all those pissy, undeveloped losers Sara saw teaching in her middle school and, now her high school. Her friends parents? Same thing – bitter losers who go from their pissy jobs to their pissy cars to drive through pissy traffic to their pissy houses. Sara cringed when her mother put a picture of her new LA condo building and neighborhood on Facebook. It was even uglier and pissier than condo buildings in North Bethesda! Big surprise her father divorced her so soon after marrying her.

No. Sara didn't want to be nasty. Her mother couldn't help it if she was just undeveloped or immature and bitter about it or something. It was sad but there was nothing Sara could do about it but put her own life together as well as she could.

To feel as sure as sure can be, she only had to ask herself this -- what choice did she have? Might as well continue winging-it with a crazy application to Bardon since her father might have to find a job somewhere else. A miserable thought, losing Gwen and Georgetown.

*   *   *   *   *

The strong, quick response from her mailing really surprised and delighted Gwen. Why hadn't she tried appealing to her contacts before? She'd always been too indirect and word-of-mouth old fashioned in her self-promotion. She told herself to wait in the past, to save her human capital until the time was right. And it seemed to be right, now.

On the third floor, sitting at her desk, she was especially excited to delve into all the possibilities of the addition to the Bardon library, daunting as it was to add onto an HH Richardson creation. She had ideas right away, about using contrasting materials and shapes to try to compliment, not compete with, the monumentally heavy brown and tan rough stone. The addition would house the school archives and have a small exhibition space for the Audubon prints, so glass was both a blessing and curse. Maybe glass facing west and large hardwood posts and beams in an interesting shape would work. What shape?

And Maria Santos added Gwen's name to a list of candidates to design the interior of a new addition to the Rose Hill Museum in Wilmington, Delaware. It was setting up the new cafe seating area and the new conference center. There would be a lot of competition, but Gwen would submit her resume. Maria, whom Gwen had known since Princeton's undergraduate architectural history class, was only one vote out of twelve board members, but Gwen could wait and see. Maybe other board members would have work for her or for Jake -- her handsome, sweet lovable Jake.

CHAPTER SEVENTEEN

October 25, Wednesday

S ara received her SSAT results and texted them to Gwen, apparently right away. Gwen knew the scores were just good enough to not eliminate Sara's chances for entry to Bardon and immediately began concocting a diplomatic text back.

> *Sara – well done. I have to wait at least a month to send Bardon a letter of recommendation. It is early days still. So we have to be patient and wait. Sorry, but we have no choice.*

> *Want to meet at The Haunt after school? At four? Agonizing as all this school stuff may be, let's not talk about just that, though, okay? Let's enjoy the present.*

Sara texted back at nine-thirty.

> *Gwen – I promise to not talk about Bardon. I never indulge in wishful thinking, or not constantly (haha). Thank you for your advice*

*and I will be calm at The Haunt. I promise. See
you at four.*

Reading that, Gwen spun her head groaning. Poor,
adorable Sara. How could she push for Sara at some of the
alternative public schools in town? She couldn't yet. Gwen
had been in and around that question for weeks and always
only came up with a strong letter of recommendation.
Gwen lectured herself -- she could only offer one letter
of recommendation, even for Bardon. So, given whatever
demographic algorithm those schools had, how much
hyperbole could the letter contain? It was beginning to drive
her nuts. She put her head down on her desk, arms folded
under and waited to relax.

That was the height of her Sara undertaking for
Wednesday morning. The rest of her time was occupied
by temperate emails to and from clients and drawings and
schematics on her computer. It was all enough of enough.
Gwen had only known Jake and Sara for six weeks and they
felt like a cyclone around her -- a beautiful, compelling
cyclone, but a bit scary, if not overwhelming.

It swept up to become four o'clock. The clouds, the lovely
dense clouds and the breeze made it feel like a precursor of
cooler, later fall. Being a Thursday meant The Haunt wasn't
full and Gwen got a table tucked against the wall. Sara showed
up with rosy cheeks and eyes wide and they faced each other,
both easily engaged.

Coffee was welcome. Gwen sat back. The cafe was
becoming her favorite place to call her own.

"It's nice to be here off season."

Sara looked around. "Fall's my favorite time of year."

Gwen agreed. "Mine too." She drank some coffee. "So, tell me, do you like to read fiction or non-fiction? Your father told me you like to read."

"Fiction. I've been trying to read War and Peace, believe it or not. But, no, last summer I read 'Nine Stories' by J.D. Salinger and 'Brave New World' by somebody. I forget his name . . .and loved both of them so much."

"Well, yeah. I think J.D. Salinger is always great and so is 'Brave New World', by Aldous Huxley. Wow."

"But, yeah, I want to read nonfiction too. I just don't know where to start. Every time I pick up some history book I feel as if I don't know what it's about enough to get into it. My father's always reading books about Japan in the nineteenth century or the British civil wars."

"Is he? Does he read novels?"

"Sometimes, I guess. He has a stack of books in his room. He says he used to read more novels and now reads more nonfiction."

Gwen loved picturing Jake in his bedroom reading but could easily be content with just his daughter for the moment. "Anyway, Sara, you have a lot of time to learn enough about various subjects to then pick up a book about them. Right?"

"So, what sort of subjects would you pick up and read about now that you couldn't have when you were my age?"

Not used to having coffee conversation with teens, Gwen had to think, but only for a few seconds. "History. I mean, once I studied architectural history I learned some basic things that led to wanting to know about other, related things. I guess I'm trying to self-educate myself in history."

Sara just stared, chewing slowly.

"Like your father's books on the British civil wars. I read 'The Cousins' Wars' by Kevin Phillips a couple of years ago. I found it at a library sale in Newburyport, believe it or not."

Gwen laughed but Sara stopped chewing and waggled her head, silenced.

"Yup. Someone I went to graduate school with lives there with her family. I only went there once for a weekend visit. Anyway, that book went into the way representational government was systematically developed by major conflicts in Britain and North America over three centuries. A lot of the legal set-ups for modern representational democracies came about as the result of those battles."

Sara stretched her shoulders, thinking out loud, "Okay. Could you text me the name of that book?"

"Sure." Gwen tapped at her phone. "I still have it somewhere."

"So old Newburyport's out though. So that's good, right?" Sara smiled with deep satisfaction.

Gwen looked up, startled, uncomprehending.

"Yeah. My father didn't tell you? They didn't hire him." Sara face caved a bit, a few nervous wrinkles around her mouth.

"No. We haven't had a chance to speak recently." Gwen felt a profound revulsion at someone somewhere rejecting Jake. And why didn't he tell her? Her insides went cold. "Okay, well, yeah, their loss, our gain. What sorts of sad fools are they anyway?"

Sara forced a short laugh, Gwen assuming she felt at least as defensive about Jake being rejected in any way. Avoiding Sara's eyes for a moment, Gwen also worried Jake would avoid her out of pride. And now, the sinking of the Newburyport public school option would only add pressure to Jake needing work and Sara needing an alternative public school. It had Gwen yearning for ways to compensate.

"You know, Sara, I'm getting all sorts of people looking for conservation work now. I think your talented father's all set."

Sara's face turned crimson, and her eyes glistened. "God, that's so great!"

"Um. Don't tell him I said that. Okay? It would sound like we were making it up or exaggerating it because of him needing the work. But yeah, between you and me, it's looking really good."

They grinned reflexively at each other as co-conspirators, nervously, both faces then directed at the floor, ceiling, other people. It took a minute to readjust but drinking their coffees and eating some pumpkin cake helped. The conversation turned to the weather and what art they liked and soon enough continued easily, both of them at ease. Gwen had never felt so connected to such a young person. After leaving the cafe they wandered around the local galleries for an hour and then went shopping. Gwen said good-bye on M Street feeling a lot of satisfaction at being able to reassure Sara, and more and more, Jake. Work was actually coming in.

*   *   *   *   *

A damp low morning sun draping heavily over Jake, by way of one window in his bedroom and the first thing he had to do, after wiping his clogged eyes, was make some coffee to wake up. He wanted to call Gwen but had to come-to first and witness Sara leaving for school.

He didn't like eating breakfast in the kitchen with Sara trying to get her food together and both of them trying to arise from sleep. Balancing a bowl of cereal and cup of coffee, he went to his studio where it was cooler and less dry than his sun draped bedroom.

He might be absolved of guilt if he were very careful to not spill and if he wiped down the counter later. Eating alone, he thought about how to organize the work for the day. He'd spray four of the collages John Forester brought in that only needed a quick removal from old mats. Then he'd poke at the two Picasso's that needed a gentle cleaning -- probably dry cleaning since there was no telling what weird adhesives Picasso used. There were some more repairs to some of the Forester works and what he had to do was finish those things in the next two days so he could start on the etchings that Betty Tang brought in and then the bank collection of very old maps.

He went to his studio doorway, responding to Sara shouting good-bye. With her back to him, she didn't see him wave but he assumed she heard him wish her a good day. The kid was surfing along on her own wave, and he could only hope it wasn't her manically determined to get into Bardon in six months. He could only hope.

Meanwhile, he was going to call Gwen, the person no longer coming into his studio. Their relationship seemed to be great for work but felt about as humanly tangible as a memory cloud. He was pretty sure she was in her office alone on Tuesday mornings. Poking around, arranging a few bits of work, he waited until nine.

He wouldn't leave a message or text. She answered.

"Hi, Gwen, it's Jake. Is this a good time?"

"Sure. How are you?"

"Great. Busy. And I know you know about Newburyport. Sara was filled with too much joy to contain it. We're all doing what she's wished for and schemed for in that way, at least."

"God, she's so funny. What a kid."

"How about you? Are you getting the sort of work you wanted?" He wanted to underscore her role their embryonic triad.

"Yeah, and it is great. I forgot how good it feels to be busy this way. It's so much calmer than not knowing what you're doing."

"Are you in your office?"

"Yeah. I am."

"Well, I'll let you get to it, but I just wanted to call early to get you, to stay in touch and tell you I'm fairly busy with work, thanks to you."

"No, it's fine. I can talk. And, by the way, I loved my afternoon out with Sara."

"Yeah, she said you went shopping. And you really shouldn't have. I mean, what the hell, Gwen."

"I know, I know. It was just a little side trip after coffee. We went to a couple of stores. I hope you don't mind me buying her those things. They were on sale and, damn Jake, it was so much fun for me. She's so adorable. Don't tell her I said that."

They both grumbled laughs. "But Gwen, see, I have to repay you. Let me take you somewhere, like Zinzers for lunch or a drink someday. I can tell you about some of the collectors I'm working for now. You're not one of them anymore." The invitation was out of him.

There was a short delay from Gwen. Then, a throaty, "Okay. I know, I'm out of stuff."

He waited for more, but when it didn't come, he said, "Exactly. So, why not tomorrow?"

"Uhh, tomorrow?"

"Yeah, you had that hankering for the National Gallery and I have a hankering for Zinzers and a talk about work.

It will have to be early or late to get a table, though. Is early good?"

"Uhh, okay. Early is good."

He was going with whatever shaky fleetness he had. "Okay. So let's meet there tomorrow at eleven-thirty? It won't be too crowded on a Friday."

*   *   *   *   *

The wind was blowing at the glass in his windows and occasionally through one or two cracks in the frames. They were the sounds Jake heard all morning as he ruminated. *He should pace himself, not lunge at Gwen. Timing was everything.* It was the third week of October pointing ominously to winter and even though Jake was doing better financially, he was unable to forget his late fall time limit. It wasn't like he had any sort of security net. Gwen had a secure future. He and Sara still lived day by day.

He walked to meet Gwen. It was a date of some kind and all he could feel was the need to surge forward.

Lunchtime Zinzers' sounds were as cozy and muffled as he could expect in a restaurant. He wondered how Gwen was feeling.

"Ever notice in movies or TV shows, people have calm conversations with each other in calm restaurants? I mean, there are noisy bar scenes in movies, but there are really calm, quiet restaurants too. Right? Ever been to one?"

Gwen wrinkled her eyes at him, thinking. "Calm, quiet restaurants? Uhm, well, there's one in New York."

They both sat upright and jostled at the irony. Gwen drank some more of her pinot noir, then leaned forward, elbows on the table. "People are used to noise. Take the racket out and most people think something's wrong. But, really,

Dewitts in Brooklyn Heights is famous for being old fashioned and very quiet and ridiculously expensive. Know it?"

Jake shook his head, trying not to imagine her there with her husband.

"Only once for me. It's an Edwardian stone townhouse and you get seated in small rooms…just a couple of tables per room. A couple of especially small rooms have only one table, but you have to reserve those way, way in advance. So, yeah, there are gorgeous, big oriental rugs on the floors and painted cork between the beams on the ceilings. So not many people and lots of stuff to absorb sounds and there you have it…hushed and private as can be. Gorgeous."

"Sounds like a private club. No music?"

"No none. Nope." She drank some more then added, "It's fairly quiet here. Not bad."

He glanced around. "Yeah, it's great. I haven't been here for years."

They turned their heads to appreciate the room they were in -- some quiet, haunting Pharoah's Dance by Miles Davis sounds coming out of somewhere. Zinzers called it their conservatory. It was a new glass addition but with reclaimed, varnished parquet oak flooring. The tables were a solid variation of French metal garden styles, and the wingback chairs managed to be elegant and stuffed and comfortable. The ceiling lights were small yellowy nineteen-nineties spotlights turned low, but the conservatory's captured natural light gave off the eternal glow only glass ceilings can give. That, and its slow pace and good, old fashioned German menu, made Zinzers one of Jake's favorite havens, when he could afford such a thing, every now and then, years ago.

Gwen already agreed copiously about it being one of her favorite restaurants when the waiter arrived. "I'm having the half portion of wurst and potato salad with the lentil soup."

Jake ordered the same thing. The waiter left and Jake
noticed Gwen studying him. He smiled. "What? No, I know,
I'm ridiculously easy to please when it comes to food."

She sat back in her tall wing back, pale blue linen slip
covered chair. "Just not in everything. Like, where you live
and how you live."

He sat back in his own tall wing back, deep crimson and
black checked linen, chair. The narrow walls of their chairs
gave them a surprising amount of privacy. The red wine was
warming him to that privacy.

"Um, I guess I can be fussy and a bit of that goes a long
way." He grimaced. "Going to Newburyport for that job made
me question why I'm always hanging around posh places. It's
where the work is that I do, I guess. But in that town it just
seemed so obvious I was caught in something in that way.
There are all sorts of locations people go to for jobs, but not
me. I have nine locations in the continental US."

"Nine?"

"I just made up that number. Maybe I have ten."

She sighed. "You have a way of bringing up prime issues.
Prime for me. God, I left the projects behind and spend all my
time designing the fanciest houses in the fanciest locations."

"You make them efficient and exciting, don't you?
Fancy? What do you mean, fussy and expensive?"

"No, I hope not. Yeah, fancy does sound fussy, I guess."

"Yeah, sort of deformed, the opposite of your stuff I've
seen online."

"Thanks, thanks. I try. You save parts of our heritage
every day."

After getting a polite, embarrassed mini nod from Jake,
she added, "Still, we do seem caught. It's like, once you get
inside the loop, you're hogtied for life."

He rolled his head in a circle and scowled at her, and they both laughed. "Damn!" he barked in a low voice. Jake didn't bother saying anything more. Hogtied might describe him, but how hogtied was Gwen? Problems with her husband? Some other problems still undisclosed?

It took them a minute to settle down. Gwen scratched at her ear. "But meanwhile, seriously, what good am I doing?"

Jake answered right away. "Helping the rich pretend they have cool, well-defined taste, while doing charity work and spreading the wealth with donations?" He squinted. "You shepherd poor kids to a better future, for them anyway. No, sorry. You're talking to a person who lives some sort of precious version of hand to mouth. I don't know what being rich feels like. You have to make more ethical choices in a day than I do in a year, is my guess."

Gwen was wincing as he said that, but a sneer escaped. "You and I have what in common?"

"Sara." He kept his left arm on the arm of his chair and leaned to the side.

Now Gwen shrank in her chair. It took her a few seconds before she spoke in a quiet voice. "It's true. God, I do adore Sara."

Jake wanted to push hard but had to be careful, relatively careful. He relaxed his muscles and lowered his tone "Well, Gwen", he raised his glass, "because of you, I have a stream of work coming in. Because of you, Sara has a female mentor. And I want more for you and me and for Sara."

Her pupils widened and she seemed to stop breathing for a few seconds. She lowered her glass. He'd been picking up a wariness from her since they sat down. Someone might see them. If he had to explain why he was taking a client out to lunch - a young and stunning client - that might amount to a three point five on the Richter Scale. If she had to explain him to someone who knew her husband, that could cause the earth to swallow her.

Their eyes were locked for what felt like five seconds, before she lifted her shoulders silently, indicating a desire to not respond to his last words.

He went on in a slow, steady voice. "I saw you in the Jonas Gallery on Wisconsin one time. I remembered after you first brought in some work to M Street Framers in September. It must have been at least four years ago that I saw you there, at the Jonas Gallery."

She sputtered, "Oh. Okay, right. I think we passed on M Street a couple of times."

He stayed still.

Gwen gazed down.

He said, "I also remember passing you on Dumbarton Street. That came back to me too."

After turning to look at the corner table ten feet away, Gwen turned back to face Jake. "I don't remember that."

He couldn't resist leering a bit, shaking his head and biting his lip. "No?"

"Were you alone? No, sorry."

"I was with Sara."

After a blank moment, she said, "So, once you started remembering these things, it all came back to you?"

"I guess." Wherever the conversation was going, he wanted to complete it, not let it conveniently diffuse. "I think I've remembered it all, but what about you?"

She said nothing. Then her head twisted to the side. "Oh, God. I saw you with Sara. You and Sara walking somewhere. You're right, I guess it was on Dumbarton Street."

Jake watched as her whole body seemed to clench. He'd been thinking about it for over a month and had a bit of a hold on their very brief encounters in the past. Gwen exerted a powerful gravitational pull, and that time on Dumbarton Street he saw the way she looked at him and Sara, like they were also exerting some sort of powerful pull. That must have been followed by him somehow blotting her out. After all, she was with a guy that time on Dumbarton Street, her husband, as it turned out. Now Gwen was struggling with something over there, silently.

He pursued. "Right, I was with Sara. We always went for walks up around there. But why? You seem upset."

Her head jerked. He had to be patient and wait. She was thinking, her face becoming more and more withdrawn.

Her voice was low and slow, "I guess I knew you had a daughter. I saw you with her...that father and daughter. Beautiful. You looked so right with each other ."

"How long ago was that? Two or three years?"

She didn't respond verbally but just crumpled a bit uncomfortably. Slouching, she shook her head, and he was worried she might cry. He turned his head around, half seeing other people. Back to her, he didn't have any words to reduce whatever turmoil she was feeling, as she avoided his face, her eyes down, almost closed.

He murmured, "Want to go?"

She barely nodded. Leaving plates of food and enough cash on the table, they walked silently, grappling with just finding their way to her car two streets away. They said nothing more than goodbye and he walked away.

*   *   *   *   *

More. The damned word shook her whole being all that night. She moaned the word to herself on and off, away from Larny. He must have noticed her sullen and distant state at dinner. Later, she couldn't sleep, finding herself wandering through downstairs rooms at three something. She was lost, half filled with instinctive fear, half titillated – lost way inside herself.

More meant mating. She knew Jake well enough. He wasn't trying to just get her into bed. The very thing that drew her to him was how well suited he was for, not just the act of making great babies, but for already being a great father. She was so damned aroused by Jake just then she decided to drink some Scotch – mumbling to herself -- this was the way women got pregnant without wanting to. The scotch numbed her fairly quickly, her arousal sifting through her brain down into the rest of her and lodging throughout her everywhere.

She tried to sleep in. When Larny was gone in the morning she wandered some more, scratched at some breakfast and sat down in the living room window seat to try to think. Of course, Jake wanted more. They'd only known each other two months but they'd been circling closer and closer around each other the whole time. Then she went on a date with him? Was she nuts? It was excruciating sitting with Jake and slowly, painfully exposing her suppressed memories of seeing him in the past. Why didn't she remember seeing him and why did she remember that way, as if he were pulling the memory out of her? It wasn't those times on M Street, walking by, or the time in the Jonas Gallery. After meeting Jake in early September those sightings were vaguely revealed in her mind. It was that time, a couple of years ago, she saw him with Sara. That was a memory exiled to deep files.

Her only chance at sanity was keeping herself busy for two hours, working on design drawings or planning meetings with potential clients. She also talked sternly to herself intermittently.

By afternoon she could think again. Her second time in the new stone bathtub, she put her head back. The temperate golden October light was finally mitigating the warm moist air outside as it pushed through the bathroom windows and stuck to the damp walls around her. She moaned in pleasure at the atmospheric combination of light and moisture. God, she loved the deep golden fall light in the Washington area especially in her gorgeous house. She loved the way her naked body looked and felt in the silky water.

Gwen's damned phone was ringing. It was in the pocket of her robe. The robe was five feet away hanging on the door hook. She'd let it ring, look at her messages later. She was getting a lot of requests for work after her mailings. In so many ways, so many things were coming her way. She looked down at herself, naked, smooth and wet and she swooned.

Self-delusion is a great aphrodisiac. That abrupt insight hit her hard. She pulled the lever to empty the tub.

The rest of the afternoon was an uneven exercise in being occupied or not knowing what to do next. Most of the time she wanted to stop ruminating about mating with Jake, so she delved into design work for hours. It worked, but only while she worked. As soon as she stopped answering emails, or phone calls or checking her preliminary calculations for the Bardon library, mating possessed her again. It was a few minutes after five. She went to the TV room on the second floor and watched a few old episodes of Friends, letting that cute, insipid universe dilute her passions for forty-five minutes. She went to the basement exercise room and ran on the treadmill.

It worked being with Larny that night, Friday night, when she was fixing dinner with him and eating and talking. She was fine. She was really fine when they made out in bed, late and fornicated the daylights out of each other, Gwen fantasizing about getting impregnated, pretending she and Jake or Larny weren't preventing that very thing.

Still, she found herself awake at three and damned well didn't want to alert Larny to her problem so she stayed as still in bed as she could, obsessed. How could she stop worrying about that unfinished lunch and unfinished conversation with Jake? Just then, it was impossible. Glowing, handsome Jake. She was always stopping things between them and running off. He had to assume she was the queen of approach-avoidance at this point. All she knew, or cared to know for now, was dredging up unexpected memories set off alarms in her. Why did she suddenly remember seeing him with Sara a couple of years ago? Why hadn't she remembered that a month ago? Maybe she half remembered back then. But why did seeing the two of them and forgetting and then remembering suddenly all bother her so much?

Did she remember her mother or her father? How could she? She'd tried in spurts all her life and always half felt she could remember something -- a vague outline of their faces. But those memories had to be constructed from the one photograph she had of them -- them very young on a park bench, smiling. Photographic memory doesn't offer a lot of creature comfort or moral reinforcement. It just sneers and jeers from too far away.

CHAPTER EIGHTEEN

October 30, Monday.

E ventually, the weekend ended. Jake's grasping for Gwen at Zinzers failed totally. He had to keep from self-destructing totally. Sara stayed in her room most of the weekend and then again on Monday, working on homework, working on her own fantasies. Jake just tried to train himself to not agonize and get work done. At least he wasn't contorted in fear he'd lost Gwen, if he worked. He did become emotionally constrained, though and, by the end of endless Monday, found himself moving along slowly. He was happy to have dinner, as usual, with Sara that night. It was great to see her and to try to talk soberly, reasonably with her.

Jake looked over as they put their dinner dishes in the dishwasher. "Meanwhile, how's life treating you?"

"Life? Fine."

"You don't bring any friends over. You don't seem to go to friends' houses. I'm a little worried you don't have much of a social life."

"It's fine."

Wiping down the counter, Jake stayed voiceless.

Sara relented. "I guess I'm just going through the motions of being in ninth grade, walking the halls of the mammoth public school, sitting in big classes, talking to friends at lunch."

That didn't reduce Jake's concerns.

Being Sara, she read his mind. "I don't know where I'm going to be going to school next year, and so, and I mean obviously I don't say anything about that to people there. Most days, I tag along with one or two people for a few lunch globs in the cafeteria, then excuse myself to do some research in the library. A couple of weeks back, Natalie and Jason teased me a few times about being a workaholic or teacher's pet. Yeah, I just smiled and shrugged and poked along to the library to read or do some homework. I'm fine. There's nothing I can do."

He was mortified by his young daughter's depressing restraint and took a second. He raised his head and breathed out, "Okay. But Sara, next year is a while away. You're not going to have friends for that long?'

"Natalie and Jason are still my friends. We text all the time and share pictures. Same as Tess. I'm blissful, Dad. Surfing the surf like a sea otter. Meanwhile, if Gwen doesn't have any more art for you, are you never going to see her again?"

That just about shattered him, but he had to withstand it. "Well, I don't know. She and I have talked on the phone about clients and things. She might bring in something someday."

"Ugh! I hope she does bring in more art. I like having coffee with her but maybe we could all go to the museum again, or another museum."

"Yeah, good. Let's see."

With nowhere positive or comforting to go Jake dried his hands on a clean dish towel and pushed his hair back with his fingers. "Anyway, surfing like a sea otter?

Sara smirked and left the kitchen, saying, "Yup. Saw some sea otters on YouTube. Night."

Jake said goodnight, turning to the sink to get a filtered glass of water. He checked that the apartment door was locked, turned out the kitchen and hall lights and walked into the studio.

The ghost of Gwen now looked down upon him but was Sara losing her too? The pathetic grasping for Bardon was Sara's last hold on Gwen? How could Sara not resent him for that? So far Sara only pushed occasionally for them to all get together, because Sara didn't know about the Zingers fiasco. The circle was Goddamned vicious, and it spun and spun as he stood in the middle of his studio -- if he needed Gwen for work in this triad-triage relationship, did it mean he had to stay away from her? Agony barely touched on how that thought made him feel.

He stretched backward, facing upward. Head down in the palms of his hands made him feel worse. He trudged into his bedroom to stand still in the middle of that room.

Was it even remotely possible to get together with Gwen and have kids with her? She had to leave her husband, but Zinzers showed him she wasn't about to do that. Maybe for the first time in his adult life, Jake wasn't subtle, and Gwen fled. Now what? Days of asking himself, *now what*, closed in on him.

He had to find a way forward. Trudging back to his studio, Jake leaned his depleted self on his worktable and forced himself to survey his workload. The John Forester prints were in the bottom drawer. He'd continue working on those the next day and probably finish by the end of the day. The middle drawer had the charcoal drawings from Gwen's friends in Foggy Bottom and were next and then the group of Audubons from Bardon. Then, the Eleanor Gibbs watercolors for the Agnew Corporation board room. Simon had to frame those when the conservation treatment was done. And Gwen

DAVID ROSS

was sending in someone Tuesday, the next morning; someone
who was bringing in two Degas pastels.

*   *   *   *   *

Jake decided to just get the Degas pastels done. It took
him two hours and their owner, Jane Mallory, was bringing
in more things the next day, Tuesday. She said she had a large
collection that she was told should be worked on -- meaning
Gwen urged her to employ Jake. That should have been great
news but there was another dimension to it. Jake was more
and more sure of it.

One o'clock Thursday came and Jake went downstairs to
answer his doorbell. Standing in front of him was the petite,
exquisite, elegant Jane. There was no way around it, Gwen
was sending a message. To demonstrate how little passion she
felt for him, Gwen decided to send over the most attractive
woman she knew. Gwen, meanwhile, would stay away from
Jake's studio and only communicate with him on issues to do
with Sara.

It was fascinating in a painfully abstract way. Jane,
wearing no wedding ring, presented herself so politely from
a careful distance. In fact, he'd seen her around town a few
times in the past, from a distance. This time, same as the last
time, they said hello and nothing else as they walked upstairs.
Like the last time, he was definitely not in the mood to engage.
They entered his studio, and his camera was switched on.

It wasn't possible to ignore her straight auburn hair
an inch above her shoulders, light blue eyes, naturally dark
eyelashes, and dark eyebrows accenting full cheeks of creamy,
naturally polished skin. It was too bad she didn't look like
an average, unwieldy, average person, like so many average
detritus collecting people. But this was Georgetown and Jane

went to Bardon with Gwen. Jane was cool and reserved and probably erudite.

"I had this room described to me by Gwen before I came here the last time. It looks like a bit of paradise." It was her easy, enunciated voice, white teeth shining, that finished the quiet bijou fusion. She made just enough direct eye contact until it seemed to register, then looked away.

He would pass the test. He was old enough to stand back, to resist getting consumed, by smiling tolerantly, being just kind enough. He muttered a few standard remarks about liking to work in the studio while he took the wrappings off her two framed Marsden Hartley watercolors. Damned if they weren't knockouts, the two fairly large views of the Atlantic across some vivid Maine shoreline.

"They're amazing. Marsden Hartley's one of my favorite artists," he said, not trying to smooth his distracted, impatient voice. What kind of collection did this woman have? He was so impressed by her bringing in the two Degas pastels. Now gorgeous Hartley watercolors?

Jane moved one step back. "Thanks. My grandfather gave them to my parents as a wedding present, along with the Degas, and some other things. My grandfather was very cool. I feel ashamed I didn't get them out of those acidic mats years ago."

"Should I get them out now?" Jake glanced at her, walking across the room to his worktable.

Getting a nod, he placed them upside down on the soft fiberboard surface of the table he used for messy chores, and cut off the brittle old backing paper, careful to preserve the old labels. He told her he'd give her those old labels to paste onto the backs of the works when they were reframed.

"It's great that I can do this at one address. And a few streets from my house," she said.

"Yeah. They use acid-free materials and handle things very carefully downstairs."

Jake pulled out the nails with his wire cutters, then removed the backing and lifted the framed work up, raising the matted watercolor out, carrying it to his counter.

"We're lucky. It isn't glued down. It's just attached with old paper hinges on top, so there's not much for me to do to this one. The watercolor's in good shape. It hasn't faded all that much." He ran his finger above the barely visible line around the edge of the watercolor where the mat had covered the paper. "It's downstairs work."

He unframed the second watercolor and the same thing was revealed.

"Okay, but please bill me for the time it took today."

"Okay. Two hours. I'll remove the acidic hinges and take the works downstairs for you. If you like, you can go down there and pick out the sort of mat board you want."

"Okay." She didn't look at him.

"But, here, let me show you your Degas pastels. We can take them downstairs now."

Jake slid open the top metal drawer and put his hand carefully beneath the first folder, then the second one, placing them on the counter. He'd removed old hinges and removed most of the adhesive residue with a bare minimum of solvent. She said she was very happy with the results, and they headed down to the frame shop, each carrying one pastel.

Jake was relieved after they nodded goodbye. He needed the work and Jane being shy should make it easier for him to know what to do -- just stand back.

*   *   *   *   *

Feeling she'd been working too hard, Gwen texted Sara suggesting they have another cup of coffee at The Haunt. Sara agreed and they met on Tuesday afternoon at four. The weather was beginning its boggy Washington end of October damp cold transformation. Sara arrived dressed in a thin wool turtleneck that happened to mimic Gwen's turtleneck. In fact, both were light gray.

They sat at the same table against the wall, after waiting for it for ten minutes, both admitting they didn't like sitting in the middle of restaurants.

"Maybe we're both introverts." Sara said, sitting down.

"I know I am. Are you? Nice sweater, by the way."

Sara grinned, sounding enthralled, "I know! I just got it online. I saw yours. Sorry. I didn't know you'd wear it today. I liked yours so much the last time."

Gwen shook her head, grinning back. "I like it so much I wear it a lot."

"I got mine on sale, sixty percent off."

"Wow. That's how to do it."

They ordered their coffee and cakes, same as before. While Gwen was laughing with Sara about ordering the same thing, she recalled her exchange with Jake on that score, at Zinzers. She didn't want to think about Jake.

"Ugh, Sara. I need this. I've been working ten-hour days on a design project and need to get away from it for a couple of hours."

"So, I won't ask you about it?"

"Oh, well, it's just a kitchen for some people a few blocks from here. I just want to get it done so I can move on to more exciting projects." Gwen was very excited to get to the addition to the Bardon library, but she didn't want to start talking about Bardon.

"Are kitchens complicated? Seems like it."

"Yes! Oh, God, Sara. There are more little issues with a kitchen than any other room in a house. You have the sink and range and so many appliances that all have to be placed just right, and clients can have some odd notions of what's right. Then, they want windows for views and natural light, so you have to explain to them that windows mean fewer places for sinks and stoves and appliances and cupboards... and then doors to other rooms and to the outside get in the way of everything. And it all costs much, much more than most people expect."

"Hmm. Sounds rough."

"No, I love it in some demented way."

"Because you're good at it and these people need you."

Gwen sat back and winced. "Thank you. Now I remember why I wanted to have coffee with you. I'm sounding negative but I'm just tired. Working for yourself can become too unstructured. That make sense?"

"Sure. My father."

Gwen winced again. There was no way to avoid Jake. "Of course. Anyway, so, how are you, instead of me grousing? Anything new?"

The carrot cake and coffee arrived, and Sara told Gwen school was fine, her grades were still all A's. Gwen was relieved Sara didn't mention Bardon, although the implication was certainly there. Gwen sidestepped that, reaching into her leather bag and handing Sara her old copy of, 'The Cousins' Wars' by Kevin Phillips.

"You can keep it. I can buy another copy."

"Thank you so much. You keep books?"

"Not all, no. I like that old one and I like to keep some on some shelves. No, I give books away all the time. Otherwise, for me, they pile up and my favorites get buried." As she was saying that Gwen began to realize how much Sara was absorbing from her. The sweater and the book might just be the more obvious points of immersion.

They ate.

Gwen couldn't help flushing with pride, half wanting to chide herself. Maybe some of the kids she brought along over the years would have become more attached this way if she spent more time with them. There were quite a few kids she guided into Bardon. She spent official time with them and then they were absorbed by others at Bardon and later some university. This relationship with Sara was more like aunt and niece, almost mother and daughter.

"We're disrupting our metabolic balances with this food." Gwen scowled and took another bite. Sara scowled back, with her mouth closed, chewing.

⋆   ⋆   ⋆   ⋆   ⋆

Simon looked tired and Jake mentioned that as he sat on one of Jake's old steel backed wooden swivel stools in the studio.

"Yeah, it's this time of year. We're crazy busy. I've been meaning to come up and visit but haven't been able to."

"You looked like you were talking to three customers at once earlier. I thought you needed a coffee break."

"Yup. I do."

"I do too, finally. I have a bunch of collectors coming in now. A bunch have more work and so I've actually been scheduling them for a few weeks down the road."

"Fantastic. What happened?"

"Gwen Minot's sending them." Jake didn't want to elaborate on that score, so he walked across the room to get a tissue to blow his nose, asking, "How is business downstairs?"

"Too busy. Yeah, it sucks right now, and I know I have to hire someone, but then things will die down after Christmas, and it takes a month at least to train anyone. Same old thing."

"Corporate socialism feeds on the conspicuous consumption of lost souls."

"Not quite my problem, my son." Head facing the ceiling, Simon made a sign of the cross in the air between them, as always showing some, not too much, appreciation for Jake's bizarre jokes. "So what else is new? How's Sara? I haven't seen her for a couple of weeks."

Jake had to think. Should he tell Simon about Bardon? He just launched into it and told him the basics about Sara applying to the boarding school that Gwen Minot went to, on full scholarship. He tried to stress the last part.

Simon pulled his head back, keeping it there. "Boarding school? Really? You want that?"

"Not really. Sara has very little chance of getting in. Yeah, it's a lose-lose deal. It came with the territory of Sara looking up to Gwen."

"Shit."

"Gwen loved it."

"You have these outstanding women coming in. That Jane Something's very, very, very comely."

Jake laughed. "Mallory."

Simon went with his audience's approval. "And Gwen Minot, wow, yeah, she's the sort of extremely-very, very cool, comely, accomplished older woman a girl like Sara would want to be like."

"Yup. That's good, right?" Jake was leaning on his counter on one hand, twisted sideways toward Simon, who was sitting eye level, five feet away.

"I guess it sucks if you don't want Sara wanting to do things like go away from home, off to some fancy school with,

I don't know…what, a bunch of obnoxious, egocentric rich kids?"

Jake knew Simon was enough of a reverse snob in a bunch of ways to ignore Jake saying Sara wouldn't get into Bardon. And Jake wanted to avoid the damned conversation but was feeling morose and also wanted to talk some things out with his old friend.

"But see, Gwen's not obnoxious or egocentric and never was close to that and there must be some kids at schools like that who aren't and there are more than enough at public schools who are." He pointed his eyes at Simon and they both paused. Jake's passion for Gwen and Sara and his new life was much too hidden inside to come out without way too much emphasis and so he had nowhere sane to go with it. Simon sat still, wooden, his arms folded pondering Jake. Some impasse halted their conversation, so Jake put his hands behind his back and leered, waiting for Simon's reaction.

Simon unfolded his arms, switching tracks on him. "You are a man trap for woman, son. Up here, waiting for them, smooth and polite, looking like you should be someone's husband or boyfriend, but you're not. That sucks them in. And, you have a sweet daughter, needing a mother. Wow!"

Jake frowned and leaned with one hand on the counter, groaning, facing down. "There are a lot of things I'm not."

"No, you're a great father. Yeah. Yeah, it all pulls them in, and it's a man trap." Simon clapped his hands.

"Okay. Give me a break," Jake pleaded in a monotone, standing up, head in hands. He peaked over as Simon was even more round-faced than usual, dimpled, filled with his own magical analysis.

"Really, Jake, you don't move. You stay so still. I know it's because you don't have the money right now. But they just can't stand it. You shouldn't be up here in this trap, waiting for them or something. They don't know what you're waiting for. Maybe you do…but they don't."

Jake had heard Simon talk like this more than a few times before, but now he told Simon he had no idea what he meant, in a strong, disgusted voice, all obviously feigned, as Jake exaggerated his slumped shoulders, head way down, walking in a circle in the middle of the room. Jake had to fend off the awful degenerate feeling inside him now. He was exposed in front of his friend. And Simon just continued unabated, his voice stronger.

"Gwen Minot's married, Jake. Tell her you're busy the next time, you and Sara. Tell her you guys go out and do things in the world, out there. You're not waiting."

CHAPTER TWENTY-ONE

November 1, Wednesday

Jake spent almost half his time organizing his work schedule with the knowledge that most people wanted to drop-off and pick-up on Saturday. That was fine except it meant he only had Sunday for Sara all day long, but she was occupied most of the time in her own private world anyway. And Sara could walk or take the bus to some event or friend's house on her own -- and did often enough to pretty much erase any concern on Jake's part that he was neglecting her. On the previous Saturday she took the bus to her friend Natalie's family's apartment to hang-out for the afternoon. It was a common sight for Jake now, watching her leave their apartment to go to a store or the library or just a walk. Still, no friends arrived, and Jake couldn't help wondering if the Bardon application process cast a pall over her current social life.

As far as palls getting cast, a week after Jake raised the prospect, or specter, of more, Gwen remained in the distance, twice sending a text about a collector who might contact him. She told him how busy she was. She also said, twice, that Jane Mallory had a huge collection. Jake just thanked Gwen. He wanted to ask her why Jane wasn't sent in sooner, but he was able to control his Gwen obsession a little. He wasn't surprised when Jane phoned him on Wednesday asking to meet with him at her townhouse on P Street in Georgetown. She wanted to show him what was hanging on her walls, to get his advice. He said he'd be there at three in the afternoon.

Jane's Northwest P Street address blended into the tight row of gorgeous Federal three story nineteenth century brick townhouses that made Georgetown sought after by tourists and lucky, wealthy dwellers.

She welcomed him in. Even the front hall was enough to grab Jake with its stairway's curving banister made of mahogany or something -- something Jake wanted to touch. And, even more beautiful and tactile, the floor was large, thick slabs of worn, brownish- gray varnished flagstone and he stood still for a moment and stared down grunting. There was a faded antique, worn, oriental runner of reds and greens flowing toward a couple of white painted closed antique doors twenty feet down the hall.

Following her, he entered the living room through a door to his right. It was one large room, longer than wide, with tall ceilings and a large fireplace in the middle of the inside wall. At the far end, French doors led to a garden room or old formal conservatory. Jane faced the wall across from the fireplace. The wall was covered in artwork, mostly small prints and drawings, but with five beautiful paintings interspersed here and there.

"Wow." Jake chuckled.

"Yeah. I need some help."

He couldn't let her sidestep the glamour of it all. "Yeah, I've been in a few houses in Georgetown and seen some great stuff, but this is really fantastic."

Jane reddened. "Thanks. I'm so spoiled I barely see it. It was my parents' house and I grew up here. They live in

Virginia now and I'm supposed to sell this. I could live in it. I just don't want to."

"Right. It's nice to have your own place." Jake took a couple of steps toward the picture wall. He had to lean over a silk, orange sofa he wanted to stare at and stroke and sit on and God only knew what. He eyed a group of very small Rembrandt etchings. "Wow."

"I know. My grandfather loved this art. My parents just left all these things hanging where my grandfather put them seventy-five years ago. My parents sort of ignored them."

"And the mats are acidic."

"Are they? I was afraid of that."

"Yeah, the old mats will leach into the artworks, as you know."

"Um. Yeah, I want to keep some and get rid of some of these things."

Jake was pointing his head as closely as he could at the seven Rembrandts and then three by Martin Schongauer. He stood straight again. "Can I take one off the wall?"

"Sure."

He raised the Schongauer, "Flight Into Egypt" off its small wall hook and looked at the back of the frame. It was a flaking mass of decomposing old backing materials. He put it back on the wall.

Pointing to the door, Jane said, "I like these old master prints, but I prefer the ones above us, in the room upstairs We can come back here." She led him back into the entry hall and up the stately, gently crunching antique stairs. Above the ground floor living room was a second living room, the same size. The fireplace was smaller, and the ceiling was a bit lower, but it was even more coated with art. The smooth chartreuse plaster walls showed off a dozen paintings, but with at least forty works on paper.

"This is the twentieth century room."

Time capsule gallery would have been Jake's description, but he just looked and tried not to drool. He walked, peered and did a quick survey. "So, your grandfather was encyclopedic and has these things arranged according to period and national origin?

"Yup."

Jake pointed at the far wall with the French cubists works and then the German Expressionists, and then some British artists like Paul Nash, Stanley Spenser and Gerald Brockhurst. Then, an American wall with a Laura Coombs Hills, a Paul Landacre, an Edward Hopper and on and on.

It was a lot of conservation work for him, potentially. "Do you have some you want me to look at right away?"

"I do. I was hoping you could take a few of these today, if that's all right. Did you bring a car? I can put them in mine if you walked."

"I walked. I've actually never owned a car." He pushed his lower lip out along with a sad, cow-eyed pout and they both grinned, not having to elaborate on whatever the weird irony was. Somehow, they needed each other, her with disposable houses and art and him with peculiar insights and skills.

Jane kept her face looking into his. "I loved my grandfather so much, but I can't live in a museum. You know?"

Jake bobbed his head. "Sure." He was thinking how happily he could live there.

"Besides," she mused. "Things in frames, hanging on walls aren't so much the art of now, are they?"

Jake coughed out a laugh and she waved both hands at him. "No-no. I'm so sorry. I just discounted you. No, I know it's still great to paint and draw and make pictures!"

"And conserve them and frame them and hang them back on walls." He laughed again and waved a hand back at her. "No, it's all right. Really, I couldn't agree more. I'm fixing things from other time periods, usually, and that's fine. The main sources of art change. Gwen and I decided that. We just haven't published our declaration, yet."

Jane's smile stiffened -- something Jake couldn't afford to ignore. "Anyway…" He turned his head back to the nearest wall of pictures, thinking he'd mouthed off and straight-armed her too much.

Jane's voice was more hesitant. "I'm going to try to get Gwen to help me design my next place. I'm thinking of a smaller house somewhere here in Georgetown. But I'll sell or give away some of the pictures."

"No siblings?"

"No. My brother was killed in Afghanistan."

Jake sank. "Oh. Sorry."

"That's okay." She withdrew, somehow arrested by her own personal history, glancing away.

Her careful, quiet style made her more alluring to Jake. Shyness could grab him. He allowed himself to keep his gaze on her and she started to weave a bit. Now, he was getting way too aroused.

But Gwen's omnipotent, omnipresent sphere of influence left no space for Jane. Wanting to move along, he said, "Anyway, yeah, I'm happy to help with the works on paper. Do you know what things you want to start with?"

She looked at him. "Well, I'd like all the works on paper unframed and conserved by you, if you don't mind."

Jake nodded. "Great."

She continued, "Could we take, say, ten works to your studio today? Then, when those are done and you have the time to do the work, I'll give you another ten? Something like that?"

"Okay. That sounds good. Why don't you choose?"

He went about pulling the ten works off the walls as she pointed at them. They made three trips downstairs and outside to her BMW. Jake sat in the passenger seat, even aroused by the plush leather, for the five-minute drive.

The activity of them bustling upstairs to his studio and then her signing his forms, listing what she was leaving, directed their energy, which was then scattered, because Jane was double parked.

She looked even more beautiful flushed. She stopped and turned to him at his apartment door. "I'll be in touch. Thanks again."

She was gone. He had to get in touch with Gwen. Jane made him want Gwen even more.

* * * * *

Cool wet air provoked her hair and caressed her face and hands as Sara's multilayered defenses kept her perfectly warm. The pale gray turtleneck was still her go-to top and her long wool skirt and ankle boots took care of the rest of her. The whisking dampness of Washington really refreshed and invigorated her in the middle of spring and in the fall. In the summer the burning humidity cooked everyone, and it coated them in ice in winter. Sara wasn't looking forward to frigid wet icy vapors soaking her clothing in a month or two – if they stayed in Georgetown that long. She loved Georgetown at the moment, walking around town, and there was no reason to ask why.

It was Wednesday, November first at four-thirty and Sara was indulging in the sights. She walked up 30th Street for fun, to be a part of it, but also to get out of the apartment and think. Looking out her window half an hour earlier she saw her father unloading a car's worth of art. What was unusual was the woman he was with. Most of the people Sara saw meeting with her father in his studio were, to be honest, not especially jaw dropping physical specimens. They weren't human dumps, usually. They just usually seemed old and worn out or something -- the opposite of Gwen. That woman with her father just then looked like a model or something. Where was Gwen, now that she ran out of art for Sara's father's business?

Sara had to come up with some way they could all get together. A day trip to Annapolis? Sara always wanted to see Annapolis.

She stepped up her walk to get more exercise and to finish it so she could get back to text Gwen. At least the sun was fading elegantly for the day and there wasn't much wind. The temperature was probably in the low sixties, so the weather couldn't be more adequate. She was going to invite Natalie over after school, but Natalie was so overweight she didn't walk any more than she had to, and there was only so much prowling on social media Sara could take. They spent the whole afternoon two weeks earlier tapping and stroking and clicking on their phones and Natalie's computer, to the point where Sara's eyes and brain dried out.

She could walk over to Wisconsin Street and prowl in some stores but didn't want to. She didn't need anything and didn't have any money anyway. She just wanted to look around her. Like the rest of Georgetown, the colors of the houses on both sides of 30th appealed to her -- every shade of green, blue, white, maroon, red, orange. A bunch of the leaves were off the trees, sprightly littering the sidewalks and streets with dabs of faded yellow, brown and red; gorgeousness she could weave through.

She stepped lively, liking the effort. If she didn't walk, she didn't get much exercise. She sat on the bench at school soccer matches, since she sucked at it and since she clearly hated pretending. *Try harder Holtz! Put some muscle into it!* That insanely angry coach hated Sara, and a few other kids, for being physically incompetent, and for not caring. Why are coaches so often so enthusiastically nuts? That woman, Tre Dongle, was probably always like that -- a bulky, spewing, sweating, emotional wreck.

Goddamn gym class was just as nuts. Stretching for half an hour and then jumping and leaping was pure humiliation. Old Lori Norman was the gym instructor, at least sixty and skinny and constantly strutting around in a sweatshirt with the words, *Fierce and Strong* printed front and back. She lectured them about yoga constantly, trying to get them to stretch in concert with their bodies in some inadequate way.

Sara would like to take actual calm yoga classes someday.

*   *   *   *   *

Gwen picked up her phone from her desk. It was a text from Sara.

> *Gwen. Just an idea. I've always wanted to go to Annapolis. I've seen pictures of it and heard it's gorgeous. I haven't mentioned this to my father yet, but he's always said he likes the place, and he needs a rest from work. Do you? Could we make a day trip there sometime soon?*
>
> *Lol Sara*

My God, that girl had ambitions and reached for them no matter what. Gwen rolled her eyes, half disturbed, half delighted. The idea of a day trip to Annapolis appealed and rankled. So much for getting some paperwork done before the Thursday deadline for that damned kitchen in Dupont Circle. So much for avoiding any thoughts of Jake.

Gwen sat back, up in her office, propped behind her beautiful arts and crafts desk, her old oak chair creaking, and tried to reason it out, comb it through, put some order to her thoughts. She told herself to wait before texting Sara back.

The office was almost too bright at times. The two skylights always aimed a lot of light into the room but this time of day, late afternoon, it irradiated the room, bouncing off walls, floors and furniture. The skylights needed shades. She made her way down two flights to make some chamomile tea, sit in her window seat and think.

She hadn't seen or spoken with Jake for over a week, apart from a couple of cold, dry texts. Maybe it was good that there were no longer easy excuses for getting together. The fact was, after him asking for more -- meaning divorce from Larny -- she panicked. Then she phoned Jane Mallory. She knew when she did it, that her calling Jane was an act of desperation; the famously beautiful Jane being such a quiet and potent svelte fatale.

Gwen hadn't sent Jane one of the architecture/ conservation promotion letters. Why? Obviously, because Gwen wanted Jake all to herself. Then she phoned Jane and pushed things forward. What things?

Now, the Annapolis text to Gwen from Sara taunted Gwen once more.

Feeling fidgety, Gwen went back up two flights to get back into her chair behind her desk. It could drive her crazy thinking about Jake being with Jane – Jane who was now divorced. And Jane had that incredible collection that Jake could work on for half a year.

223

Gwen finished her tea. Just about everyone avoided Jane in school and Jane, being naturally conservative in style, and somehow unsure of herself, hid in a shell, avoiding people's eyes. Jane was clearly unusually great looking but somehow didn't fit in. She was a bit of a loose end, despite being rich and beautiful. It might have been her quiet formality. It might have been that she looked like a WASP of old, of the old Bardon School. Gwen didn't have anything to do with her and didn't know anyone who did. There were a few kids who hung around her. They seemed to be loose ends too. Gwen felt bad about that when she met Jane years later, in town. From conversations in the last few years, Gwen learned that Jane had very accomplished and arrogant relatives who ignored her -- a Philadelphia art museum director for a grandfather and parents heading divisions of the State Department. Gwen got fairly close to Jane eight years earlier, when she and Larny moved to Georgetown -- Jane in that fantastic, eccentric house she grew up in. When Jane would complain about the fussy old museum-like place, Gwen would tell her to move and Jane would sigh, filled with guilt and admiration for her ancestors or something. Now Jake could help her sort through the art and maybe Jane could move on.

Yeah, Jake and Jane would move on together, with Sara. Gwen did want to go to Annapolis.

Sara, that sounds like a really good idea. Let me think about my schedule and talk to your father about it. One or both of us will get back to you.

Lol to u 2. Gwen.

CHAPTER TWENTY

November 3, Friday

The perfect hint of perfume circling, Jane stood before him writing a check, dressed in a staggering knee length, dark blue velvet dress. She was holding a thin trench coat. She looked and smelled and probably tasted and would definitely feel, as soft and lusciously feminine as anything Mother Earth provides. Handing him the check for the Hartleys, she clearly saw his eyes inflate because she blushed and stepped back.

"I'm dressed to go to a party on 28th Street. It's people from work."

"Oh." Jake was having a hard time not stepping forward as she stepped back. He could barely think and said nothing, standing still.

That pulled her forward verbally. "I'm sort of dreading it. It'll mostly be boring attorneys standing around not even trying to be coy about how much more powerful they are then each other."

"Wow. Sounds bleak."

Jane's blushing continued. "Yeah, want to go?"

He laughed, then took a second. "Uh, really?"

"Um." She grumbled sheepishly, very red-faced. "Sorry, I know I just said it would be awful. I just need someone to help me keep the creeps at bay. We could leave after an hour, and I'll buy you dinner for the favor?"

It was a bit after four in the afternoon, Friday and Sara was in her room. Jake could feel his whole body harden. His chest muscles heaved up and out just enough to be discernible. It was plenty discernible to him, but he saw that Jane, her eyes inflated now, was visually taking him in.

He nodded. "Great."

Mumbling about what he had to wear and Jane telling him any old suit would be more than formal enough, Jake disappeared into his room, his heart whomping. What was he doing? It felt like cheating on Gwen, even just going to dinner with another woman, and he knew how disjointed that logic was.

Would a bit of jealousy help dislodge Gwen, dislodge her from her damned marriage?

He nervously texted Sara.

> *I'm going out to a party. Can you take care of yourself here? Apart from the great leftovers from yesterday, there are a couple of frozen entrees in the freezer. I'll be back no later than eight, probably earlier. Okay?*

Why did he feel ashamed telling Sara that? Why didn't he want to introduce Jane to Sara? Sara would see Jane as serious competition for Gwen, even though she wasn't. The whole thing was making his stomach twist. His put on a white shirt and blue and red striped tie, his old dark blue silk suit and his black Mucks on his feet. The fact that he looked like a lawyer from the Kennedy years seemed perversely appropriate.

He said that last part to Jane and she stared, stuck, seeming to like what she was looking at. "It looks extremely cool." She glanced away and they headed out. Ahead of him, walking down the stairs, she added. "Cool will fly over the heads of the money grubs we're about to see."

Jake liked the compliment but was reaching distractedly into his jacket pocket in response to his phone vibrating.

OK. See you later.

Jake would have to ignore the internecine war in his head. Sara had to be able to eat one dinner by herself, but it was his first time leaving her alone in the apartment. He'd text Simon and ask him to text Sara later.

That stirred look on Jane's face when he presented himself dressed-up to her, remained a shared hormone stirrer. Nothing said, they moved along. The walk only kept his blood pumping more, bubbling like an expresso maker. It took them five minutes. They entered a large, early twentieth century shingle styled town townhouse. A profusion of natural light from large windows everywhere mixed with the hum of voices and the scent of alcohol, all frothing around them until they stopped in the middle of the large open plan kitchen-diner. Someone rehabilitated the bejesus out of the interior.

They were offered some red wine by a young jacketless guy in black-tie formal wear. Jane was waved at and even hugged enthusiastically, despite her quiet lack of joining in. But she was extremely-easily the best-looking person in the room and Jake was almost feeling giddy. Someone named Lester Cardimone arrived as Jane and Jake stopped zigzagging into the living room area. He hugged Jane, who blanched, then reddened and then introduced Jake.

Lester was a partner in the same firm Jane had some part in and he owned the house around them. When asked,

Jake told him what he did. Lester laughed. "I knew you were too well groomed to be an attorney."

Jake grunted a laugh to be polite and Lester asked him if he knew about Jane's art collection. As Jake nodded and began to answer, Lester suddenly apologized and waved and yelled to a new guest. Lester left them.

"He's a tennis buddy of my ex-husband. He won't come back."

Jake nodded, with some apprehension.

Jane shook her head. "My ex-husband isn't here. He's a financial adviser and surely at a much more lucrative party in New York."

"So, but how am I so well groomed?"

Jane, flushed unremittingly, hunched her shoulders and lowered her voice. "Oh, no. Lester just gets nervous if someone looks, uh, elegant without it being about money."

"Okay."

She coughed into her hand, trying to clear herself and the life around them, up. "Yeah, it's always seemed to me there are two ways to present yourself in this country. Either you dress like a teenage hipster, or you dress like the money you have, or don't have. Lester couldn't read you."

"Money or hipness. That's it in life?"

She chuckled for a second. "Uh, well, I mean, there are all sorts of variations. I actually came up with that theory after spending a year abroad in college. So I was twenty."

"Hmm. Well, I think you actually nailed it when you were twenty."

Jane's glass of wine was half finished, just like Jake's, and he could assume she was feeling as warm inside as he was. They were smiling endlessly. "Where'd you go abroad?"

"London."

Jake nodded, mumbling about spending three weeks there years ago and loving it. He looked around. There were men and women in suits and in other clothes that weren't usually seen on the street or in restaurants. They were the professional outfits he saw in expensive shop windows that managed to avoid style. He said that to Jane in a low voice. "Expensive anti-style is what it looks like to me."

She beamed, whispering. "Yup. These are major money makers, but it's not smart to care about how you look." She looked like she was going to add to her contempt for the wealthy professionals around them but seemed to know there was nowhere good to go with it. She and Jake just bit their lips and glanced around. A woman near them with very short hair parted on the side, had on a shapeless zip-up sweater and dark baggy pants. She was talking to a man in a cheaply made dark brown suit with a light gray shirt and yellow and brown-gray tie, all visually decomposing. The other woman with them had on a management black skirt, white shirt and high heels, seen hundreds of millions of times for what seemed like thousands of years.

He faced Jane again, Jane being a Vaughan Williams symphony in blue velvet. Jake was tempted to tell her how beautiful she looked in her quiet, perfectly tailored dress, but not that tempted. "So, despite appearances, you're a lawyer… or, sorry, an attorney?"

"I'm an attorney, a lawyer." She ducked her head as this came out.

"No, that's fantastic, if you like it. What sort of law?"

"Actually, I specialize in non-profit law. I've sort of ended up in that and I do like it."

"Hm, well, that's interesting. So, what, non-profits like new museums?"

"If I can, very rarely, or anyone who needs to incorporate, you know, legally set-up not-for-profit organization status and needs to define it correctly and make sure it gets the right designation, the right tax designation."

"Great. Well, so it sounds like you've found a profession you like. A lot of people don't."

"Um. It took a while to get to the sort of law I'd like to practice and to work up a clientele, but, yeah, it's seeming really good now." She sipped some more.

"You know, I really liked that theory you came up with. Gwen comes up with seriously profound insights like that too. Is that why you're friends?"

Jane wrinkled her forehead and took a sip. "Um, I guess that's it. That and living nearby and our husbands working together. Plus, we went to high school together, Gwen and I did."

He felt a cold breeze of separation encircle him. Maybe that was Jane's aim after he introduced Gwen's name. Sure enough, the news that Gwen's husband and Jane's ex-husband were business associates in some way rattled him. It wasn't like two hostile guys were an army, but they were rich and powerful in some way and there he was in a house filled with their fellow travelers, not his. It didn't take much lately for him to feel disarmed.

He noticed Jane's face concentrating on him, on his estrangement.

After another sip of wine, she said. "So, you chose the arts at a time when most people were selling their souls. Are you a saint or a prophet or something?"

He laughed. "Not that I know of. No direct orders from God, yet. I'm waiting."

"You're not a communist, are you?"

Now Jake really laughed, and she laughed with him. He coughed into his non-wine-glass-holding hand. "No, I'm not a communist or an anarchist or a nihilist or even a Unitarian. I'm for whatever supports self-government and free enterprise…the freedom of enterprise and the enterprise of the free. How about you? Are you a communist, trying to recruit me?"

"Not that I know of. And I'm not waiting for orders, so I'm not any of those things you listed."

"Were you as transformed by Bardon as Gwen?" It shot out of him for so many reasons. He felt mortified for sounding puerile, reinforced by the repulsed look on Jane's face, so he quickly added, "She's told my daughter, Sara and me, stories."

"I guess. I also know about your daughter, Sara. Gwen told me a lot about her. So, do you three spend a lot of time together?"

He shrugged.

"I've just noticed Gwen talking about Sara a lot, as I said."

"Yeah. I think Gwen and Sara have bonded. But it's impossible to not bond with Sara, if she'll let you. And Sara thinks the world of Gwen."

They both drank some more from their second glasses of wine and Jake seldom drank much so he was beginning to feel top heavy. The voices around them sounded like intoxicated birds of prey, but when he said that in a low voice to Jane, she didn't react at all.

She shimmied in a couple of small private movements, from the inside out. Then she said. "I think I get why Gwen's been talking about Sara so much lately."

Jake didn't want more words and he should have been excited by how profoundly well-developed this Jane was, but he began to feel afraid of something. He knew a large portion of that fear came from the widening chasm this date was creating between Gwen and him. He realized he was probably staring at Jane, and barely getting any oxygen, so he made an effort to snap-to a bit. When she finished her wine, he did too.

He leaned back restlessly. He made a few very small twists with his head.

Jane looked hard at him and then away, thinking in a pause. Her eyes were burning.

Trying to sober up he raised his eyebrows obligingly at her. She apparently noticed that and asked, "Is there something I should know?"

He found himself muttering, "No. Not really."

Jane drew inward, something he could tell she was expert at. He just gazed at the floor, feeling ashamed. He was the one with the blood rushing to his face now.

"She's married." It was all he wanted to say.

Nothing was said for a few no-trust, metastasized seconds.

Her head was turned, her facing the closed sliding doors and the boring backyard beyond. She said, "She is my best friend. Maybe we should rethink that dinner."

Jake stood still. "Sorry. Yeah, I…" He hated feeling like such a spineless degenerate, but there was still nothing he wanted to say, no bridge he wanted to burn, except maybe the one to Jane. She looked a little horrified and Jake knew he had to fight any implication Gwen was cheating on her husband.

"Nothing's happened. Nothing."

Jane shifted sideways as she walked past him and headed to the hallway.

He had to follow. After long entangled moments of depositing their wine glasses on the nearest flat space and not speaking or looking at each other, they headed for the door.

Outside on the shady sidewalk, Jane lowered her head in contempt. She took in enough air to possibly cool her anger.

There was a moment of just that before she gave him her statement.

"Yeah, see, I think I see. Gwen likes the father-daughter scene. She was always the one debating whether to have kids."

Jane walked away.

*   *   *   *   *

Jake woke up Saturday and drank a lot of water, wanting to cleanse himself of at least some of the wine and Jane parching from the day before. Breakfast was over and Sara was out visiting Natalie, so he went into his studio. He looked at his phone for his appointments -- two in the morning. Next was appraising his workload. There were about three weeks of things to do.

Obviously, he had to reconcile losing Jane's business with his desperate needs. It was the price of being in love with Gwen his single on-going benefactor. It was the price of having Sara so determined to make Gwen her replacement mother.

Jake would get other work, through Gwen at least, he hoped. How long should he live in hope? Was he nuts thinking Gwen sent Jane around as a test? So what if he passed that damned test? He told himself to just get his work done. He had no choice but to work and wait.

That same Saturday, now afternoon, sitting on his tall steel stool in the dry midday light, leaning over a Paul Klee collage, Jake's phone rang. He had to sit back and upright, stretching his right leg out so he could reach into his pocket.

"Hi."

"Hi, Jake? It's Simon."

Jake was going to joke that he knew that, but Simon spoke first. "Did you hear the news? Did you hear anything?"

"What? Anything what?"

"Uh, about Emma."

"Emma?"

"Jesus. Sorry, Jake. I'm really sorry, but an old neighbor of hers from Bethesda just called me. She said she read that Emma was shot. She got mugged last night or something. She was out with friends, and they all left a restaurant and Emma was alone in a parking lot. Something like that. She was killed, Jake. Jesus, sorry. Nan said that and she sent me an article some mutual friends had on Facebook. I don't know..."

"Killed?"

"That's what Nan said, and she sent me the article, just a short article in the LA Times online."

"Who?"

"What? Uh, Nan's someone who used to house-sit for us and babysit for Becky and me and for Emma. Yeah, she said she wanted me to know. Shit. She sent me the link. Really sorry, Jake."

Silence.

"I can send it to you, Jake. I'll send it."

*   *   *   *   *

Five minutes to four. The time from hearing the news and reading about it, around one-thirty, to Sara walking in the door, was open ended. She was at a friend's house. His thoughts were quick and slow, involuntary. He stopped trying to think before he started trying to think. He waited. He had to text her. She might come home soon, but it could be hours.

Sara, are you going to be home soon?

He waited, again. Not long.

Yeah, the bus was late. I'm not that late.

His mouth tasted like tooth decay or something, even after he drank some water. He didn't ask Sara when she'd be home. Nothing changed the waiting, not moving around, not sitting. It was ten after four. Where was she? Looking out one more time, she wasn't on the sidewalk outside his bedroom window.

The door clanked downstairs. His chest clamped down and he waited, standing in the hallway, ten feet from the apartment door. After the shuffling of feet, the door pushed open.

She stared. "You left the door unlocked. What? Why are you standing there? What's wrong?"

He pointed with his head, turning toward the studio. "Uh, come in here, Sara, please?"

One hand on the back of his steel stool, he faced her as she stopped a few feet inside the studio doorway.

"Some awful news. Your mother was shot in a robbery in LA." He walked to Sara. "It was last night and I'm so sorry, but she was killed." He waited and when she looked like his words hit home, he stepped forward and hugged her.

THREE

CHAPTER TWENTY-ONE

November 5, Sunday

Sara opened her eyes to the dark. Her window shades were down, and she had on her clothes from school. Her clock said it was nine-thirty-six. The horrific rebound hit her -- her mother was shot and killed. Her mother was dead? No! Sara tried but wasn't able to twist away from the words, then the facts. Sitting up didn't help. Nothing did. Part of the gnawing inside her was having to urinate, part of it was hunger. Most of it was a mass of acid burning away. Who the hell-on-earth would shoot her mother?! Why?!

She didn't want to know and did want to, and she wanted to shoot that person, but was afraid to even think that way. Who did it? How could she ever stop hating, hating, hating, hating, hating, hating, hating, hating! She pounded and pushed at her mattress, grunting and moaning.

Slowly, she forced herself to stand up, wobbling.

She'd have to go out of her room. She couldn't see her father. It was too much. She sank to the floor. Her poor father. Her poor father. Poor father. Sobbing weakened her. She was weak from hunger and sobbing. It was all adding horror and rage. Everything was. Her poor father hugged her and brought her into her room after he told her. She saw his tears, holding back, telling her he would check on her. He said he'd bring her food and did. He sat next to her for at least an hour. Where was he now? Seeing him would unleash more horror, anger and sobbing.

She listened at her door. Nothing. There was almost no light through the cracks. Very carefully, quietly opening it, she crept to the bathroom, seeing her father's light beneath the cracks in his closed bedroom door.

Out of the bathroom, she crept to the kitchen and slowly opened the refrigerator. A covered plate of salad sat next to a small bowl of dressing. Her father had that there for her and she had to hold back the tears. She had water in her room. Her father gave her that earlier, putting it on her chest of drawers when she couldn't look at him. Now she took the salad into her room, with a slice of oat bread with almond butter.

*　*　*　*　*

Jake

Funeral arrangements will be as follows:
Wednesday, November 8th

11 am - Montclaire Funeral Home Chapel, 2198 Veteran Avenue, Culver City, Los Angeles

12:30 am – Roseland Cemetery – 1447 Coscove Blvd., Culver City

Rick and I will be there, along with Samantha and Sean. Also, our mother and stepfather and Luke, our father. At this point, I'm not sure who else might make it.

Cindy

Yeah, his connection with Emma was sour and distant for so many years, and now it was a morbid imprint, fixed and dismal, but Cindy didn't have sign out with just her name. Cindy, who was never exactly friendly with Jake or Emma, was probably put out that she was stuck making long distance funeral arrangements. And those damned arrangements were for a funeral all the way the hell out in California in three days? The poor woman was only out there for five months. Jake tried to be magnanimous, but it was all so tortured out of any real shape. He remembered Emma always saying Cindy didn't ever want to leave Richmond, Virginia. Now, they were all going to rush out to bury Emma three thousand miles away.

Jake somehow managed to find a halfway decent rate on a flight to LA for Tuesday and texted the information to Sara. Sara seemed a little bit less sad today, after a day of miserable, solitary mourning in her room. Jake found himself sleeping a lot, after the first night of no sleep. The sickening, waking nightmares attacking him Saturday night were so awful he was taking erratic naps all day Sunday. Awake, he couldn't shake his worries about Sara. What was a miserable rejection when her mother hightailed it had collapsed into her mother getting brutalized? Now Sara couldn't even be angry at Emma? The local LA news account Jake read online only said the shooting happened next to her car, that the attacker or attackers stole her wallet and phone and shot her. The grotesque viciousness of the act played again and again in Jake's mind. His fury came and went with his exhaustion.

The police had no suspects yet. There were no surveillance cameras near the scene and no witnesses. Someone heard two shots and called the police. So, there might never be anyone accused of the shooting? Agonizing as that thought was, footage from a camera would have been much too gruesome for Jake and Sara to even contemplate.

What could Jake do? Could he just be there for Sara, watching and hoping for some of what people call closure? How the hell does that work? You finally get totally exhausted?

*   *   *   *   *

So many hours of plodding through colossal airports and squeezing into tight airplanes and taxis finally led to Jake and Sara lying, worn ragged, in twin beds trying to sleep in Los Angeles. The Hampton Inn was only four miles from the Funeral Home. *Funeral Home,* Jake drifted, lying in a stupor. Is a funeral home an art gallery, the corpses exhibition objects of death? He'd decide tomorrow.

Morning came as a surprise. He didn't remember sleeping. It was 9:39. He took a shower and shaved. Sara took a shower as he went downstairs and got milk. Back in the room he made some coffee and got the organic cereal out of his small suitcase. He ate some, then got dressed in the bathroom while Sara got dressed in the room. He ate some more, and she only nibbled. Almost no words were employed by either of them.

They waited in the lobby for an Uber. The Montclaire Funeral home would have been the same as any large, stucco-white, two-story building on the busy street, except for its large sign on the lawn and its long driveway lined with black limousines. There were very tall, straight palm trees with nothing but endless, narrow trunks and only a few palm leaves crowning the top. They seemed to be common to LA. Everything was draped with perfect, warm sunlight.

A few groups of people walked in ahead of them, people Jake knew were unrelated to him or Emma and heading to their own rooms inside. Following those people to the entrance on the side of the building Jake nodded at two ushers in cheap dark suits who were gesturing passively for them to go inside. Inside a large, pacified vestibule with mauve stucco ceilings and walls and white ceramic tile, an usher murmured that he was sorry for their loss as he asked their names and pointed to an open doorway. There were a few other doorways down two corridors. Jake expected a room with a casket and some people standing around, greeting guests. Instead, they entered a continuation of the colors and textures of the vestibule and hallway – a forty by forty-foot room with a temporary arrangement of chairs and a small pulpit. The dry stuffy air smelled of floor cleaner.

Sara and Jake sat behind the front row of people already there. Some of Emma's relatives turned and nodded, looking at Sara and giving sad smiles. Sara was stiff, taut. Jake wondered when she'd cry.

They all waited, inactivated, caught in the riddle of commercialized mourning. Jake was struck by how few people there were --seven, including Jake and Sara, in a room built to hold ten times that number. And when they were normally engaged at home, half of those people had little or no contact with each other from what Jake knew.

He assumed Emma was cremated, so that was why there was no casket. God, he hated the horrendous shifting all around him, inchoate space available to honor the person who wasn't there. He sat trying not to cough, hearing Sara's breathing.

When he was making arrangements for the flight to LA, Jake asked himself if he should say something at the funeral, and he always came around to, no. He had rejected Emma so many years before and Cindy and her mother hated him. He did ask Sara if she wanted to say anything. He said it was up to her and he didn't say why. He didn't have to say why it was up to her. She knew. That was on Monday, the day before their flight. He asked her to think about it. Twenty-four hours later, ready to leave their apartment for the airport, Sara said, no. There was nothing she could say.

She added, "I'll say something to you someday."

Now, it was five past eleven. There was a generic minister notable only by her clerical collar standing to the left side of the chapel-like room and Jake guessed the funeral home people were hoping more people might arrive to fill the fifty or so folding chairs. After whispering to the usher, the minister walked to the pulpit that was level with the chairs.

"Hello. We gather here today to mourn the loss of Emma. It's a tragic loss much too soon that will be hard on the many people who loved her. A vivacious, generous, loving mother and sister and daughter, she inspired all those lucky enough to share time and place with her."

Sara was slightly shaking next to him now. Jake turned to see tears dripping. He put his arm around her, and she moaned and stayed slumped, looking down. She had a small package of paper tissues and Jake had two more packages in his suit jacket pocket. The minister spoke on in her bland, staged-formal way. The woman was paid to pretend she had some connection with Emma. She was mentioning names, reading the sheet of paper on the cheap pulpit. Jake was mentioned and Sara, "her dearest daughter."

Jake should have been ready for that but wasn't. He wanted to stop it now, shut the woman up, or leave with Sara, but obviously couldn't. It was too late anyway. Sara had gone from looking down, to aiming her face away. The minister introduced Emma's father, Luke. Jake looked up, never having seen him.

He was tall, around six-two, with patches of hair, lightly dyed a reddish-gray-brown, on the sides and bald on top. He looked stuffed into his navy-blue blazer and brown khakis even though he wasn't much overweight. It might have been the strain of mourning the death of his daughter bloating his insides.

He cleared his throat but still spoke in a deep, hesitant, creaky voice. "Emma never knew when to quit. When she was a kid we nicknamed her Pug and I think that just about summed her up. Her mother and I gave up making rules for her. I don't think she noticed." His voice trembled getting the last bit out and the blotches on his cheeks were growing darker and spreading over his face.

He cleared his throat, then made a point of holding onto the unstable, little pulpit and not looking at anyone. "We had no say in her move out here but knew she'd make a go of it." Tears ran down his face. Hands still on the shaky pulpit, arms stretched, he leaned down. After a minute, he coughed into his fist. He shook his head, walked away and sat down.

The lapse in integrity was too obvious for even the most desperate family member to miss. Luke left the family when Emma was ten and had little to do with her life. Bret, the stepfather just filled space and paid some bills according to Emma, and sat there now, filling space, very wide body stiff, using his shoulder to prop up Emma's mother who was almost as wide, just shorter, wedged, face-first into Bret's arm, not moving.

Cindy, who had been crying, now slowly made her way to the pulpit. She looked fundamentally the same as the first time Jake met her. She was still bony all over, including her face. Her long, fluffy hair was dyed some ginger blonde color and her face was blotchy, stretched thin from her recent grief. She had on a dark gray dress.

"Well, I told her to not come out here." Tears poured from Cindy. Her jaw clenched, her face rigid and her back straight, she stopped. Jake felt his whole insides automatically convulse. His heaves were silent, but he had a hard time breathing. Why was he surprised by all the actual grief in the little group?

Cindy imitated her father's technique of holding onto the pulpit. "But she never listened to her older sister." Another bout with control, with her shaking her head. She stood looking down for half a minute.

"An independent spirit was stolen from us." Cindy bowed, bent by emotion. It swept up the rest of them as bodies trembled and people cried, including Jake and Sara. Cindy sat down, unable to say anything more. Jake couldn't help but wonder how much of the grief in the room was based on fear, fear from the sudden, easy violence of Emma's death. He knew he couldn't shake away the fact that it was an act of savage hatred, just one little pull on a trigger and someone is dead.

The generic minister walked, gradually, to the pulpit. Maybe her flushed face and awkward movements showed some genuine sadness.

"Bless you all and bless the spirit of Emma. Thank you."

Jake was glad she kept it so brief, as if she were trained to know that was all that group could handle. Maybe she had a bunch more quick rituals to complete.

* * * * *

Sara was walking out next to her father. Why couldn't they walk faster, up that stupid little central aisle? She was so, so tired of crying and had to get out and get some air and real light. The fake ceremony in that Goddamned fake chapel wasn't even real enough to call a freak show.

Aunt Cindy and Grandpa were leering and veering toward them from behind and Sara might puke. And, shit, her father started slowing down and, he was shaking their hands?!

Pissy old Aunt Cindy, who never had anything to do with Sara, now had her hand on her shoulder. Sara's father was stuck shaking his head solemnly alongside Grandpa, all of them shuffling along, so fucking inadequately.

In a stage whisper, twisting her neck, looking at Sara intensely, with pink liquid fueled eyes. "It's so great to see you, Sara. You holding up?" Aunt Cindy's whole being seemed clammy. Her hair smelled like hot, rotting seaweed.

Sara had to fake it in order to get rid of the clawing old wreck. She nodded sincerely. "Yup." They were almost at the doorway, but that was just to the vestibule and then they'd have to walk, clinging to each other another thirty feet to the gaping, open doorway spilling life-cheering sunlight in. The outside free world was there.

"Ugh, it's so hard. It's so not easy, but you'll be great. Your mother thought the world of you."

Every muscle in Sara's body jammed. She stopped walking. Aunt Cindy hugged her. "Oh, Sara, she knew you were so strong. She knew it, Sara. She always knew you could make it on your own."

Sara began to quake. Aunt Cindy began hugging her again and Sara pulled away and ran.

The old men guards at the door watched her run by, and they probably still watched her stand, trembling, hunched over at the weird tall tree on the sidewalk. She probably looked like she'd have a heart attack. She just wanted to try to relax, end the California funeral ordeal.

With her bio-grandfather and Aunt Cindy and her grandmother and lardass old boyfriend or husband or whatever he was, standing next to the limos and mumbling things, glancing over at Sara, her father walked down the driveway quickly.

"Sara? You okay?" He stood two feet away.

"Yeah. Sorry."

"No. That's fine."

Thank God her father didn't cling. He never did that pissy, leaning all over a person emotional thing that Sara hated. He turned away from the five relatives waiting twenty feet away just as freak-face Aunt Cindy shouted, "Uh, we're all going in the limousine to the cemetery. Okay?"

Sara felt her body shake again. She looked down and rocked her head back and forth. That took a minute.

Facing the ground, Sara had her say, through her teeth, quietly. "Those people want to say that they're connected to us now, for two minutes, but they're not and never were. Mom never had anything to do with anyone in Richmond and they had nothing to do with her. Now, they want to wail about Mom's independent spirit? Fuck. She's independent now."

Her father's face had looked gray and sad for days, but suddenly blood filled it.

"Jesus, Sara. Okay. Uh, look. Let's go to the cemetery in a cab. Let's just follow through though, okay? We'll be home tonight. Okay?"

Sara looked at him. Their own cab? She nodded, finally feeling some clean air enter her lungs. She'd owe him for this.

CHAPTER TWENTY-TWO

A fter an endless night's struggle with sleep, slowly sitting up, Gwen felt all life's worst emotions set like so much cement inside her. The weight wanted to crush her, so she had to get up and heft herself through the morning routine of eating some sort of breakfast and saying goodbye to Larny. Her reluctance to make the call had to be explained by that crushing weight because even an hour later, the effort of thumbing her phone was difficult.

Sara answered. "Hi."

Gwen had to try. "Sara. I'm so sorry. Ugh…"

"Thanks."

"Um, how are you doing?"

"I'm okay." Sara coughed away from her phone. "I was really upset after we got the news, for a few days."

Sara sounded somewhere beyond upset, trying to rein in her reactions. That was fine up to a point. "I honestly don't know what to say, Sara. Yeah, I just want you know I'm available for you, anywhere, anytime."

Sara's hushed breathing sounded like she was sifting through what Gwen said. Gwen waited.

Sara murmured, "Um, I guess there aren't words to describe how we feel when something like this happens."

Gwen paused. Her pity for Sara had to really be seriously channeled. "Yeah, well Sara, it's hard to make any sense out of it. Ugh, God, I'm just so sorry Sara."

"It's okay."

Gwen moaned, tears all over her hands and face. Sara's gentle voice pierced her. Gwen had to fortify herself somehow, catch her breath, keep her disgust for Emma's violent death from escaping. They stayed quiet for a minute, Gwen still fortifying herself so she could attempt to fortify Sara. Standing in the center of her living room, Gwen began to walk, looking at her shoes, one placed directly in front of the other, straight down the middle of a long, wide floorboard.

"Sara, let me tell you something." Getting silence back, Gwen plunged. "Uh, look, do you still want to go to Bardon? I'm so sorry if it seems crazy to bring it up now. I just think there's an important reason to."

No answer. No sounds, then, "Uh, Bardon? Yeah, I still want to."

Sara's weak, distracted voice might have been off-putting, but Gwen felt highly obliged to push forward. "Okay, yeah, well you need some time to get through a bunch of things here but let me just mention a possibility. I think I can push for you there now. Please, please forgive me for sounding unfeeling about what's happened, but I just think you might benefit from some reassurance, and also some people other than your father and me being there for you. I needed that when I was your age and I got it and I want you to have it… if you want it."

Nothing but some sort of faint oscillation from Sara's side for a moment, then a confused, faraway voice saying, "Oh, but what do you mean?" Her volume still faint, "You think I could get in?"

"Um, I do. Do you understand?"

"Sort of. Not really."

"Sara, I was just in no position to actually push for you. It's almost impossible for me to get into it, but that doesn't matter. At this point I can push if you want me to. You have to understand, it's not just me feeling bad about what's happened. It's actually a new angle that would probably get you in. I just wanted to tell you that, you know, to relieve you of one source of pressure. But, Sara, there's time. Take your time to wade through it. It's not necessarily what you should be thinking about just now. Right?"

"Right."

Gwen stopped there, knowing she was pushing too hard, but feeling like she was desperately digging away at rubble to rescue Sara. How could Sara ever survive under the weight of a mother who abandoned her and then became a murder victim?

Gwen wanted to suggest Sara talk to a therapist but knew that had to wait. Gwen gritted her teeth, still walking, head down, one foot in front of the other along one floorboard, then swiveling at the wall and walking one foot in front of the other back along the next floorboard. No one uttered a sound.

Gwen stopped walking and sighed. "Well, I will always be there for you, and so will your father. So will a bunch of people later."

"Great. Thank you."

"I love you, Sara. I know you know that."

Sara made a muffled sound and both of them cried and gasped for air for a couple of minutes.

Tear-filled eyes, Gwen sat in her window seat. Sara didn't seem able to add anything. Gwen knew Sara was crying, probably holding the phone away, but Gwen couldn't think of anything to say, except strategic grumbled good-byes. "I'm afraid I have to go. I have a lot of work to do, fortunately. We can have coffee very soon. Okay? I'll call or email."

"Yeah."

"Okay, bye."

Gwen leaned over and put her phone on the floor, put her head back and focused, hard. She had work to do to really help Sara, not just weep with her. That phone conversation was necessary but felt so disgustingly short of the mark. Sara would have to go through some sort of contorted mourning ordeal for her crazy mother. And Gwen felt no damned waves of compassion for Emma. Emma's nasty death was just a lose-lose situation for Sara. It would take more than a teenaged epoch for Sara to sort that out, unless she had some serious help.

Yup, Sara would have to be the middle-class exception to the rule of only reaching out and helping poor minority kids. Sara could easily be presented to Bardon, and later major universities, as *in need*. Sara's burdens would turn into her advantages – Gwen would make sure of that. It would be easy for Gwen. But why was it so hard to raise children these days? Gwen had no idea and hit the mantle with the palm of her hand, determined to not get distracted by fear or frustration.

No, after days of fury at the plight of Sara, Gwen was no longer letting her emotions crush her insides. Sara needed her and Gwen had to rally herself. She'd take a nap later. Her lack of sleep the night before meant she'd be less productive up in her office, but Gwen stood and headed upstairs to do what she could. People were relying on her.

As soon as she sat at her desk she realized she couldn't concentrate on building designs or client needs. Barely seated for half a minute, she stood up to go downstairs to take that nap she needed.

Lying flat on her back, hands to her sides, eyes closed, trying to rest, Gwen was too aware she wanted to text Jake. It felt like an ache inside. She'd force herself to wait a day, make him wait and want it even more to give her leverage. He had to stop fearing Bardon, stop aiming at how much they all needed each other and aim instead at fitting the right parts together for his daughter.

*   *   *   *   *

As always, Jake had to keep working. There were bills to be paid. He walked to the end of the counter and reviewed the work calendar on his wall. There were things he had to work on for John Forester. Only a third of that collection was finished.

He reached beneath the far end of his counter and opened the top drawer of his flat metal filing cabinet. There was the Jean Arp etching on transparent, delicately thin paper -- or he could work on the Max Ernst. He pulled out the Ernst. Delicate pieces might be more than he could manage at that point.

As he leaned over the drawing to examine what seemed like old someone's old dirty fingerprints, he calculated the time needed to reduce the smudges at three hours. There was the noise from down the hallway of Sara opening her door and going into the kitchen. He stopped all movement and listened. The refrigerator door opened and, after a few seconds, closed. A cupboard opened and closed. A drawer opened and closed. Silverware and dishes clattered. She went back into her room.

He'd knock on her door in a couple of hours and see how she was doing and negotiate some dinner options. They hadn't cooked together and eaten on the pullout table in her room for six days - since getting the horrible news.

* * * * *

Her father was outside her door asking about dinner. Sara didn't want to but finally had to be sociable.

"Okay, I'll be right there, Dad. Just a salad for me."

Working on issues of food and dishes in the small kitchen was irritating, but Sara knew it wasn't any easier for her father. They did make their way quietly across the hallway into her room and sat at the table. Eating in cumbersome silence for a few minutes, Sara let loose.

"Boys get lost in their own thug aggression and refuse to grow up and girls get lost in their own endless emotions and turn into sour crazy bitches. I hate them all."

Her father's eyes bugged out. Sara began to laugh, but a flood of ideas washed over that impulse.

"I didn't want to get damaged when Mom left. I didn't want to get damaged by her when I was a little kid. But these stupid things kept happening around me, mostly to do with her, my one and only mother. The goofball boyfriends? The extremely dated fashion choices that didn't even fit her? The total lack of actual information? She never read anything and spent every waking moment on social media, gushing about pictures of herself or some friend's new car or kitten. But who was the Goddamned fucking damaged psycho-who shot her? Of course, I want to shoot him, fifty times." Her face filling with blood, she tried not to feed on her fury, groaning through clenched teeth. "And that can't be a constructive, healthy approach to life."

Her father groaned. "No."

Sara sneezed and blew her nose in her paper napkin. She crackled, "Meanwhile, I'm assuming it was a guy, but I'm beyond crying and too tired to whine. And when I first moved here last June the look of pity on your face was enough to make me feel damaged and I was only fourteen." She took a break and sat back, aware her father was still waiting for a reasonable verbal calm to come so he could contribute in some way.

Jake just groaned again and Sara knew she had to show him some kindness. "Sorry, but the last six months have been such a pain in...I mean, I'm not stupid. I knew I suddenly had a psycho rap sheet, and I was supposed to be an emotional wreck because I was abandoned by my mother. But, Dad, I always wanted to live here anyway, and I was always so much more connected to you and then, Gwen came along and, oh my God, it was all perfect. I just don't want Mom to wipe out all that...may she rest in peace."

Jake's head trembled just visibly. "No, Sara, nothing will get wiped out. Your mother meant well. I don't know."

Sara saw there was nowhere he could he go just then without just stirring the mess even more. She folded her arms and mumbled. "Um."

He sat up more. "I'm sorry you've felt, what, bottled-up? But, and you're not damaged, are you? You do have some solid underpinnings, right? Things that can't be removed."

"Um, unless there's a war or depression and it's the End of Days."

"Jesus!" Jake coughed and glared at her. They both laughed loudly, and it took a minute to stop.

He shook his head at her. "Where the hell did you even hear the phrase, *End of Days*? God, Sara."

"On the internet. I read all sorts of things on my computer."

"Damn, Sara. You're fifteen, not sixty."

"I'm a researcher, Dad. I wade through the internet, and I avoid the brain damaged, or culture damaged shit. Sorry, I know you're letting me use nasty disrespectful language because you feel sorry for me. Anyway, no, I've been doing more and more research."

"Research?"

"Yup. I figure since everything around us is getting more and more tossed around, like the world's an insane salad spinner with voices yelling at us to invent ourselves constantly...Jesus, whew, I might as well get some information."

"Information?"

"I know that sounds a little broad. No, I'm serious. I watch documentaries now, all the time. I didn't go to school this week and I learned a few things. What's with the British? Why do they make so many great documentaries?"

"Like what?"

"Gwen told me about them. Actually, Grandpa told me about one. Things like a BBC documentary about the Russian Revolution, then all the Communist purges before and then after the Second World War. Yeah, why do I know they won't teach us that in school? But, yeah, one on how people cooked food hundreds of years ago in different parts of the world. How they made clothes. One on electricity."

Her father didn't say anything.

"I stopped crying last week and spent hours and hours doing that stuff online. I know it sounds nuts, but sorry, I just don't think it is. You, what? You think I should talk to someone and get it all out...release my rage?"

"Might be good for you to at least talk to someone. Talk to Gwen? You know you can talk to me."

"Yeah, I don't want to right now. I mean, this talk is fine, but you know what I think? I think time's too precious to waste on spinning around stuff. I plan on going back into my room and finishing a history book Gwen gave me. That's real. Going around with some rage about Mom dying isn't. Sorry, it isn't. I'm extremely sorry she died. If you or Gwen died, I'd, Jesus, I'd be a mess. I'd wail in the streets for years. No, sorry, I know. I'll see an old picture of Mom or just be reminded of her by something and feel extremely sad and I hate the pathetic psycho bastard or bastards who shot her. But I just think I have some research to do. I'm only fifteen and the internet has a lot to teach me, Dad."

*　*　*　*　*

His dinner conversation with Sara didn't reassure him. Brilliant Sara had enough guts and integrity to deal with one hell of a lot, but her mother's sad two stage disappearing act? All he could do was stand by Sara's side, relatively ready.

Maybe prompted by Sara, he watched a slightly paranoid documentary on YouTube about corporations and governments getting hacked by international gangs and then read a book for a while. Before turning out the light he checked his phone. No messages from Gwen. Why the hell not? But, he felt conflicted about talking to her about Emma's death anyway. He didn't owe Emma much, but he had to respect her memory to some extent, sad as her memory was.

Emma's pathos aside, it was impossible for him to relate his attraction for Gwen to the grotesque reality overtaking Sara and him. Bankruptcy loomed and Gwen was a distant figure. Should he email her? He would tomorrow.

There was a listing on the job site he looked at occasionally. A conservation center in a town called Golden, Colorado had an opening, and it all – town and Center --

looked very good, and it was thousands of miles out there near Denver. He went to bed.

He turned onto his side knowing trying to sleep would only make his endless fears expand. What could he do for Sara or for himself? Since Emma was killed, even midday, his brain centered on a blistering fear of Sara having no mother, no one but penniless him.

If he ever did find a job somewhere out there, Sara might think he was taking her away from her new and perfect mother, Gwen.

After two hours of self-torture, beaten, Jake collapsed into sleep.

CHAPTER TWENTY-THREE

November 10, Friday

Jake,

Just an email, Jake. First to say how sorry I am about Emma's death. Sara texted me and we talked on the phone.

I hope you're well, under the circumstances. Speaking of Sara, I'm seriously worried about her. I don't have to tell you how many complicated conflicts life has suddenly thrust at her. She does have you and she has me, but I'm worried she's too good at reassuring herself that she's strong and can handle things on her own. I think she needs more than you and me and her own brilliant self. I think she needs a professional therapist to help her through all this. It certainly wouldn't hurt.

This leads me to my second idea. I think I can push for Sara at Bardon. Without getting into it too much in this email, I can just say Sara will get a very sympathetic audience at Bardon now.

Spring term, Jake? She could stay at home, and I'd drive her there once a week for exams or whatever. Apart from all the other support Bardon offers, she'd have immediate, free, access to Jenny Frome, the school psychologist. Jenny's a friend of mine and I think she's a fantastic person and highly professional.

Sorry if I'm overstepping my role as a friend of yours and a mentor to Sara. I've just had this brewing since I heard about the loss of Sara's mother. Please let me know what you think.

Gwen

Gwen clicked send after a cursory review. Her adrenaline was keeping pace with her determination to help Sara.

Jake wanted more? Well, Gwen could now easily lean on the humane side of Kate Moffet and Jean Smot in admissions to get Sara into Bardon –– that would be a lot more.

* * * * *

Jake read Gwen's email a few times, more and more seized by his dependence on Gwen to provide him work and Sara, the world. It was overwhelmingly enticing but it smacked of something so damned irrational too.

Sara actually going to Bardon?! So, suddenly Gwen might have a way of getting her into that school, even with a full scholarship and all that, because now Sara could fit some *disadvantaged* category?

Jake couldn't even go for a walk. He found himself pacing in his room, then the studio. The obvious question blared --did he even want Sara going to Bardon?! His walking around his apartment picked up pace. He hadn't spent a lot of time considering it, assuming Sara had no chance of getting in. And Spring term? Christ, that was only a few months away. Even if she lived at home during the spring, she'd ship off in the fall and be gone. He didn't want to answer Gwen's email right away and he really hoped she hadn't made any promises to Sara. Sara would flip-out ecstatically, all her dreams coming true.

He stopped walking. His pledge to find more work or move roared inside him. He'd been assuming he had no choice – he had to move to get a job. Now, Bardon meant he didn't even have that choice? He couldn't move? Gwen knew that, didn't she, and that Bardon or no Bardon, he had to make an income?

He'd spent much too much time questioning himself, and, instead, now got some work done. Small tangible solutions in the present meant the day ground on and on.

It would be an uneventful dinner with Sara if he stayed away from the main subject. He decided to let her finish eating. As a father and daughter, they were just about buoyant enough to not need much filler conversation.

And he had to get to the main subject. "Any plans for the weekend?"

Sara shrugged, then, sarcastically, "You?"

He ignored the implicit joke about their current somber isolation. "I do. Tomorrow, Saturday, I'm meeting some people in the studio at eleven-thirty and at one."

Sara was sitting back, finished eating. He told her about Gwen's email. When she stayed motionless and focused on her empty plate, he repeated the two points of the email –

living at home but going to Bardon after Christmas break and getting professional counseling there.

"Why does she think I need to talk to a psychologist or therapist or whatever they are? I don't get that. I mean, I get it. I get the logic, but I'm just surprised she thinks it's so important."

"Um. It couldn't do any harm, could it? She did it and a bunch of kids there do it."

Unanswered for a moment, Sara chewed on her bottom lip and twisted her head to one side, then the other. Then she sucked in and blew out some air. "Bardon next term. Wow. That's amazing! She didn't say that on the phone...Gwen didn't. Sorry, I was going to tell you she said she could get me in. I was just so amazed I couldn't believe it."

Jake hesitated, then asked. "You want to go there, do this?"

Tapping her back teeth almost comically and yet looking lost in solemn thought. "Wow, go to Bardon sooner. In a couple of months? Sure, assuming they'd work me into classes and whatever."

His heart singed with anxiety, Jake barely managed to get words out. "Uh, ask Gwen questions like that, I guess, Sara. I didn't answer her email. I wanted to wait for you."

"Should I email her, or call her or something? Damn, sooner might be even better. Damn!" Sara's energy was picking up.

"If you want to go, call her. Maybe after you've thought about it."

Sara's eyes settled on him for a second or two longer than usual. He tried to not show his sour state of mind but that was very hard.

"What do you think?" She asked.

He should have expected that question but in his panicked mindset all afternoon, his endless questions didn't end anywhere.

He sat back. "Yeah, well, I don't know. I was really uncomfortable with you going away so soon and that was when we were talking about nine months from now. But Gwen's making a lot of sense about you talking to a therapist there, now. I know you're really smart and strong and mature, Sara. But I'd like you to talk to a therapist. Hell, I should talk to one."

"Maybe you should."

"Maybe I will…but you first." He didn't smile.

"I'm getting that you don't want me to go to Bardon, that you're just going along. Right?"

"Yeah, I'd rather not have you go away, ever, but seriously, not as soon as nine months from now. It feels too soon. But, yeah, therapy's free there, like everything else and Gwen says the woman there's very nice and very professional. Big surprise." He regretted that last quip right away.

"Big surprise?"

"No, it's just that Bardon is amazing and it's offering all this phenomenal stuff to you."

Sara's already alert expression intensified as she reddened and sat forward staring at her plate. Then she stood up. "Wow."

"Think about it. Take your time."

"Okay."

They did the dishes swiftly, mumbling some chit-chat, but mostly without talking. Just as swiftly, Sara disappeared into her room.

* * * * *

Sara knew she wouldn't take her time. She knew Gwen and her father just said that to keep her thinking they weren't controlling her – the primal fear of the teenager. It was all very scary, but so damned exciting too. Bardon, all hers? All paid for? Fuck!

She'd have a hard time not phoning Gwen. It was Thursday night, almost seven. Or maybe she should just send Gwen a text, or maybe an email. It was hard to stand in one place and she didn't want to anyway. She couldn't sit down. Bardon. Bardon very soon. She'd be part of the coolest place on earth -- actually right after Christmas break.

No more pissy, inadequate public school. Screw the therapy whatever. She didn't care about that one way or another. Sure, she'd whine about herself to someone for an hour a week. Why not? Sounded like fun.

She looked down at her floor. She knew the reason she wasn't calling Gwen wasn't because she wanted to think about it all. She would think about it, but at that moment she was just a bit nervous and didn't want to mess up whatever she wanted to say to Gwen, screw-up her questions.

What questions? She didn't know. She grabbed her phone sitting on her desk, feet on her chair, back to her window. She had to text Gwen.

> *Gwen. My father told me about your idea of me going to Bardon next term and talking to their therapist. I want to think about it, but it sounds great to me.*
>
> *Lol Sara*

Her heart was pounding so hard she thought she might pass out. She had to sit in her chair and put her head on her arm, like she did in kindergarten at nap time. She heard her phone buzz and looked up, around the room. It was on the floor.

Hi Sara,

I'm on my way out so I can't talk but maybe you could ask your father about a trip to Bardon tomorrow? I could pick up both of you around 9, if you'd like. That way we could all talk about it and meet with a couple of people there.

Love, Gwen

Sitting on her bed, Sara's head began to take on more and more weight. So much for taking time to think about things.

Sara got onto the floor to lie face up, trying to calm the hell down. Gwen was in some kind of big rush if she wanted to drive to Bardon the next day. Why? She wanted Sara to see that therapist? Her father just made it pretty clear he didn't want her even going to Bardon, and the trip tomorrow would seal the deal? Sara squirmed uncomfortably when she thought of telling him about Gwen's plan. Why not wait a week or two? Meanwhile, her father had to meet with clients. He couldn't go and if Sara went without him, that would make her feel like a major pissy brat.

Sara wished she'd waited and hadn't sent that text to Gwen. She hated to but she had to tell her father. This time she paused. No, she couldn't tell him.

Gwen,

*Thanks, but unfortunately my father told
me earlier that he has some appointments
tomorrow. I don't want to go without him.
Maybe in a week or two?*

*   *   *   *   *

Gwen was in much too much of a state to think about
anything but Larny. He'd been watching her grieving and
lamenting about Sara for days and Gwen really had to explain
things, explain selected things, before he thought she was
losing her mind.

Larny was putting on a sweater.

She chirped, "The restaurant's air conditioning can get
testy?"

He turned and forced a frown. "Yeah. I'm taking no
chances."

She was dressed and ready to go and was aware he
noticed that but said nothing. He looked tense.

They made their way down to the garage and got in his
car. It was an early that Saab he loved and spent a lot of money
maintaining, but it was his only financial indulgence. He built
a financial services company from scratch that employed
over fifty people and that made multimillions for years.
Gwen loved the way Larny wasn't at all materialistic except
in houses, conveniently, and she always wondered if he were
just indulging her desires with houses. Hell, with investments
worth over seventy million, they could afford a few houses.

Flap Jackson's Cafe was looking and feeling just about
right as they sat in their favorite back corner booth. It was an
early favorite of theirs -- a comfort food joint on H Street near

Union Market they went to right before and right after they were married, when they were living off borrowed money.

They both gazed around but Larny looked homed in on something else, something inside himself. He saw her staring and deflected her, saying, "Yeah, it looks exactly the same, but the menu doesn't. The neighborhood doesn't."

Gwen gurgled a laugh. "God, but it's been what? Nine years? Dilapidated, boarded up buildings sometimes get gentrified in nine years."

They got two local microbrewery beers and ordered an Alaskan salmon and organic sweet potato salad for Gwen and a veggie steak sandwich for Larny.

Gwen couldn't resist. "Organic veggie steak on organic sourdough toast? What's happened to the neighborhood?"

"I know. And it comes with organic mashed potatoes with celery root."

Laughing, they were clearly feigning too much fun. Still, Gwen couldn't guess what he suspected her topic was for the casual night out. They took a couple of sips of very tasty beer.

"You have something to say, don't you?" Larny's countenance became more fortified, verging on grim. He sat very still.

So she sat straight, blinking away all stray thoughts. "I do. I've been thinking…for a while, as you know…about kids. I just feel I have to tell you I don't want to, and we're in our late thirties so I thought we should discuss it."

His body tensed and his face sharpened even more. "Wow, yeah. I thought that was the topic, somehow."

"Really?"

"Yeah."

They stopped speaking for a minute. Usually, that was his way to stay sober, to not reduce a decision to anything remotely frivolous. They barely breathed, their eyes occasionally finding each other but not for long. Gwen hoped Larrny would not let any extraneous emotion mar the importance of what she was proposing to not do. She hoped, with any luck, there'd be time enough in the future to let it settle into their pores.

She said, "I know you know how thoroughly I've weighed this."

He nodded once. "Yeah."

His restrained responses began to unnerve her. She didn't want to be the only voice, so she waited.

"Will the kids at Bardon be your kids?" Larny's voice was as sincerely plaintive as she'd ever heard from anyone. But that was not what she wanted to hear just then.

"Uhh, I guess. I love all that involvement." She clenched her teeth. "It doesn't leave much for you in that way. I get Bardon and you get employees and committee meetings." She knew her attempt to lighten the load could smack of falseness. She was becoming discombobulated.

"No, well, anyway…" Larny's restraint was more preoccupied, his voice quiet and labored. "It takes two to make kids. But it helps if both are sure they want to raise them."

"It helps the kids especially."

That seemed to shut Larny down again. He sat biting his lip.

"Oh, God, I hate this Larny. I can't make this decision for both of us. You really want kids or a kid? Same as before? Same as the last time we talked about it?"

His chest rose slowly. "Yeah, but wow, not if you really don't. I thought you might change your mind over time." He leaned back in his chair, his eyebrows raised. "But, maybe I was lying to myself."

They hadn't talked about it for a few years, maybe as many as four years, and the conversation was never complete.

Gwen knew that but seeing Larny's dark eyes and shifting shoulders over there, less and less with her, she worried he was feeling more resolute now.

"I hate it. I do. We have everything together. And I hate you thinking I'm a phobic mess and can't have kids because of my disaster of a childhood. I'm supposed to face those early traumas and stop reliving them and all that, but my whole life has been exactly that…me not reliving that crap."

"Gwen, Gwen, Jesus, you never seem to me to be anything close to a phobic mess and I think I spend a fair amount of time with you, and I am a decent judge of character. We all have things we're afraid of. Jesus, I'm sure I'm filled with phobias, and I know I didn't have anything close to gangs constantly shooting up the neighborhood as a kid, or parents who were never parents at all. So, I guess there's not much I can add to what I've said over the years."

Yup, Gwen had heard all that before from Larny. Hell, she'd heard that from friends and therapists, almost always people who had few if any traumas in their lives. She just stayed on pause this time and Larny shifted in his seat again, leaning back, speaking in a low voice.

"This couple. This father and daughter. What are they to you?"

Her insides compressed. Her heart stopped. "What do you mean?" It was exactly what she wanted to avoid at that moment – anything to do with them.

He watched her.

"It's just Sara. I told you, her mother was shot!"

"Um." He looked away from her. He knew her inside and out and she could feel herself conveying guilt like never before in her life.

He leaned his arms on the seat of his chair in some highly uncharacteristic, insulted state. The seconds crept by.

He leaned forward and murmured, "They're your readymade family. I can't compete with that."

That did it. Gwen wagged her head, bloodless, wordlessly begging him to not think that. But when he sat back and kept his arms locked on his chair and looked to the side of her, she put her head in her hands and shook in horror, tearless. She barely heard what Larny was saying to the server as Larny reached across the table to get Gwen's attention. It was something about asking if she wanted to leave. The heaving inside her chest and brain continued while they made their way out. It continued during the ride home. She wanted to tell Larny she was inert, speechless because she felt bad that he would think such a thing, but that felt so damned false. That would insult Larny even more. God, why did she come so undone so suddenly in front of him?. It reinforced any suspicions he might have. How did he read her so Goddamned accurately?

She calmed down sitting in her window seat in her living room. Larny stood leaning against the mantel, holding a scotch. She was not going to drink. She was not going to pull a Zinzer and run away.

She burbled the words, "I'm sorry, sorry, let's have this talk. I'm not a wreck who can't move on in life."

Larny looked straight at her. "Um, Gwen, you said you don't want to have kids, but you've been moving on with this father and daughter."

"Moving on with them? What? What the hell do you mean?"

"What are you doing tomorrow?"

"Yeah, I have to take Sara to Bardon. I told you."

"So you're moving on with them, the almost established family, only lacking you." He put his hand up to block a response as he walked without his drink, out of the room.

Watching him walk away to the library, Gwen was in shock but forced herself not to push back. She half wanted to protest, to yell at his back that she hadn't earned that distrust, hadn't done anything but talk to Jake. And Sara was just a kid, a kid who needed help. She shook with anger and sat still. How the hell did her life suddenly descend into this? She stood up and headed to the kitchen. Anymore vague apologies from her would only hurt Larny more and then he'd hurt her back. She had to give it some time, let the guilt and suspicions die from lack of air. She fumbled around the kitchen alone, failing to coordinate anything like a meal and went upstairs to bed.

Larny never joined her. It was their first major fight, and she was horrified and lay staring astonished at the walls and ceiling for hours. She had to save her marriage whatever she did. Larny meant everything to her. That fact came around again and again. Jake and Sara didn't come around in the same way. Obviously, everything changed when Sara's mother was killed. That was a trauma revisited for Gwen. She knew it was that, but what was she supposed to do at this point? She had to face the fact that Larny felt spurned. She caused that. She did. But he had to face the fact that she couldn't have kids.

And Gwen was just not able to dismiss Jake and Sara, or Sara anyway. Jake, no. She was slightly repulsed by the thought of him now. How did she let some attraction to him come between Larny and her? Jesus, what a ridiculous, awful person she was and stupid too. Of course, Larny knew she was obsessing over the gorgeous father and daughter. Larny wasn't stupid.

She had to rid herself of Jake and make that clear to Larny. Maybe given some time she could rid herself of both Jake and Sara, but she had to finish setting up Sara in Bardon before she did anything else. It wouldn't take long. She couldn't just abandon the poor kid.

CHAPTER TWENTY-FOUR

November 13, Monday

Her father barely tried to hide his anger. Sara noticed that when she couldn't stop herself from telling him about Gwen wanting to drive to Bardon as soon as possible. He just raised his shoulders and didn't reply to her. She knew – when he went silent, he was upset. Still, somehow, she managed to convince him and Gwen, three days away, Monday, would work for everyone. And they were off, Gwen driving west in her plush leather interior Mercedes.

Sara specifically told herself to bring a watch so she wouldn't look at her phone when she wanted to know the time. Did she? No, of course not! *Avoid your phone, dipshit*, would have to be her mantra now. Mature, enlightened people don't stare at their stupid phones all the time. She was happy she insisted on sitting in the backseat though because she didn't want to make forced conversation with Gwen, who definitely seemed less there than usual. Was that true? Gwen and her father were only making forced conversation up there. And when they did talk, they looked out windows, not at each other.

It didn't help that everyone was worried about her, except her. This hurried visit and parachuting Sara into Bardon in the middle of the school year was fairly drastic and a lot of trouble for a lot of people.

She wasn't tired, just a little on edge, so she certainly shouldn't engage in forced conversation with anyone, so she leaned her head against the door and closed her eyes.

*   *   *   *   *

Twisting her rear-view mirror to look at sleeping Sara, Gwen exhaled, head still looking forward, "Jake, I forgot to mention, Carlos Mendez will be available to speak with you while Sara's meeting with school Head June Jacobs and some teachers. Carlos is Director of Curriculum…you know, in case you have any questions about courses Sara will take. Sara will meet with him at some point today too."

"Okay. And we'll be there a couple of hours?"

"Yeah, I think." She wondered why that was his question – after all this trouble she was going to for Sara and for him.

He didn't add anything, and Gwen was irritated by the discomfort level, so after a minute she added, "Do you have any concerns about courses?"

"Uh, no. Sara and I looked at the suggested curriculum last night and it looked very good."

"Bardon sent it?"

"Yeah, an email attachment from Carlos Mendez."

Gwen tried to relax. She was feeling so hyper-involved in her life and the life of those around her. The whole Jake and Sara effort worked against her core curriculum with her husband, who, for a few days now, showed how much he wanted to avoid her. The distance between Larny and her was lightyears away from their usual intimacy.

She had to say something to Jake, who, now, for an unhappy congruence of reasons Gwen could no longer include in her daily dose of problems. He looked about as angst filled over there as she was feeling. "You could go to the museum while you wait for Sara. I'm going to do a couple of things at the library. I have to talk to them about an addition they want to put on."

She told Jake about that project for two minutes.

Driving along, exasperatingly out of monologue, Gwen just wished she were finished carrying all the damned guilt about this effort. All she could do was be done with it soon. Then she could turn her attention to Larny and her.

*　*　*　*　*

He walked around the Bardon Art Museum alone, trying to use up his two hours, first taking his time looking at the special exhibition of Susan Lui paintings done from sketches and photographs of her trip to her family's hometown in China -- portraits of relatives and neighbors. Susan Lui went to Bardon years before and then Columbia and then stayed in New York.

Being Monday, students were occupied, so apart from a gaggle of them getting a tour from a teacher for half an hour, Jake was the sole visitor to the museum, and it was going to be a long haul. He'd do it because he wanted to help Sara, but it was bleak, being stuck alone wandering. For some insane reason, now if he thought about Gwen being there, he couldn't stand it. He hated it. There was a horrible, miserable one-way dependency between him and Gwen. Sara and Gwen had a great connection, growing greater by the day. But *Gwen Minot of Bardon* was apparently all that was available for him, and he was going to have to like it.

The walls of the museum were a sort of plum color upstairs, where he decided to walk through again. Normally he loved museums, but the collection around him was an organ of the world-shaking body named Bardon School. Jake wanted the best for his daughter without their world being shaken.

Maybe he could go outside and look around. But he didn't want to. He started to feel his anger grow inside him. It was a struggle. When was the last time he had an irrational public fit? Never as an adult. There was the time he stood on his desk senior year in high school. He just wanted the teacher to stop moaning on about Betty Smith's A Tree Grows In Brooklyn. The teacher was a dolt but that was only part of the reason Jake stood, rocking precariously on the small desk, moaning loudly, doing an expressive rendition of the teacher, Mr. Cunningham. The real reason was Jake wanted to get the girl sitting next to him to laugh. She did. She was bored too.

It wasn't funny now. Jake had to sit down and stop thinking about that, or anything like it. There was a cushioned bench in the gallery of William Holman Hunt drawings and wood engravings. Normally, he'd love staring at those beautiful Hunts. Now he sat forward, elbows on his knees and tried to calm down by closing his eyes. No one would see him. There was only the occasional sound of a distant voice somewhere in the building. The occasional guard wandered by. He checked his watch just a minute ago, but he did it again, almost an hour and a half since arriving and probably another half hour before lunch, whatever that would entail. His earlier fifteen-minute meeting with Carlos Mendez to discuss Sara's classes was fine, great. Sara would be shimmied in at whatever pace worked for Sara. All first-year students had that flexibility. It was part of the humane wizardry of the school.

At lunch conversation flowed and food was consumed, and Jake felt warmed by the loving embrace of the kids and adults around him. It was hard to tell how Sara was reacting. Her flushed look could be read any number of ways.

A number of thanks and byes, along with social media connections and phone numbers, got exchanged.

Gwen was leaning on her fancy, big, soft-but-supportive-inside Mercedes, reading her phone. The shady breezes around her were inviting as Sara and Jake approached, but not much else invited. Gwen's mystique seemed far removed.

"Hi. Good visit?" She opened the driver's door, disappearing.

Sara said yes to the air, and inside the car, minimally outlined the occurrences of the day as Jake sank in and listened. Gwen didn't probe, letting Sara peter out, saying she was exhausted. Gwen forced a light laugh and asked Jake if his day was good and he, also with few words, said it was. Grinning with pat irony, Gwen put on Miles Davis, *In A Silent Way*, suggesting Sara could sleep. He wanted to sleep too, but Jake forced himself to stare at the road and once or twice make a statement about the weather or traffic.

Eventually, Gwen dropped them off. By the time he was alone in his studio Jake rebounded just enough to feel stable, fine. He couldn't get over how extreme his reactions were to the school back there in Delaware. As for Gwen, he just couldn't help his resentment. Bardon was a convenient obsession for her. It wasn't for him, and he wondered if it would own Sara. Major institutions had a way of permanently branding people. As he stood and leaned forward with both hands on his long, black soapstone counter, looking down, he hissed, "It's the ideal school. It's the epitome of institutional excellence, from its appearance to its caring people to its results. What could be better for Sara?"

CHAPTER TWENTY-FIVE

Tuesday, November 14

Sara did not want to go to school. Telling her father that should have caused a parental pushback, but it didn't. Sad lines all over his face, her father's voice firmed up and he said, "You do have to start going on a regular basis again, but okay, I'll call the school and explain again about your mother."

Fortunately, he left her to eat her cereal in her room, Sara sitting uncomfortably at her desk, her big shade down blocking any outside view. She missed a few days the week before and the trip to Bardon took up the day before, and before she could stand going to the humongous public government-institutional high school again she'd have to settle down. The jitters seized her in weak moments since the weekend. They got worse and worse until being there at Bardon she thought she might split a gut or whatever you do when you burst open.

Gwen didn't have much to do with that Bardon visit, except, of course, she set it all up. Then, Sara never saw her again, except in the pissy car ride home when Gwen said nothing and played some wacko jazz to cut out conversation -- not something there was a lot of anyway up in the front seats. What? Was Gwen finished with Sara's father? Was she finished polishing up another sad girl project? Was Gwen moving on? Sara had to try not to get too smashed up about it.

But no surrogate motherhood for Gwen and Sara?

She couldn't finish the cereal and it was her favorite organic oats and cranberries and almonds and chia seeds granola. Why were her thought details so gnarly lately? Sara hated the details on top of details and details, feeling like microbes eating her insides.

Lying on her back on her bed, her eyes closed themselves impulsively, so she opened them. Bardon was great and maybe it was scaring her for some reason, but there weren't any good reasons for that, so she just had to try to relax about it. That school therapist, Jenny Frome, had to be the nicest, gentlest person in the world or something and she let Sara say pretty much nothing most of that hour. She gave Sara a hug at the end and Sara knew it was because of Sara losing her mother, losing and losing her.

Bardon feeling sorry for her -- just then, lying in bed, Sara couldn't get herself to open that can of worms.

Now, she'd have detailed pictures of cans of worms on her mind.

* * * * *

Gwen could feel herself sink into the evening's wine enhanced complacency, sitting there not saying too much. In her earlier, stiff conversation with her one and only husband she obviously had to avoid any mention of the past day spent with Jake and Sara and concentrate on her Bardon library job. Larny flowed reasonably well along not asking about Sara or Jake, only asking questions about the proposed design plans.

Now, at ten in the evening, she was a bit more lit than usual, especially for a weeknight. They were in the library, her across from Larny, both looking through books they pulled off the shelves. She settled on a heafty 1996 Philadelphia Museum of Art exhibition catalogue for a Cezanne exhibition. She just wanted to flip through some glossy pages, indulge in a picture feast glaze over.

God, it hit her hard inside somewhere. There were those damned videos Jake had. The flirting was recorded, and the flirting was so damned overt at times –all that sex and romance foreplay being filmed sickened her now. Jake, who was plainly put off by her these days, wouldn't ever use them against her, would he? Of course not. He was too sane and decent. Plus, he owed her, more and more now that she was offering so much to Sara and him.

Larny got up from his antique leather club chair. "I'm off to bed. Very busy day tomorrow."

"Great. I'll be up soon."

Why did it seem Larny was reading her mind, even more these days than in the past? It was nuts to think he read her thoughts just then. She was just strung out and had to calm down. In a few weeks Bardon would make Sara's admission formal and regimen routine, more and more on her own.

* * * * *

Predictions of Thanksgiving were a barrage of ads all over the internet and in shop windows. He could almost smell the feast and barely afford it. Sara might be set for a long time, maybe life, but he was going to be trampled by bills. He had to try to get a job and still be close enough to Bardon.

Sitting in his bedroom armchair holding his laptop, an hour after dinner, he started searching the usual sites for art conservation jobs. He wouldn't tell Sara. He was only looking, and Sara had enough worries. At dinner he insisted she go to school the next day and she sulked in silence most of the rest of the meal.

There was a job in that weird private studio in New York City that everyone knew was disreputable. It was a scam for a large, mediocre art gallery, where desperate or just untrained conservators restored damaged art, with the public none the wiser. There were always sweat shop jobs like that. They didn't even pay well.

There was a job in a museum in Texas – some small museum outside Houston. At eighty thousand, the salary was good, but they seemed to be saying the conservator had to mat and frame and, "look after" paintings, works on paper, furniture and sculpture in the collection. The job outside Denver, in Golden, was still posted and looked great. But again, it was so damned far away. Golden Colorado looked so good online, and the salary was good.

There wasn't anything listed within four hundred miles. He searched more obscure, little classified ads. Actually, Pittsburgh had a listing for a paper conservator in a two-person private studio. It was near the Carnegie Art Museum. Jake got excited. He really liked Pittsburgh and he loved that museum. Dale Cosgrove was the paintings conservator who was listing the job. No salary was mentioned, but Jake jumped into it. He wrote an email and enclosed his resume and letters of recommendation. He sent it off at a little after eleven-thirty and went to bed.

Sure enough, in the morning Sara was sour faced and thin lipped as she left the apartment. Jake telling her anything about the damage done already by her missing almost two weeks of school would not reduce her burden, so he said nothing, and she said nothing, and she was on her way. He had the last of the ten gorgeous prints from Jane Mallory's collection to finish. He had a few more works brought in by John Forester and a few other works. He got to Jane's works, just to get them done.

Checking his computer at ten-thirty there was an email from Dale Cosgrove.

> *Jake – thanks for your email and resume. It all looks very good. Could we talk – Zoom – later this morning? I would like to fill the position soon.*

Jake's eyes bulged and his heart pumped a few extra times. He hadn't planned on a quick positive answer, probably because he hadn't applied for a job, other than the Newburyport hostile one, in many years.

He stood and tried to think. What should he say? What should he ask? Who was this Dale Cosgrove?

He grabbed his computer and did a search, finally finding the name: *Dale Cosgrove, Paintings Conservator. Oswego State College BA in Business Administration. Eight years internship with Lasky Olittshy, Paintings Conservator, Albany, New York. Twelve years Chief Conservator, Cosgrove Preservation Services, 17 Winthrop Avenue, Pittsburgh, PA.*

Jake should have looked it up last night before sending his email.

There it was on Facebook – Cosgrove Preservation Services. The long and the short of it was one guy provided consultation services for collectors. He probably hired helpers when he could. Dale connected collectors with dealers and galleries and restored anything in need of a bit of fixing up. Fixing up usually meant altering the hell out of original works of art.

It was a sham. The guy wasn't trained professionally and probably worked out of his apartment. Jake had to fight off the shoddy reputation of working alone above a frame shop, but Jake had professional training and lots of it. Still, the threat of being labeled unprofessional or shoddy by the people in blue chip institutions, like museums and non-profit centers, plagued Jake. It was one reason he had to find an institutional job now.

He hated immediately turning down something as vital as a job, offhandedly, so he took a walk around his apartment and did some chin-ups on his door frame. Then he splashed some cold water on his face, which always helped him relax. Jake didn't answer Dale Cosgrove. Instead, he phoned the Carnegie Museum of Art. After a phonic turnstile or two he got through to a curatorial department.

"Yeah, my name's Jake Holtz. I'm looking for a private paintings conservator in Pittsburgh you could recommend."

"We don't actually recommend any one art conservator. We have a list we could email you."

"That would be great. Thanks. Uh, is a Dale Cosgrove on that list? I'm asking because his name came up when I was searching online earlier."

"Uhm, no he isn't."

"Oh, it says he's located near the museum."

"Right, well we have three names of paintings conservators who do private work in the Pittsburgh area who are professionally trained. Would you like me to email the list to you?"

He told her yes, gave her his email address and said a polite thank you, good-bye. As far as Jake knew -- and he asked friends to call and ask once a year - he was on the Washington and Baltimore art museums' lists of private art conservators, for what it was worth.

He sent an email back.

Dale – thank you very much. Just this morning I was offered a position somewhere else. Again, thank you and best wishes.

Jake Holtz

Right, Jake had a job in the wild blue yonder. Dale might be a petty con artist, but Dale was making enough money to hire an assistant. Jake got back to work. Searching online for jobs was a Goddamned nitpicking, mind-jarring pursuit he'd have to save for nighttime. Anyway, Pittsburgh was a bit too far away from Sara and Bardon.

*   *   *   *   *

It was Thursday morning with Sara just off to school in as melancholy a state as he'd ever seen. Sara's two previous days at school didn't seem great, from the few words he begged out of her. *"Most public schools are just huge, grim, inadequate institutions the state makes people go to, Dad."* That was grumbled at dinner the night before. It was her first and last summing up for that day. He wanted to remind her he, and just about everyone he knew, went to public schools, but decided to wait.

Out of desperation for his slightly strung-out daughter, Jake resorted to sitting himself down to email Gwen. Gwen was the one orchestrating Sara's future and Sara needed some serious emotional support. Any bitter separation he felt for Gwen now had to be contained. Okay, he was ready. He had enough strength to do that for ten minutes. An email would be more formal and distant than a text.

Hi Gwen. Hope you're well. I'm afraid Sara's having a problem with going to school these days. She stayed home for a couple of weeks after her mother's funeral, and that only made sense, but I had to practically pry her out of her room yesterday and today and she left home looking very gray.

I wonder if you two having some coffee at The Haunt would help.

Thanks. Jake

Jake, hi. Sorry to hear about Sara and school. I could talk with her, sure, but it also makes me wonder if she shouldn't meet with Jenny Frome at Bardon again. I'm going there Saturday and could take Sara. Jenny's a professional who deals with Sara's age group. I'm not. What do you think?

Gwen

Okay, good. I'll ask Sara when she gets home from school, and she can let you know. Thanks.

Jake could no longer tell Gwen what he thought.

CHAPTER TWENTY-SIX

Saturday, November 18

Bardon was coming closer and closer. Gwen was right next to her, driving, and Gwen was the pubescent girls' guide to Bardon and a life of independence, from everything but Bardon. It might be scary, but Sara figured if she could handle the internet, she could handle schools and colleges.

Sara poked her head forward, looking up out the windshield saying, "The sky's thinner blue as the sun's faster retreating."

"Okay. That's an interesting description." Very likely worried Sara was hallucinating, Gwen's face stiffened.

"My father said that this morning. He was just trying to say something poetic and soothing to his high wire act daughter."

"High wire act? You've always seemed to be firmly planted and steady to me."

Sara saw Gwen's concern take over the driver's side of the car. Gwen barely knew Sara.

"I think I am…steady. That's what I was trying to say to you the first time we had coffee at The Haunt. But I get that I should talk to a therapist. I do."

"It's just a way of working out what's on your mind, Sara. I wasn't the only kid at school who needed someone to talk to when I was your age. Most of them did. I still do. I see a therapist once a week, sometimes with very little to talk about."

"Really? Hm."

"Yup."

"Kind of like how people used to talk to ministers or rabbis or priests or whatever in the past, right? Not to mention parents. Or neighbors."

Gwen's head jerked just a bit as she glanced at Sara. "Yeah, I know."

"Wow. But who listens to ministers or rabbis anymore? You know what I saw online a few days ago."

"What."

"Just about all our universities were set up by religious groups. Private schools, same thing. Bardon was started by Anglicans, right?"

"Yeah."

"Anything Anglican going on at Bardon now?"

"Not exactly, no. We use the Chapel for things."

"What things?"

"Uh, well, students give their own talks there to other students. First year orientation is held there."

"Wow. That's depressing."

"Is it? Why?"

"I don't know. It just sounds like it was something major…I mean major enough to create all these major places, and now it's nothing."

"Oh, no, Sara, it's not nothing. Students use the place all the time and there are still people who practice some religious faith."

"But not really at places like Bardon anymore."

"Yeah, I get that. Bardon has to…uh, what's the phrase… move on with the way the world's changed…accommodate everyone. I know that can sound sort of…"

"Hopelessly inclusive?"

Gwen scowled and Sara laughed. "Sorry. I remember you saying that the first time I met you."

Gwen bugged her eyes at the highway, sighing, "I think I said, self-inclusive…about working alone."

"Yeah, funny that. No matter what we do, we all exclude someone. I read that online. Anyway, know what else I read online?"

"What?" Gwen, dramatizing her wonder at Sara's sudden rush of incites, bugged her eyes at the highway again.

"Some scientist talked about something called, the biological imperative, which I remembered was in my biology book, but this scientist online made sense out of it for me. So, basically, the biological imperative is two things linked together. First, there's the survival of the individual and then the survival of the group through reproduction. All animals survive that way, or they die off. Right? I love that. It's why I sometimes love science."

"Okay. That's very interesting. You said you wanted to study science. So, you like biology? You're taking biology in your current school now?"

At that point in the conversation Sara could ignore Gwen's attempt at diversion. "Yeah, sort of. It's a good course, but they wouldn't ever teach that. No, I watched a talk online. Yeah, it's so basic and yet so important…all we creatures have to stay alive so we can make more creatures. Or we don't survive. Of course, half the effort is in protecting and guiding the creatures when they're young, right? And Bardon is some complicated way of doing that because more and more people are only doing the first part, surviving, not the second part.

And that's what you're doing, right? The second part. It's when you help kids like me."

Gwen didn't respond with words. She just bobbed her head very slowly. A few minutes before her focus had been on the road, only peeking at Sara occasionally. It didn't surprise Sara that Gwen's eyes were now gripping the road.

In a slow, restrained voice Gwen said, "So, anyway, Sara, you like talking with Jenny Frome, right?"

Yeah, I do. Yeah, she's really great."

*　*　*　*　*

Dinner was late. It was almost seven-thirty before Sara came in the door. Jake was hungry for food and for information.

"You didn't have to wait." Sara took off her sweater, placing it on a kitchen chair.

"It's fine. I ate a late lunch."

They made their way with plates of salad, baked sweet potatoes and broiled haddock, across the hallway into her room and sat at the table Jake had already set.

"Eat, but then tell me how your day was." He started eating.

Recently recalcitrant, Sara now seemed anxious to say something to him. She was sitting erectly and bouncing just a bit.

"You should talk to Gwen, Dad. She and Jenny Frome are cooking up some things that you should talk to them about."

"What things?" Jake wasn't sure he could handle more cooked-up things.

"Can't you just talk to Gwen about it? Or are you two on the outs or something? I'm getting the feeling that's it."

He didn't want to go near his outs with Gwen, not with Sara. "No, things are fine. She's just busy these days and she ran out of art to bring in a month ago. What should I talk to her about?"

"They think I should stay at home, not go to the hated public high school anymore. Bardon will supply me with materials to study and I'll work here and just go there, to Bardon, once a week to get tutored and take exams or whatever. That way I'll be in better shape to fit in there in January for spring term."

The words were abundantly clear. He had no way to add to them.

Sara compensated. "I know. It's amazing how much they're willing to do for me. But, damn, it sounds great to me. I'm a little nervous I'll fail all their exams, especially since the other kids have been studying the same stuff together for a couple of months."

Now, all he could do was start to comply. "Yeah, no, Sara, you can more than handle whatever the classes are. Unless there are some subjects that are entirely new to you. But, what about the public school? It's a law that you have to go to school."

"Uh, Gwen met with Mason Randolf the Principal. Yeah, believe it or not, Gwen went in there yesterday and met with him and there are some forms that we have to fill out or whatever. But it's all set, if you agree. I want this. I think it's great. I really do."

Jake sat teeming. Gwen did what, without talking to him first? Was she ever planning to tell him?

Sara stopped eating. Her flat face showed him how stern his own expression might be. "Sorry, I know Dad. It all came together in like one afternoon. Jenny Frome said she wanted to talk with me before she endorsed the idea and Gwen said she was waiting for that too. I guess they just had it as a possibility, depending on what I looked and sounded like in my session with Jenny."

"Um. They could have included me at some point in the last twenty-four hours, before they suggested it to you."

Sara's eyes drooped. She licked her dry lips. "You don't like the idea? Why? It's so great."

"Yeah, okay Sara. I guess it's great, but this is me hearing bits about it after the fact from you. What the hell!?"

He seldom lost control of his emotions with Sara. He had to now, since he had plenty of reason to be pissed-off -- just not at Sara. He was really getting angrier and angrier as he sat there, at Gwen. And who the hell said this damned Jenny Frome could decide Sara's future?

Sara was over there saying something to him about Gwen and Jenny Frome claiming they'd get in touch with him on Monday. He ate a bit more, then headed for the kitchen with his plate, with Sara following. He knew she was worried he'd have a fit of some kind and spoil everything, so he tried to calm himself.

"It's fine Sara. Let's do it, if it's all legal and official. I just don't…never mind. We can talk about it some other time."

He got away from his daughter, telling her he'd put away the dishes later, after she filled and ran the dishwasher. Standing fast and concentrated in the middle of his large bedroom, he centered on his fury.

He waited for fourteen years to get Sara away from the clammy claws of Emma. Emma, who constantly tried to get Sara out of the house so she could party with some boyfriend, finally got herself out of the house permanently, just in time for Jake to dry up financially.

Bad enough Gwen wanted nothing to do with him, but now she was making it clear he had no role left in Sara's life.

It was a living nightmare. Gwen was judging him, playing the role of the Old Testament Solomon and Jake had to prove he was the real parent and choose Bardon for his daughter.

*   *   *   *   *

The limp gray light idled outside Gwen's expansive Georgian windows. Trees could barely hold onto their dry, brittle multicolored leaves and the sun barely flickered from somewhere else every now and then. The weather was supposed to be vivid late November briskness – sharp, distant sun rays through cool damp wind and trees. It wasn't vivid at all.

Knowing she had to call Jake and try to explain and then try to apologize, put a mean edge on Gwen's Monday morning. The day before, Sunday, same thing.

Gwen thought Jake was now more insecure because of the death, the killing, of his only daughter's only mother. There was no one else around to blame, just him, standing there hoping for work. Sara would look at him and remember a lot of useless things Emma did while he could do next to nothing to help. But then, no one, including Gwen, could shake it -- soon, Sara would be in a separate world, some ultimately better place from him and she'd stay away. And there was no real way for Gwen to help him.

Gwen plowed straight into the phone call.

"Jake, I don't know how to explain. I'm sorry I didn't phone you on Friday. All I can say is things took off on their own. Obviously, I knew, once Sara heard about it all, she'd be hooked. I did tell her in the car ride home that it was up to you and her, not just her."

"Um. Sara's thrilled."

"Really, I should have called you."

"Yeah, I would have really preferred that."

After Gwen reluctantly received Jake's mild scorn, she groaned, one of her long self-mocking groans. "Let me tell you how it all developed, weirdly. I decided to go see Mason Randolf, the principal at her school. I'd been to the school once before telling one of his assistants about the scholarship program I represented at Bardon. I got sort of brushed off the way I so often do. Some elaborate, expensive damned private school where kids board sounds like a hostile alien world at best. It takes a while to really describe Bardon, right? This time I told Mason Randolf's secretary it was about one of their students, that it was urgent and that I'd only take five minutes of his time. Yeah, then I had coffee with him and two assistants for forty-five minutes, Jake. When he saw I was black and came from the streets of Baltimore, I was okay and he wanted to know about the Bardon program. Sara was then quickly dismissed - *yeah, great, she can go to Bardon right away. Sorry her mother was shot. We have a bunch of kids here whose parents have been shot.* And they want another few freshman kids there to be considered for Bardon too."

Gwen didn't hear anything on the other end and continued. "So, I was late picking up Sara and made a point of not telling her about my meeting with her principal, but I made the mistake of hurriedly telling Jenny Frome before she sat down with Sara. And, I sort of said it wasn't a done deal, but I think she thought I meant Sara had to be consulted or something. Then Sara just seemed so bored and alienated by her current high school that Jenny apparently concluded Sara would be a lot happier to do this -- stay at home for the next few months and ease her way into Spring Term. Jake, Sara probably already sees herself as a Bardon student, not a part of that urban public school. You know?"

"Yeah, I know. It all makes perfect sense."

"Sorry it happened so quickly."

"It's fine. I hope. I'm a little stunned by it all."

"But if you don't think Sara should go to Bardon so soon, obviously you can say that."

There was blankness on the other side of Gwen's phone conversation.

"Jake?"

"Yeah, to be honest, it's just one of those things. I never could say no to Bardon. And Gwen, it's true. Words cannot describe how fantastic Bardon is, so I just never had a choice."

Gwen's felt a festering irritation with the sad man she'd only met two and a half months before. She no longer felt any connection. In fact, he wasn't trying to connect. It frustrated her. She worried he'd become an impediment for the next few years for Sara. And Gwen did not need a dead weight hanging on her whenever she charted Sara's future -- as in university applications.

Gwen shook off the frustration. Once Sara was boarding, in just two months, Gwen could step back. It was what Larny wanted. It was what she wanted. She knew she had to stop promising so much to strangers.

Now, irritatingly but conveniently, when she waited for the right words to say, Jake gruffly said, "Anyway, I have to go."

CHAPTER TWENTY-SEVEN

Tuesday, November 21

Bobby Joplin came and got Jane's artworks. Jake was surprised Jane didn't come herself, but only surprised, or in denial, for two seconds. Jane was finished with Jake. Apparently, in some perverse way, big, lanky, thirty-something Bobby was a Jake substitute who announced in a southern drawl that he did odd jobs for Jane. Jake asked what odd jobs? While loading up the van he was told Bobby and his wife cleaned Jane's house, did minor repairs, supervised plumbers and electricians, and got groceries and household items. Jane was able to steer clear of the messier paraphernalia of life – all the little stuff. For Jake, it made his transaction awkward-free. The check would be in the mail.

That was that. He walked into the studio. He had to have a conversation with Simon, and he had to have it as soon as possible. The worst part of it was Jake had just told Simon two days before that Sara was, in fact, going to that boarding school in two months, for free. He stressed the fact that it was all paid for. That ripe message was texted, so Jake was spared whatever sour faces Simon made while grunt-texting back, '*Okay. Good luck.*'

This time when Jake grabbed his phone from his studio counter, he couldn't just text.

"Simon, can you talk for a minute?"

A two second pause. "Yeah, on the phone?"

"Yeah. Simon, the conservation work's still not coming in enough. It's better than a few months ago, but not enough to really do the trick, or whatever. I'll apply for conservation jobs around here but in the meantime, what about me doing some work in the frame shop if you need someone?"

Another pause. "Uh, like matting and framing?"

"Yeah, only if you need someone. This is the busy season, right?"

"Yup. Yeah, Jake…" Simon lowered his voice and Jake could tell he was walking to a more private spot. "Really?"

"Yeah. Simon, I know, you've been telling me for years to not sully my hands with any work down in the frame shop. The hell with that. Maybe I can learn to do something a little more useful. I have to do something."

"Okay. So, obviously, we're talking about part-time, right?"

"Yeah, maybe fifteen or twenty hours a week. I mean, I have no idea if I'll suddenly get a job, but it's not looking good. And I have to stay in the general area. Yeah, about that many hours a week for a while? And minimum wage. Hell, I'd have to be trained." Jake was sorry he even hinted at Sara's school constraints on him. He'd meant to totally avoid that.

"No, that's fine. I just worry about you going nuts doing matting and framing. You don't mind working for minimum wage? I could pay you a bit more."

"I can't afford to go nuts and no, Simon, thanks. Look, I'll try to do a good job, but pay me what you pay novices. Hell, I may not exactly be an ace at matting and framing."

"You'll pick it up. Okay. We do need help and part-time is good. When would you start?"

"Tomorrow, Wednesday, if that works for you? Nine, when you open?"

"Okay."

Good-byes were uttered, a little abruptly by Jake, as embarrassed as he'd ever been in his adult life. He was fairly sure Simon's hesitant voice sounded sorry for his ageing, failing friend. Basically, Jake just had to endure some people around him feeling ashamed of his fall from grace. But he had sealed the deal and could move along and maybe make enough money to pay his bills. Sara's brilliant life was going to be all paid for by someone or something else.

* * * * *

Jake was downstairs at eight-thirty and so was Simon drinking some coffee and reading over some receipts. Jake said hello walking to the front counter where Simon was standing.

"Hey, Jake. Want some coffee?"

"No, thanks. I had some."

"You're early. The rest of them won't be here for half an hour."

Simon walked to the wall switches to light up the place, then back to Jake.

They stood staring at each other, then down.

"How are Becky and the kids. I haven't seen them for, what, almost a year?" Jake was too occupied with Sara in the last six months to even ask Simon that question.

"Great, great. Tania likes eleventh grade and Carl's new at it but likes Lehigh University...so far."

"Yeah? Carl's studying engineering, right?"

"Right. He doesn't know what kind of engineering yet, but he has a lot of time."

"Anyway, Simon, don't let me get in your way. I'll read my phone until the others get here."

Simon stood bending at the waist, his folded his arms, then back looking up at the ceiling and then around as he mumbled perversely about not knowing if he should turn on the air conditioning or the heat. "Whatever kills the musty air in here." He walked back to his spot by the marble counter at the front of the frame shop.

Jake remained resting his hip on a worktable and poked at his phone. Ten minutes of that and he had to use the bathroom in the back corner. As he got to the same worktable, Sean came in the front door. He said hello to Simon as he meandered toward Jake, not making eye contact.

Jake introduced himself, shaking Sean's hand and starting to explain his being there but Sean stopped him. "Yeah, Simon told us."

Sean made his way to the bathroom looking annoyed about something. Fiona came in and then Luis and it was more of the same lack of eye contact and annoyed fiddling with the arrangement of stools and mat knives. Jake aimed at Fiona, ten feet away. "I guess you're going to supervise me."

She turned, wooden, snarling, "Sure. Great. Yup, you're gonna just follow me around all day and I'll explain what I'm doing?"

"Okay."

"What's this some way to add this to your resume? You'll say you also know how to mat and frame?"

There was no time for Jake to negotiate a relationship with these three youths, so he just shrugged. Sean was back and he and Luis, giving each other slightly peeved askance glances, started heading for a computer against the wall. Jake, like a stray gorilla, tried to not get in their way. There was a work list typed onto a computer screen on the shelf along one wall. Each project had a priority number, a due date and a check list of what was required. Fiona supervised the assignments, deciding who did what and when, so she read over the morning's work schedule and told Sean and Luis to mat and frame the four Miro prints owned by some insurance company. Then Fiona walked Jake around explaining where tools and matting and framing materials were stored. He didn't tell her he already knew that from working on his own tiny collection over the years, after hours.

Sean and Luis wore street clothes, both in jeans and black T shirts. Fiona was in a tan corduroy jumpsuit. Jake had barely tried to tone down his mammoth age gap in his khakis and tan button-down cotton shirt. Luis and Sean stayed busy while Fiona went to the sixty-inch-wide metal drawers and pulled out a group of family photographs needing mats and frames. She said Jake could watch her complete that order.

"The customer check list shows they want off-white 4ply mat board. See?" Her voice toneless, her face stale, her going through the motions, Fiona pointed at the receipt Simon had filled in with Julie Thatcher, the owner of the eight by ten snapshot photographs. "There's bright white, warm white, off white and then you get into the creams and other colors. Most people choose the warmer whites, especially for photographs like these."

Fiona cast a very reluctant, wary look at Jake, who nodded. She pulled out an aluminum ruler from a shelf beneath the table. "That's where we keep the smaller ruler and the yard sticks. I measure everything a few times, you know, because it takes more time and materials to fix mistakes. Then I write down the dimensions on a pad I keep here." She grunted just audibly, reaching for a small pad of paper on a shelf to the left of the rulers and yard sticks.

Every feature of her work process was described, and Jake nodded along. Most of it was obvious, but he had to yield to her interpretation of training the old weird version of a new guy. She spent twenty minutes on the mat cutting unit that was attached to the wall.

Around ten-thirty Jake got to cutting a mat for a reproduction of a Cezanne still life. He took his time, and it was okay. Fiona shrugged, looking unimpressed. She gave him another reproduction, this time of a Tissot and Jake did it slowly, but correctly.

Fiona worked up enough patience to demonstrate how to cut glass and plexi and frame things after lunch. Then he had fifteen more reproductions to mat, all belonging to a financial firm in Dupont Circle. Jake told himself along the way he'd only have to put up with being so bored and diminished two days a week.

* * * * *

It was the day before Thanksgiving, a big family celebration coming up for their family of two, Sara noted to herself all week. She was more and more pointed in that direction. Then, filled with pissy irony, after an email appeared from a delivery company, Sara heard the doorbell ring downstairs. She reluctantly trundled down to collect what were some of the last material remains of her life with her mother. Aunt Cindy sent an email too, a week before. There was no choice in the matter, the boxes contained what Aunt Cindy described as memorabilia. Sara hated the idea of that, whatever that was. After all, Sara chose whatever she wanted to bring with her when she moved out of North Bethesda five months before. That was it. She didn't want anything more.

No, with the sky getting thinner and the sun retreating, on Wednesday, the twenty-second of November, Sara had some sorting to do. Gwen would be there in forty-five minutes to drive Sara to Bardon.

The two cardboard boxes were only something like eighteen by twenty-five inches wide and ten inches deep and not very heavy. With some curiosity, Sara carried them upstairs, put them on her bedroom floor, tore off the tape of one and opened it. On top of some clothes was an eight by ten sheet of white paper with the handwritten words: *I guessed your mother kept some of your clothes. If not yours, you can give them away.* Sara recognized immediately the skirts and jeans as her mother's, not hers. She pawed down through and that was it, nothing more. What a sick joke. Aunt Cindy thought the stupid, ugly clothes might belong to Sara when she was thirteen or fourteen, not her mother. Meanwhile, they were all at least a size too big. Sara closed that depressing box. She tore open the second one half dreading what dreary memories in it might release. There was a laptop computer under more clothes and two framed photographs, one hideous sixth grade school picture of Sara and one of her mother taken at some beach years before, looking as seductive – and for Sara, looking sad and desperate -- as possible. Sara closed the box, contents inside, and went to the bathroom to wash up and get ready for Gwen. Unkempt memories could be dealt with some other time. In the meantime, Sara was feeling an aggression growing inside.

Sara was swept away in the solid, luxurious hunk of a Mercedes on time, half an hour after the closing of her box opening little ceremony. Sara sat silently for ten minutes, wanting to adjust to the spotty, partly cloudy day and wanting to let Gwen finish with pleasantries.

"Uh, Gwen? So you know, my father's working in the frame shop a couple of days a week."

That stopped Gwen from poking at the car's climate control. "What? Really?"

"Yeah. He started a couple of days ago. He didn't tell me until the night before."

Both hands on the steering wheel, Gwen didn't look at Sara. "Hm. So, did he say anything about why?"

"Just that he wasn't getting enough conservation work and something about wanting to learn how to mat and frame."

Gwen looked disheartened, stuck in some inner debate that she wanted to keep to herself. Sara looked away. They drove and looked ahead, until time and space had to be filled and Gwen asked Sara stilted questions about her homework assignments and tests. Sara answered that homework was done and, in her backpack, and yes, she studied for two days for the Algebra and Biology exams she was about to take. They listened to some inadequate poppy jazz from Gwen's radio that Sara blocked as well as she could, trying not to worry about her tests coming up, her alone in that room on the second floor of the library.

Feeling testy Sara said, "So, I've given up on War and Peace for now. I'm almost finished reading the original book, Frankenstein."

Gwen looked startled but said nothing.

"Ever read it by any chance?"

"No."

"Really old fashioned...the style is...but I love it. The author, Mary Shelley, had a horrible time trying to have children, uh, and in the middle of that misery wrote Frankenstein about some mad scientist creating an eight-foot human in a lab who people think is a monster, so he becomes one." Sara laughed darkly. "I mean, damn, so her own baby died, so she created an eight-foot baby in a lab?!"

Gwen looked at Sara dully, shaking her head, swallowing while Sara laughed until Gwen mouthed a weak, barely audible, "Okay. I don't know what to say. Okay..."

Sara knew that it wasn't actually funny. It was as pissy a thing to say as possible to Gwen at that moment, and that was what she wanted – some way to push and pull at Gwen.

Settling down from laughing, Sara turned to look out her side window, asking, "What have you been reading recently?"

The rest of the drive was partly filled with radio noise and Gwen chatting about the book she was reading on climate change and a few other distracting things -- just nothing more about Sara's Bardon-deleted father.

∗ ∗ ∗ ∗ ∗

Gwen had the question at that point. But she could only let it dangle dangerously for the next day and a half. She needed the act of holding on, gripping something deep inside herself for the rest of Saturday and all of Sunday -- almost two days of standard stuff of eating Japanese food from Cosmos, and not even half-hardheartedly reading and answering emails and texts, and very skittishly talking to Mary and Jason, her cleaners. She couldn't leave the house.

The deadly question swung over her like a knife edged pendulum. The awful question had to be avoided until it couldn't be. There was a deadly cold wind blowing through her when there she was on Monday at eight-thirty in the morning, sitting on her velvet window seat, aching dry eyes aimed blindly at the long planks on her floor in the bright sunny room. She let the voice inside her say what had to be said. Larny was somewhere else. He said on Saturday morning he just had to get away to think. When she tried to answer his question about whether or not she had stopped seeing Jake and Sara, he wouldn't wait for her lengthy explanation. He had to go, he said, suitcase in hand. He'd text her. Then his car pulled out of the garage and down the street.

She repeated that -- Larny was gone.

Gwen stood up and asked the question -- what did she do? What the hell did she do?

CHAPTER TWENTY-EIGHT

Saturday, December 2nd

The weekend drive to Bardon with Gwen was as inadequate as any drive anywhere ever, but Sara knew Gwen was gone. Whatever interest Gwen had in Sara was from some sort of complicated institutional distance, as solid as eye floaters. As for Gwen and her father, that was as over as over gets and Sara had to admit she knew why.

Her father was looking sad and needy to Gwen now. Sara concluded the message of the week before, that her father was working part-time in the frame shop, finally totally put off the woman. He was losing his Georgetown art conservation business and there wasn't anything Gwen, or anyone else, could do about it.

Yup, Sara saw it all so clearly now – she'd have Bardon in her life, but not Gwen or her father.

Meanwhile, the dull drive to Bardon was driving Sara crazy. Finally, turning the stupid music down, Gwen, looking more like a statue of herself, asked Sara how things were going with Jenny Frome.

"Fine. Great."

"You like her? She is very nice, isn't she? The school loves her."

"And she loves the school absolutely."

Gwen glanced at Sara, just a tiny bit closely, then turned away and onward they drove with pointless conversation their goal.

Sara was very happy to be finished with the two hours of tests. That awkward lunch between the tests, sitting with some students Sara's age was only bearable because it had to be rushed. Sara only had thirty minutes before the next test and then her appointment with Jenny Frome in that new steel and glass office in the contemporary building on the outer ring of the campus.

Sitting very comfortably in the gently reclined steel and leather chair, Sara was tired but contented. In fact, she felt extremely accomplished. Sitting in a matching armchair with her small, almost invisible notepad on her lap, was silver-haired Jenny Frome. It was notable silver hair because it was dyed a very fine, even tone and was thin and straight and cut with perfectly straight bangs half an inch above her eyebrows and then behind her ears, chin length. Her skin was fairly smooth for an older person. Sara guessed she was in her thirties, maybe forties. Add the woman's gray eyes and high cheek bones and Sara imagined, for ridiculous fun, Jenny grew up in the Alps and skied to school as a kid.

To start things, she asked Sara about the tests.

"Um, I think I did pretty well on them, especially biology."

"Where do you take the tests?"

"In the library, on the second floor."

"In one of the conference rooms?"

"Yeah, I guess, or a study room, a small one."

"You don't mind being alone, taking these tests?"

"It's just for now. No, I know I have to finish up things."

They shut off their voices – Jenny Frome's eternally soft one and Sara's edgy-twangy one -- for a minute. Sara knew, usually these blanks were meant to be filled by her, to explore her inner voices or something. Sometimes Jenny wrote down notes. Like this time.

"Last week you told me you haven't made any friends here yet. Would you like to spend some weekends here and go to parties." As usual, Jenny purred when she spoke and always half smiled.

"Uh, no. Thanks."

"No?"

Another shift to blankness.

"So, Sara, tell me. How do you feel about Bardon now that you've become a bit more involved."

"Oh, well, yeah, it's a great school."

Jenny's smile faded just slightly. "Is there anything you particularly like, don't like."

"I don't like the chapel being used by older students to lecture younger students."

Jenny's smile tightened just a bit, her voice purring more strongly. "Oh, do you mean the first-year orientation program?"

"Um."

"What don't you like about it?"

"I just prefer older, actual teachers teaching subjects and don't like a bunch of students telling other students what's right and what's wrong."

Jenny very gently jerked her head sideways. "Oh, right and wrong? Well, is that what it is? Or is it about the values and culture of the community here? Where have you read or seen information about the orientation program, Sara?"

This was the most in-depth conversation Sara had had with this school therapist.

"Online."

"Online. From our website, you mean?"

"Right."

"Oh, well you may find it's more to your liking when you participate in it. It's not a graded course or anything. No pressure."

"No pressure to conform?"

Again, Jenny's head tilted automatically. "Oh, I don't think so. No. It's meant to welcome new students."

"For a whole term? Three hours a week?"

"Oh, well, I think it allows students to voice opinions away from the prying eyes and ears of teachers. You know?"

The purring was driving Sara nuts.

"Um, in the chapel? Why the chapel?"

"Uh, I don't know. Why? Does that bother you in some way?"

Sara sighed. "It does. A bunch of kids given the holy site on campus to turn up the volume on their stupid hang-ups? And we all know the loudest, most obnoxious students will dominate. What the hell do they know about right and wrong, about any culture anywhere? Why did the adults give up the holy site?"

Jenny made a condescending little soft gasp. "Holy site?"

"Yup. The original heart and soul of the Bardon culture these know nothings are supposed to be lecturing each other about. And I'm not even religious, by the way."

Jenny nodded slowly, professionally pacing herself. "No. Okay, that's fine. It sounds like you've thought a lot about this."

Sara had only begun to spill some guts. "Yeah, but it's not actually the point right now. My father's the point for me."

Smiling and sitting very still, Jenny actually looked excited, like she was more and more ready for some serious stuff now. She might just have a nutzoid teen on her hands. Just what she trained for, for so many years.

"Your father?"

"Yes."

Blank. No words added by anyone.

Jenny had to say, "Do you have something you want to talk about Sara?"

"I found out...uh, about six months ago...that my father could probably get a decent paying job he might halfway like somewhere out there in the country. I was listening at the door when he was talking to Simon, our landlord. I mean, I only listened for a minute, and stopped in the hallway and went back to my room. I mean, I've known for a long time my father did all that for me. He gave up on moving for jobs because of me."

"Right. Was that because he wanted what was best for you, do you think?"

Sara hesitated. Jenny was now stating what Jenny thought, softly, but sternly, no light in her smile anymore. It meant Sara could be really pushy because pushy Jenny started it. After sitting back Sara said, "Some things aren't up to us. A whole lot of things aren't up to my father. I knew that when I heard him talking about jobs, but it's just taken me six months to admit it. So, what's best for me is being with my father for now."

She could see Jenny was taking her time, leaning back, disciplined. Sara watched, knowing despite all appearances, you were either with Jenny or against her.

"Hmm. How do you think then, Sara, your feelings of wanting to stay near your father might relate to recent events in your life?"

There it was, the question Sara wanted. "I love my father and respect him and I don't want any school coming between us."

"Can a school enhance a family? We have all sorts of families here that benefit from working with us and us with them."

"Good. And thanks, but not us. You can't actually give us what we really need."

The discussion was actually over whether Jenny and company knew it or not. Sara and her father had a long Thanksgiving dinner conversation nine days before. After finally convincing him she didn't want to go to Bardon, he applied for a job in Golden Colorado, Zooming and all, and was just offered a job. Sara was looking forward to researching schools in the Denver/Golden area.

With Bardon gone, Sara, father and all, had to make it on her own. She knew that. It was a bit scary, but she just knew it was the way it had to be. With a bit of luck there were more Georgetowns in her future. And maybe even more therapy -- if she got around to it.

David Ross was born in Brooklyn, New York. He went to Syracuse University and Tufts University and then spent two years at Oxford University's Ashmolean Museum.

He wrote three novels while raising two children with his wife, Judith –*The Saleswoman and the Househusband, That Boy's Facts of Life and Sara's Money's Gone.*

David lives with his wife in West Sussex, England.

Printed in Great Britain
by Amazon

41665861R00175